I0563721

The Journal

of

Djuna Malik

Liza Wieland

Livingston Press
THe University of West Alabama

Library of Congress Control Number: 2025044331

Typesetting and page layout: Kelly West
Proofreading: Brooke Barger,
Savannah Beams, Kelly West

Cover and back cover art and layout: Kelly West

This is a work of fiction. Any resemblance
to persons living or dead, events, or locales is coincidental.
Livingston Press is part of The University of West Alabama,
and thereby has non-profit status.
Donations are tax-deductible.

6 5 4 3 2 1

The Journal

of

Djuna Malik

for my students

I.

Near the end of the flight from Dublin to America, my dead father woke me. I opened my eyes, waited for the blur to clear. No sign of him, only the empty middle seat, rows of other passengers, the backs of their heads. Across the aisle, a man snoring behind his eye mask and a woman blued to ghostly by the light from her laptop screen. Outside, the world was all soft darkness, like velvet if you could pass your hand through the window to touch it. Clear as a bell, Da's voice had just said, "Liam, picture a girl."

We were continuing a chat that had been going on ever since I stumbled my way into a university job and bought my ticket to Raleigh, in North Carolina. We were trying to work out how I might teach anything useful to American eighteen-year-olds. You'll be brilliant, he'd said, you're a natural. You've always got your nose in a book, haven't you. Like your brother.

Like all of us, Da, I'd said.

What'll you give them, then, he wanted to know.

There's a required reading list.

Ah, he said, but you tell them to read everything. That's the great secret, reading it all. The news, sure, but biscuit packages, recipes, whatever swims into view. *People* magazine even. Their roommates' diaries if it comes to that.

That's a terrible idea, Da!

Just take care how you make the suggestion.

I won't be making it at all.

Pity, then. One of the main social functions of a diary is precisely to be read by other people. An American said that.

Who? I said.

Susan Sontag, wasn't it? One of your favorites.

Sure she didn't mean it.

In the seventies, he said, after everything went off the rails, the teachers were falling all over themselves assigning diaries. At first to talk about Bloody Sunday, *process*, they said. I heard the writing was brilliant.

But you didn't assign them.

I didn't think I could bear it. Their private lives. All that rambling on.

But it wouldn't have to be rambling. You could give them ideas, direct their attention.

I believe you could, he said. Starting with something small.

A single person, a bit of mystery, something to be filled in. Tell them, picture this. Imagine that. Go from there.

As so often happened, my dad brought me around to an idea by seeming to dismiss it.

I could see a faint lavender glow on the horizon, just ahead of the airplane. I thought, maybe somewhat oddly, of the hem of a woman's dress. In an hour and a half, we would be landing. I closed my eyes, and there it was again, Da's voice, a bit cracked, as if he were moved by some strong emotion. "Liam," he said, "really what I mean is this: let them teach you."

#1

Picture a girl alone on a road.

Nisha Malik is sitting behind the steering wheel. The car is parked on the service road behind the CVS. It's 6 in the evening, and she's just come off her shift in the pharmacy. The wind today charges fiercely from the north, a scream in its mouth. She can hear the wailing rattle along the doors of the storage shed at the back of the parking lot. Beside it are two blue rolling carts that don't move at all. They are serene and beautiful in their stillness, the blue of imagined seas, becalmed. Ancient. Nisha watches them for a long time to make sure. The radio broadcasts the President talking about either Mexico or China, it's hard to tell which. "We'll see what happens," he says. He sounds like someone addressing an audience of children, about to read them a fairy story. She presses the dial to turn off his voice. Then, without knowing she'll do it, she flips down the sun visor and slides open the cover of the mirror. Like the politics here in Pamlico county, it slides to the right.

There's her face encircled by the edges of the dupatta she sometimes wears. Coal black eyes, skin the umber everyone here recognizes as immigrant brown. Her sister Djuna wondered when that shade would be added to the Crayola 64 box. Nisha's not frowning, but the twin worry lines above her nose suggest grave concern. From squinting into the sun all those years, from actual worry. More lines around her mouth. They look like scars.

"I think you're still alive somewhere," she tells her reflection. "Or present at least. I can't help it. How can I keep you here?" Then she slides the cover closed, leans to rest her forehead on the steering wheel. "Since I can't I bring you back."

She taps the dial again, and another radio voice fills the car, announcing the end of the North Atlantic hurricane season. But here in eastern North Carolina, the forecaster says, we won't really be able to relax until late December.

That there is calm after a storm is a lie people tell to sell you damaged goods or to make you look away from their sleight of hand, look away from the wreckage.

The sun on the water here like paparazzi flash. Or like the two mismatched cities—Mumbai and Boston—that Nisha has seen from an airplane. She came here for water, to live beside water, slake some visual thirst. And she got what she wanted. Water, water everywhere, as far as the eye could see from certain windows in the house, from certain seats in the main room that was kitchen and dining and living. Water moving mindlessly west or east depending on the wind.

Sometimes moving higher, over the dock, into the yard, into the house. Brackish water, salty as tears, half salt, so that everything it finds to soak or submerge never really dries out completely, never seems right, never gets back to normal. Into the house, into the chairs and sofa, to the walls, into the bed.

Into the marriage. Never gets back to normal, never seems right.

What sort of spell would set things right?

A spell from a children's story no one's ever told, never even dreamed of. Once upon a time, there were Indians in North Carolina. From India.

Nisha removes the pins from the dupatta, pulls it off her head, lays it out on the passenger seat. She promised her mother to wear it sometimes, but she can't here. Not after what happened to her sister. She's too afraid.

Nisha wasn't there, but she believes she heard the shots. One bullet each, to the head. That's what she hears, even after she's told it didn't happen that way. She couldn't bring herself to imagine the screaming though, which would later lead her to believe there wasn't any. Maybe Djuna said *No* or asked *Why.* Maybe Kasim said *Don't.* Maybe his sister Sariah tried to get to the back door and the neighbor told her calmly to come back to the living room, and she did. The *living room* is what they called it in the newspapers. Nisha got stuck on that irony for a while.

Djuna died in the kitchen. Maybe. Or not.

Nisha heard the shots, she'll realize later, because someone was hunting out of season in Green's Creek or in the slough closest to the house her husband lived in. She was there to take her winter clothes. In August, she had moved out quickly, without thinking of what she'd need later. The window was open because it was October. She thought about the shots: this wasn't any kind of season, not deer or dove. Trout and spot and red drum were starting to leave the river for their cold weather stillness in the tributaries. Nisha imagined these creatures in suspension, like bees and spiders you sometimes see encased in amber, floating there. As soon as she arrived at the house, Michael had gone to pull out the crab pot, but there were six good sized blues and so he left it. Leaves had just started to fall, except for the pecan tree. The last half-dozen tomatoes, bright red against yellowing leaves. All of this departure silent, except for the gunshots.

The day before, Nisha had seen a snake moving slowly across the dirt road a quarter mile from the house. She drove around it, then returned to try to take a picture. She thought at first the snake was dead, or maybe sun-struck. She tried to remember what the pattern meant—not diamonds, like on a rattlesnake, but a repetition of filigree ovals. When she got back, the snake was just disappearing into the ditch. She looked it up later: copperhead. Moving into hibernation, stealthily below the cattails and into the pasture.

Later, it was hard not to make that into a metaphor or an omen.

Her cell phone chimed. A Chapel Hill number she didn't recognize.

"Nisha Malik?"

"Yes?"

"This is Anne Kelly. I'm the Associate Dean of Students at Carolina."

Oh no, Nisha thought.

"There's been a situation involving Djuna. A shooting off campus. She's been hurt. You'll want to come right away."

"A shooting?"

"You'll want to come right now."

"Yes. Yes, of course. We're three hours away."

"I understand. UNC Medical Center. Emergency. I'll meet you there. You can text me at this number, and I'll be in touch also."

"Is she all right?"

"She's badly hurt. Please hang up now and come right away."

"We will. Right now."

Michael was standing in the doorway. "What?" he said. And then again, louder.

"A shooting. Djuna. This person." Nisha held up her hands, made fists and then unmade them, as if that would help explain. "In the dean's office. She said go to the Medical Center. Do you know where that is?"

"It's in the middle of campus. I can get there."

Then they were in the car. The road seemed especially, eerily empty. Nisha remembered the snake. Michael was driving. He was a good driver. Steady.

Nisha texted everyone she could think of. Michael didn't speak. The story of what happened began to take shape in little green and blue speech bubbles. Marcy, Daniel, Larsen. Names she knew from phone conversations. An argument in the neighborhood. The man next door, Devin Graham, had found reasons to complain about parking, trash bins, a dog barking. They didn't own a dog. Couldn't be. Djuna got along with everyone. Her housemates Kasim and Saria, were brother and sister, he was older, in med school. Who else did Djuna know? It all seemed like a dream now—the dreamer wants to wake up, call out, but can't. Can't move either, can't stop repeating some embarrassing bit of behavior. Djuna had said most of the neighbors were students, though. She liked all of them, really. She said everybody had a story. Perfect strangers often told her about their lives. Maybe someday, she would be a writer.

Certain stretches of Highway 70 toward Kinston run through farmland or blank land, acres people seemed to be keeping for some terrible future, fenced aggressively, no roads in or through. Now only daylight fading to darkness.

Too much quiet time to think, though supposedly Nisha was connected to all those people she was texting, and riding twelve inches away from Michael:

Djuna as a baby. Seventeen years ago, in Mumbai. Nisha old enough to be her mother. And then, after their mother was killed in the Taj Hotel attack, she was.

"We should have moved with her to Chapel Hill," Nisha said to Michael.

Instead, she thought, we clung to our precious river view and that illusion of real estate. Selfishly, stupidly. No one owns the river. The cheeky fishermen who troll between our docks know that.

"Maybe we would still be living together." Michael said.

***

"I'll only be three hours away, Djuna," Nisha said, in May. "I can get there if you need me."

"Would you leave this?" Djuna extended her left arm out, toward the view, like an American game show hostess.

"If you wanted me to, I would," Nisha said.

16

Michael came into the room. "And you get to visit us here whenever you want," he said. "Chill out and eat fresh crab. Fish."

Djuna made a face.

"OK. Not fish. Hang with your sister. Talk about what assholes white men are."

Djuna looked at Nisha, a frightened question in her eyes. Nisha shook her head.

"We don't do that, Michael," Djuna said. "We like white men. We like that they make hard decisions so we don't have to."

"Don't bait him, Djuna."

"Speaking of bait," Michael said. "I'm going to fish."

"Catch me a flounder," Nisha said.

"It's too early for flounder."

Nisha didn't believe Michael meant to slam the door. She thought it must have been the wind.

***

Now Michael's hands on the steering wheel. Whitened fingernails reflecting the dashboard lights. Little moons inside the car, haloed over the wheel. That was all Nisha could see.

"They think she's in surgery," Nisha said. "But they're not sure. Marcy texted."

"Surgery," Michael said. "That sounds like it could be good. At least it means she's…."

"I'm going to try texting Kasim again," Nisha said.

"You haven't heard from him yet? That's strange."

"Marcy hasn't mentioned anything about him. Or his sister."

Something about saying that out loud.

"Oh no," Nisha whispered. And then she knew: Kasim was dead. Nisha knew as if she had seen his body with her own eyes, the stark contrast between his face and the white sheet pulled up over his throat.

She couldn't unsee it.

There is a split second before the news, then there is the knowing, the *information* and after that comes cliché. Cliché claims the life: nothing will ever be the same. She didn't suffer. She went straight to heaven, if you believe there is such a place.

But there's more. Because the bullets had lodged in her frontal cortex and her spinal cord, this cliché: it's a mercy. She would have been paralyzed, she would have lived only in a persistent vegetative state.

Nisha wanted it back, that split second before, but at the same time, she wondered if there had been any such moment. How could there have been a *before* when she'd known deep in her heart that Kasim was dead. Is that where a person knows such things? In the heart? And if Kasim was dead, surely his sister was too, surely, they were all three dead.

The past tense is always something of a charade in the telling of a story, a ruse. Claiming to know what's already happened, pretending to have the authority to declare that these things have absolutely transpired. As the president says, we'll see.

One last text from Anne Kelly, as they exited I-40: She's in surgery. Go to emergency. That was it. Impossible to discern tone or intention. Michael knew the roads, so Nisha didn't have to watch or navigate. Instead she tried to feel Djuna in the world—she believed she could do that, discern a presence, a warmth, breath. Not for Kasim. When she said his name in her head, or his sister's name, *Sariah*, she felt blank, like she couldn't understand the sound the letters made, as if the name came zooming at her in Cyrillic or Chinese ideograms.

The University campus is cut in half by a road called Manning. Above, the stately, leafy green campus, the original brick buildings, the mown lawns. Below, the medical center and Djuna's body.

Djuna was an exceptionally good sleeper. Last fall, when she was studying American poetry, she joked "Sleeping is an art. I do it exceptionally well. I do it so it feels…" and then she made up all sorts of last lines.

No. She wasn't asleep. She was unconscious. Sleeping Djuna. The parody made Nisha cry out.

"The nurse thinks the surgery may take a while," Michael said.

Why did people think consolation was repeating what you already knew?

"Ma'am?" A police officer stood by the nurse's station, his service revolver the largest thing about him. A nightstick. Closed pouches along the belt containing—what? What else did he need besides a club and a gun?

"Ma'am," he said again. "Are you the sister?"

"Yes." She felt enraged, suddenly, by the definite article. "*Djuna Malik's* sister. Give her a name, please."

"Can I ask you a few questions? Let's just step into the hallway."

"Now?" Nisha said. "Can't you see…. I just got here." She glanced up at Michael. "We haven't even seen a doctor yet."

"It's fine," Michael said. "He's here to help."

"I want a lawyer," Nisha said. She wasn't sure where the words had come from. Instinct.

"Nisha, that's not necessary," Michael said.

"No, I think it is necessary. I might say something wrong. I might…. I just can't talk to you right now."

"Sir," Michael said, turning away. "What do you want to know?"

"Stop it, Michael. I want to call our attorney. Or text him or something."

"We don't have an attorney."

"Demorest. Who did our wills."

Did the police officer roll his eyes? "We just want to know if your sister had complained of any trouble with the neighbors. That's all. It's really just a yes or no."

"Yes," Michael said. "The one who worked for—a cable company, I think. He didn't like them."

"Devin Graham?" Nisha said. "He didn't do this."

"I think maybe he did," Michael said.

Nisha stood up. "That's enough," she said. She walked away, to the nurses' station. "Please." She looked at the nurse's hospital badge, her wedding ring. "Mrs. Achebo," she said. "When can I see my sister? Djuna Malik."

Mrs. Achebo looked into her computer screen, tapped a keyboard. "She's still in surgery, Ma'am." She glanced up, beyond Nisha to Michael and the police officer, still talking, their backs to her. "I can give you a quieter place to wait." Mrs. Achebo stood up, beckoned. "Come with me."

Nisha followed her through the waiting area and then down a narrow hallway. It felt like a submarine passage, underwater, removed from outside air. Mrs. Achebo opened the door, stood aside and let Nisha pass into the small sitting room.

"You can wait here, Mrs. Malik," she said. "I'll let the surgeon know."

Mrs. Malik. That was their mother. Such a person did not now exist in this world.

"Thank you. But no one else please. Not even—"

"No one else. I'll make sure." Mrs. Achebo pulled the door closed.

A chair for the doctor. A sofa for the family. A window that didn't open. This is where the awful news is delivered. The air felt thick with sorrow and disbelief. The view was the hospital roof and the south campus dormitories. Where Djuna should have lived. She wanted something more like family, she'd said. She wanted better food, her own food, the familiar smells of cooking. She wanted people who understood eating low on the food chain, did not think it was an exotic form of dieting. A *cleanse.* She knew there was a certain kind of American college girl she did not want to share living spaces with.

"Why did I let her live off campus?" Nisha asked the hospital roof, the trees beyond, the baseball diamond. "Why, why, why?"

***

"You're not my mother," Djuna had said when they argued about it. And then they both wept.

"She would have wanted you to stay in the dorms," Nisha had said.

"She would want me to assimilate!"

"That's not the right word. And you know she didn't really want that. She just didn't want us to close ourselves off."

"How am I closing myself off? I'm in classes all day. I have a job in the library, so I'll see pretty much every undergraduate at the University. I'll probably eat half my meals on campus. I know myself. I will want some quiet. Not everybody is like you, Nisha. Citizen of the world with a billion friends."

"I like quiet too."

"Just let me try it."

"I can't really stop you."

"Of course you can. You can stop writing the checks."

"It's Mommy's and Daddy's money. I'm just the trustee. You can go to the estate and petition."

"I can?"

"Any time."

"But I want you to approve."

Somewhere outside the room, Nisha knew, two things were happening. Michael was looking for her and Djuna was unconscious. Nisha texted him: I need to be alone for a few minutes. He texted back Why? Nisha turned her phone over so that the screen went dark. Michael would understand or he wouldn't. She pictured him falling away into darkness the way it happened in the movies when an astronaut became untethered from the mothership.

The mothership. She would try to tether her mind to Djuna's. Their mother had said something about that before she was killed: we are all tied together, we three women, and nothing can ever undo that knot. Nisha closed her eyes and pictured Djuna asleep. The image came easily—she had been watching Djuna asleep a few weeks ago, in the car, driving to Chapel Hill, the face turned half away, the late afternoon sun illuminating her skin, the shadows under her eyes lightened somewhat. The perfection of sleeping, the illusion of peace.

That version of Djuna she tried to hold in her mind. Asleep for now, the girl who would wake slowly, like a cranky machine, but whole and eventually happy.

"Rest," Nisha whispered. She closed her eyes. "The surgeon will fix it. The surgeon knows what to do."

When Djuna slept, she did not ever move. She did not talk in her sleep or twitch. Sometimes an earbud would dislodge, and Nisha could hear the lullaby—lately *The 1975* or the soundtrack to *Les Misérables* or *Hamilton* or *The Sound of Music*. Orphans who make good, do good in the world.

Nisha imagined herself as the sound in Djuna's head. You'll be okay. You'll come out of this. You're not ready to leave this world. Mommy doesn't want you yet. Mommy won't want you for another seventy or eighty years. Or more. Or ever. She wished she could say all this to Djuna's body. She could go ask the nurse again, but then Michael would fly back into orbit, tethered again to his same arguments and questions. Better to stay here for now.

But she could not sustain it, the image of Djuna peacefully asleep. The picture in her mind gave way to tubes and machines and blood. Nisha opened her eyes.

What did they give you to look at in here? Nothing to read. A painted sunrise over the ocean. The Chapel Hill cupola, the Old Well, an impressionist rendering, pentimento, half of the image erased to reveal something like clouds and flower petals. On the wall opposite the window, a copse of trees, sunlight filtering through the leaves. Vaguely hopeful, all three of these. No people in them, though. Vast silences.

Djuna had maybe tried to talk to Devin Graham. She would have done that, tried to make peace. Maybe she had said to Kasim and his sister, Let me go talk to him, and they had believed in the magic of Djuna. She would have let herself out the front door and picked her way across the adjoining lawns, her mind and heart opened like a flower. The hem of her jeans would have been damp with dew by the time she reached the porch. She pressed the bell once, not insistent, not angry. No answer. Maybe she waited, then turned to look over her shoulder. He was home, Devin was, his truck was in the driveway. She waited, counted to twenty, pressed the bell again. She heard stirring inside, the shriek of a chair pushed back, a pause while he picked up his gun. The door thrown open. She might have said, We can work this out, or Can we talk about this.

She would have walked carefully backward to stand in the street. Nisha pictured her that way: the emptiness of the road seeming to rush away from Djuna in both directions. She might be saying, We're really sorry. Or she might not have had time to say anything at all before he shot her.

That can't be how it happened.

That was the problem with these paintings, Nisha thought. The real world has people in it. A lot of people. This was the problem with the world too. The people have different ideas about how to live, and then they fight about them.

Then the neighbor stepped over Djuna's body, lying there on his front porch or in the road, and he strode back the way she had come across the lawns. Maybe his feet touched the grass in exactly the same spots as Djuna's had. He opened their front door and marched his wet shoes into Kasim's house and shot Kasim and his sister in the living room, where they were sitting on the couch, waiting for Djuna to call them to dinner.

A knock on the door like a slow heartbeat, then silence.

"Nisha." She could hear the awful news in Michael's voice. "The surgeon wants to talk to you."

The wailing afterwards was so loud and so long it seemed the sound came from the hospital building, out of the walls and floors, the drywall, the pipes, the wiring, the invisible Internet signal. Nisha was both inside and surrounded by this crying, even though she wanted her sister's wrecked body all to herself, even when she sent Michael away, climbed onto the gurney, held Djuna in her arms. She did not know how she would ever leave this room, return to silence. Someone would have to drag her away, carry her out. The wailing would do that, Mrs. Achebo seemed to be telling her, Mrs. Achebo's howling, as she stood beside the gurney, keeping herself between Nisha and all the others who would try to silence them, take them away.

#2

You don't know what you don't know.

Even from the far edge of the crowd, I could see what was happening and the way it would all end. The protesters had encased the monument in a sleeve-like banner. Christo, you might think of the wrapped Reichstag, though smaller. But this wasn't art. This was a great, grave trick, a *monumental* ruse. Pretend Silent Sam is not here. Pretend it's already true, what the words on the banner say: SILENT SAM MUST GO. Inside the sleeve, the lads were attaching ropes to the statue, around the soldier's neck, then his chest and around his legs, the way a Negro slave might have been bound just before he was sold or whipped or hanged. Outside the sleeve, fifteen or twenty people, mostly young, mostly students, shouted *Silent Sam must go! Whose University? Our University! Down with racists!* This shouting and movement behind the sleeve went on for about an hour and a half, while a crowd formed, drifted apart, reassembled, kaleidoscopic it would have been if you could see it from beyond and through one eye. Students were just back from summer break, fall term classes would begin the next morning. The campus was buzzing, nearly frantic with many different sorts of anticipation. The night was warm but not stifling. The sun set, followed by a moment of silence, an exhale. The protest seemed to be over.

Suddenly, then, came a kind of flurry and confusion at the base of the monument. Lads holding ropes appeared, it seemed out of nowhere. The briefest pause. Inside it the sound of labored breathing almost amplified, and then the statue fell through the paper, face-first into the dirt. It was like a dramatic magic trick performed so fast it causes a kind of cataclysm in your brain. It's like you got lost in time and space.

I heard a barmaid in Dublin say this about her own cocktails: some drinks, you order them, and then they are there in the glass, then gone, and confuse you into the memory of them. I tried so hard to understand what she meant. Her specialty was a Pot O'Gold, garnished with edible gold flakes and microgreens. I fell for her magic every time.

The whole quad erupted in cheering, whooping, applause.

I cheered along with them. I didn't know which was my own voice, mingling and ricocheting between Graham Memorial and Hyde Hall. Some people stepped forward and spit on the statue, on the back of the soldier's head. Others tried to bury the head in the sandy soil of North Carolina. In the half-light of cell phones, the statue looked like a real fallen man, dead, stiff, totally still.

Campus police arrived and slowly waded through the crowd to the base of the monument. They did not speak to or touch anyone. They turned and faced the protesters. Three of them were white and one was Black. The Black policeman was smiling.

I stepped away and walked toward Rosemary Street, back to my little rented bungalow. I was swirled inside a crowd of students, a living, moving sleeve. I wondered if any of them would turn up in my classes the next day or Wednesday. Then I was home, this unfamiliar place, furnished according to someone else's taste for someone not planning to stay long. Tree frogs chirped out of the darkness. You wondered how their small green bodies could make such a bloody racket. No other sound. Two blocks from campus, you couldn't tell if anyone knew what had just happened to the monument.

Five days later, the Confederacy play-actors called The Proud Boys arrived on campus, wanting, I suppose, another confrontation like they had in Charlottesville. The police massed, in riot gear. Instead of feeling protected, the kids called them pigs and chanted, Why are you in riot gear? We don't have no riot here. But it got ugly in short order. A black student set fire to a Confederate flag on the steps of South Building, and the police immediately put handcuffs on him.

There looked to be a sort of bleak parfait of people involved—black students pressed up against the front of the building, a layer of police in dark blue, a wider layer of others, mostly white people, in brightly colored summer clothes. I thought an aerial view might provide a kind of apocalyptic spectrum, scrambled though, the eye moving from black to indigo to vivid confusion. People were shouting, Let him go. I wondered if the police hadn't actually saved the flag-burner's life by arresting him.

I stood off to the left, halfway down the steps. I had met all of my classes twice by that time but had not seen anyone who looked familiar. I felt a little bit sad about that—I wanted to have this event to talk about with the students. The crowd surged forward from below, and I was knocked to my right and looked down. The young woman standing just beside me seemed familiar—and I remembered she had an unusual name, but not what it was. She smiled up at me, gave a little wave. She said something I couldn't hear and turned away. I followed her and caught up as she moved to the edge of the crowd.

"You're in my literature class," I said. "And you're called--?"

"Djuna Malik."

"Right. What do you think of all this, Djuna Malik?"

"Both sides behaving badly," she said. "I think it's pretty damaging to everyone."

"Interesting. Maybe I'll ask your class to write about it next week."

"I'm not sure we're going to have anything to say."

"Too soon?"

"Too soon and too young. Sometimes...." She looked around us, lowered her voice. "I actually felt a little bad for the statue. People piling dirt on it. Spitting."

"That's interesting." I hoped no one had overheard.

"I wish more people would listen instead of yelling."

"I do as well," I said. "What it is we should listen to? Or whom?"

"I don't know," she said. "Books?" She smiled as though she had made a joke. Which maybe she had.

"That seems like a good idea. As this is an institution of higher learning." I pointed toward the library in front of us.

"So, are faculty allowed to be here?"

I had not given this a thought. "I hope so."

"Probably no one noticed you anyway," she said. "You have that tall person James Comey thing going on. Seen but not seen."

She turned away, toward the center of campus, unfortunately called The Pit. I felt a strange, vague alarm rising from the middle of my chest.

Seen but not seen. Seeing but pretending not to. Or the reverse. The story of my life, wasn't it.

The room where I met the Introduction to Literature class was in the basement of Bingham, but seemed less like a bunker than a nest, a place you might feel protected, even warm. Or maybe this was the students sitting hunched in their seats like ruffled fledglings, slightly unkempt and a bit frightened. I'd met them twice now, but still had no sense of who they were. Djuna Malik sat in the front row, just below a high window, so that the light washed over her head, keeping her in shadow. She was always the first to arrive. Until she wasn't.

"So much going on last week," I began. "I'm sure you noticed. Raising many, many questions. The big ones seem to be: first, is what happened on campus Saturday what you'd call domestic terrorism?"

Silent. All of them. A vacuum to be filled. "The people with Confederate flags. The Proud Boys."

"That's what they want," a student said. "To terrorize us. That's what the Ku Klux Klan was."

"I'm sorry I don't know your names yet."

"William," the student said.

"Anyone else?"

They waited.

"And so another question," I said. "Pulling down the monument. Is it damage to public property or is it justice?"

"It's both," Djuna Malik said. "But you want to know which is more important."

"Ah, but you've changed the question, haven't you?"

"I think everything needs to change," another student said. I did somehow know her name was Taylor. "All the questions."

"And the people too." The name of this student I couldn't recall. I thought I should give up trying to remember their names and then having to interrupt to ask. "Literally change. I mean like the ones in power now go away and let new ones in."

"It's going to happen," Djuna said.

"You feel changed, do you?" I asked them.

Most did. Said they did.

"Is some damage necessary for change then?"

Silence again. No one wanted to answer this question. Not so early in the term anyway.

"I'm changed by damage," I said. "Truly. I am. I'm Irish. We don't call our history, history. We call it *troubles*."

I let that get in their heads. "I've just had a thought. I won't be able to teach this class the way I was supposed to, will I now? The way it's been taught for the last two hundred years. By men like Silent Sam."

What did I mean by that? Why didn't anyone ask? Instead, twenty-five first year students waited, their cell phones set on silent, but buzzing away, their hive calling them to fly back. They sat impatient but trusting. *Stop that*, I wanted to tell them. *Don't give me any credit. I don't know very much more than you do.*

"Did anyone notice the other part of the statue? Below Silent Sam, the image carved in?"

"We're first-years," Taylor said. "We just got here."

"It's a woman. She's meant to represent the state of North Carolina. She's telling a student what to do, which is drop his books and join the Confederacy."

"You don't want to think too hard about that," William said.

"Or do you? I think we should. Here's the arrangement then. We're not a literature class." I was talking now without thinking. It was my Da's voice got in my head again. "We're a book club."

They gaped at me. Or not even. How had they come to perfect that blank stare in only eighteen years?

Except Djuna Malik, who was smiling.

"Well, I know what you're thinking, don't I. Your *mothers* are in book clubs. They drink Chablis and talk about your fathers."

"Or they talk politics," a young woman said. "Don't stereotype just because you're not American."

"In Ireland, actually," I said, "we have book clubs too. My mam used to be in one, and she talked about my dad. Or so she said. But you're right. I'll be careful about stereotyping."

The air in the room seemed to move a bit, in what direction, I wasn't sure.

"But we are going to talk about the book. Or the poem. We'll do poetry too. Stop with the long faces there. I'm Irish. Did ya think there'd be no poetry?" I was putting on the accent pretty heavy. "Everything is fair game. If you don't like a book, you can say that, but you have to explain why. You have to *read* the book. If you come to class, and you talk, and it's clear to me you've read the book, and you do the in-class writing, you'll get an A. That's my contract with you."

"No essays?" Taylor said. "I thought this was a literature class."

"Twenty minutes free writing every day, and more for homework. From prompts I'll give. By the end of the term, you'll practically have a novel yourselves."

"No research paper?"

"No."

The students looked at each other the way the Von Trapp children do in *The Sound of Music* when Maria says she's never been a governess before.

"This is great," Djuna said. "The Troubles Book Club."

"So what kind of trouble are we talking about? What's the worst you can think of? What kind of trouble can't be undone? Follows you everywhere, forever?"

The atmosphere shifted further. Then a cloud passed over the sun, and the room darkened. Something strange happened then: the class laughed at this sudden darkness, the timing of it.

"Death," Djuna said.

"Right," the boy named William said.

I said I agreed. My voice wobbled.

What I want to tell these students, the ones who didn't know already, is that the dead will never leave you alone. They walk beside you as you go about your daily routine, as you stumble to Lenoir in the morning or sleep in Wilson Library in the afternoon or stagger back to the dorm late at night from some bar on Franklin Street.

"But I had a strange thought recently, about the dead. What color are they? Are the Negro dead still Negro? Are the whites still white? Of course they are. Are they happy? Have they mended fences with other dead? Of course they have. Because we make it so. The dead can't exist without the living."

I wasn't entirely sure what I was talking about. Still, I thought I could hear their thoughts turning like rusty gears.

"So there's the first prompt. What color are your dead?"

These class looked at me as if I'd lost my mind. And sure, maybe

I have.

I gazed back at them, and thought, as I still do sometimes, that the students are their own dead. The notion strikes me as odd when I'm having it, always, even though it's occurred to me before. But they look so lost and unloved sometimes, even as they're beginning the most exciting period of their lives. They all look motherless.

And then you find out that one of them actually *is*. Motherless. She knows first-hand that the dead will never leave you alone. And her dead are brown, she tells me. She knows more than probably anyone else in this classroom, in most classrooms that she enters hour after long, lonely hour, day after excruciating day.

She knows more than I do.

Djuna Malik.

Whatever she knows, I want to know it too.

"Are you any relation to *the* Liam McFadden?"

The question lies in wait, like a snake or some darker, more dangerous creature. Over the years, I have perfected some replies. Not perfected. Assembled. As in put together badly with a very modest set of tools:

Yes.

No.

I *am the* Liam McFadden.

None of what you've heard is true.

Every bit of what you've heard is true.

I'll tell you if you tell me whether you're any relation to *the* (insert interlocutor's name). This reply clearly has limited usefulness—you're out of luck if you don't know the name or have drunk so much that you've forgotten it.

Why do you want to know?

Did he owe you money?

Sometimes, I just stare back. This works to greatest effect in dimly lit places such as pubs, a pub being where most people gather the courage to ask the question in the first place.

And then there are the responses, equally various:

What was he like?

That must have been pretty wild.

I've read everything he wrote.

(So have I).

After one of these exchanges, there is almost no way to have a civilized conversation. My father hobbles me in death as he did in life.

"That must have been really, really hard," Djuna Malik said.

She had come to see me during my office hours, just after the book club discussion. We sat in my sun-splashed office in Greenlaw, which I had not yet had time to decorate—or that's what I told myself. I didn't know what I would hang on the walls, not really. Clean white plaster and the tops of trees and whatever shadows the sky made were good enough. I told myself the walls were like the blank page—inviting and scary.

"To be his son, I mean."

I knew I was staring at Djuna Malik in a terribly pathetic sort of way. I closed my eyes.

"We read *The Widening Sky* in high school. I guess everybody did," she said. "He was a great writer."

"Do you want to be a writer?" I asked her.

"I am a writer. Like you said about my last prompt."

"I did, yes. I'm glad you read the comments."

"Do *you* want to be a writer?" she asked.

Where did she get such bravery? I would have given the world to know the answer to this question.

"I used to."

"But not anymore." She wasn't asking. The room seemed to turn cold.

"We're meant to be talking about *your* writing, are we not?"

"Yes." Djuna leaned over to rummage in her backpack. "I wanted to ask you about this comment." She laid the bluebook on the desk between us. I saw that she'd written the word *journal* on the cover in black ink. She opened the bluebook and turned it toward me, flipped back three pages. "What does this mean?" She tapped her long index finger on the single word *more*.

"It means I like what you've written there and wish you'd keep on in the same way."

"What part?"

"The description of what they're doing, the other people sitting beside you. I can see them. I want to keep seeing them."

"I was making it up. No one was really doing any of those things."

"I know. I was in the same room when you were writing it, wasn't I." We both looked up and around as if we were surprised to be in my office and not that classroom. "It's a bit surreal. It's as if everyone in the room was dreaming their separate dreams and acting them out totally unaware of what anyone else was doing. And you made that quite vivid."

"So more of that?"

"Yes."

"All right then." Djuna slid the bluebook across the desk and slipped it into her backpack. She zipped up the pack decisively and stood. The chair made an painful squeal and we both grimaced.

"See you in class," I said.

"I like the book club idea, by the way. I mean, I know it's slightly cheesy, but it works. It doesn't seem like some fashionable teaching gimmick. My housemate's teacher is making them write a literacy autobiography, whatever that is."

"Seems a bit precious."

She had a wondrous smile—I swear the room lit up, warmed up—even if it is the worst cliché, that's what happened. "I love it," she said, "when people use 'precious' like that. The irony is so...*quiet.*"

She slipped her arms through the straps of her pack, walked to the door. She turned back then and gave me a little wave.

The irony is so quiet.

My father, *the* Liam McFadden, would have adored her.

***

What is it parents want when they give a child exactly their same name? I don't really mean *parents*. You don't hear of women, mothers, doing this very often. So one ought to ask the question this way: why? Why does the father do it? Pride, is that it? Can't be. Too soon for pride—what if the namesake turns out badly? Is it some hoarse, primal cry for immortality? Or an awkward lunge in that direction? You would think a son who shared his father's name would know why, but this particular son really hasn't a clue.

And what about the other children, the other son—in my case the notorious Shamus McFadden. Shamus of the hot temper and huge appetites, Shamus the writer who never wrote much, the lover who never loved, the scholar who refused to be schooled, the brother who never bothered. This last, it's not true. He bothered plenty. He was good to us when he was home, when he was not distracted by a little bit of fame. I was just there trying my hand at being him, waxing poetic. And see? Didn't I miss the mark? But who could help but wax poetic over such a terrible, delightful person. And God, how I miss him. I miss him like fuck-all. Every bloody day.

The McFadden boys are both great writers, all our teachers said, but that Shamus has his father's gifts. They said it the Irish way: he didn't lick it off a stone.

I always wondered what our father felt about that. Might he have wanted his gifts back? Might jealousy have played some part in their terrible end?

I ask these questions daily, and I try to atone. Ask these questions in my evening prayers alone in the rented house just off Franklin Street in Chapel Hill, North Carolina, cloaked in humid darkness, having marked fifty first-year papers from my other classes, having written on each paper a long love-letter about the English language, and isn't she an elusive, frightfully rough paramour? All those hours and words I might have devoted to my own story or novel.

"These young people," Liam McFadden the elder said some years ago, "if only they would work harder." He looked over at his sons. Scowled. Winked.

One of the sons did work harder. The namesake. The other did not. Because Shamus had so much talent, he did not have to work, did he? And wicked blue eyes, a confusion of dark hair that seemed to make women want to untangle it, untangle his clothes, untangle *him*. He appeared to be at home in the world and in his body, completely at ease. Stayed out and slept in. His first poems published when he was 19. The world seemed more astonished that his last name was like the famous writer's name. And yet, the exact same name, belonging to me, the son who published stories a few years later, seemed to the world far less consequential.

Of my work, the world said very little. Maybe I confused them. Maybe people thought oh, that's just Liam again. I bet I've already read that one, sure.

I can offer a million reasons why I didn't get the same attention Shamus did. Except for the real reason, the nub of the problem: I wasn't as good, was I? So for a while I found other work in the world. School, my mam's decline. Anger of the simmering sort. For when Da went for drinks at Neary's, he took Shamus, and I stayed home with our mam. Shamus was more fun. When my father went to visit Bob Hennessy, he took me, because I was more helpful, and Mam stayed home alone.

Bob Hennessy was my dad's oldest friend. Their mothers were school chums who adored each other, married the same year, and gave birth to their sons six weeks apart, Liam in July, Bobby in August. The boys went to Christian Brothers Secondary together, then to Trinity. Bob went to work in publishing and then for *The Irish Times*, and Dad wrote novels and started teaching. They married nice girls, those being my mam and her great pal Nancy, who were themselves close as sisters, and moved to opposite ends of the city, Bob to Ballsbridge and Dad to Ringsend. But they liked to meet about midway in between, at Mass at St. Mary's in Haddington Road and go for a pint at Smyth's after.

Just after his 59th birthday, Bob Hennessy suffered a massive stroke. Dad couldn't believe it and he went into one of his greatest rages. It was as if Almighty God had insulted his friend in the worst way. And I suppose this was true. I said it out loud one day, explaining my refusal to go to Mass anymore--how could God insult Bob Hennessy like this, which caused Dad to put down the book he was reading and take off his glasses and look at me in a way I'd never—I almost can't think about it. *Notice me.* Then he stood up and called to Shamus, and they went out to Neary's.

But that notice stayed there in his study, shimmering in the room, a living object almost. The front door clicked shut, Dad's and Shamus's voices faded down the front walk and into the street. Other rooms in the house settled into the near-silence of their engines and systems. I knew my mother was upstairs in her green tufted chair, either asleep or crying softly about sadness she did not explain. Sometimes she howled with unintelligible grief. It broke our hearts, this start of her journey into dementia. But now, in the study, the thunderclap of my father's attention echoed. I sat there for maybe a quarter hour feeling the exhilarating shatter of it. Then I got up to wake Mam and make us a pot of tea.

The next day, Saturday, after a very late breakfast, Da said I was to accompany him on an important errand. We would walk, he said. It was far but not impossible. The air would do me good, and truly it was a glorious day, clear blue skies, not too hot, the sort of weather that puts everyone in a grand mood. We walked vaguely south, a ways along the River Dodder. On the way, my father asked about my studies. Would I go to America after Trinity, as I had always hoped? Where would I go? New York? But I might find that too competitive, too disheartening. Boston would be the same. Chicago, then? He did not mention San Francisco, having some years before attempted to talk me out of admiration for Kerouac and Ginsberg (Shamus and I drove our parents mad reciting "Howl" at full volume, from memory) and the incomparably sexy Grace Slick. I thought once or twice to ask where we were walking to, but my father's hundred visions and revisions of my future crowded out everything else. I should go somewhere more surprising, where I wouldn't be one of a million scholars with accents, somewhere more quiet, where I would stand out. The South. I admired the same writers he did: Faulkner, Fitzgerald, Eliot. All American southerners, more or less.

Yes, I said eagerly, like a puppy. Yes, you're right, of course. You've hit the nail on the head.

So I was somewhat surprised to glance up ahead and find we had walked into Bob Hennessy's neighborhood, with its grand houses and yards big as pastures. I had been here before, many times over the years, but always by car or by taxi.

"Oh," I said. "You've brought me to see Bob."

My father let out a grim little laugh. "Only it's not really him."

I wanted to ask why he'd brought me, but Bob's wife, Nancy,

had already come out of the house. She opened her arms to my father and wept a little but recovered quickly and reached up to give me a kiss on the cheek. She asked after my mother. She was a beautiful woman, dark-haired, green-eyed. That she managed the Life and Style section of the *Times* wouldn't surprise anyone. She led us inside and to the closed door of the room I knew to be the downstairs guest bedroom. We'd stayed there once or twice when a party lasted into the wee hours.

"There's tea things out," Nancy said.

"Go have some fun," my father said.

"What's that?" Nancy said, shaking her head. "Thank you so much, Liam." She winked at me. "Liams."

She reached for the doorknob, but my father caught her hand and spun her slowly around, slowly, as if they were dancing in a dream, until she faced away from the door. She let go my father's hand and walked toward the staircase.

Before he opened the bedroom door, my father gave me a look I can't forget: both stern and sad, reluctant and loving, the complete distillation, or so I imagine, of fatherhood.

The room was badly lit by two weak lamps. The drapes were closed. We saw the outline of Bob Hennessy in a wheelchair, drawn up close to a low table.

"Well, this won't do," my dad said. "Liam, open those drapes, please."

I did as I was asked. Two tall windows faced onto the garden. Early afternoon sunlight flooded the room. I turned to see Bob Hennessy blink, shake his head. I thought he might stand up out of the wheelchair and start talking. I thought my dad had cured him. Why shouldn't he have that sort of power?

Bob looked at us, but he didn't move or speak. He was very pale, his whole face drooping as if the flesh had all of a sudden given way to gravity. He seemed to be sleeping with his eyes open, a sight that was at first unusual and then progressively more frightening the longer I looked.

My dad sat down on the sofa and patted the cushion beside him. I sat. I said, "Hello, Bob."

"Yes," my father said to me, quietly. "That's how it goes." Then he began to do something I'd never once seen him do: he poured tea. A cup for me, a cup for himself, and a cup for Bob. He asked Bob if he wanted tea. Then he said, "Oh I am a perfect jackass, sure. I forgot you despise tea. Never mind."

We had our tea. My father talked about his classes, about his new novel, about the publisher. He asked Bob questions that were really statements cleverly disguised as questions: "You're quite satisfied with your publisher, aren't you, Bob? I know you've always said so."

"Liam, tell Bob about your plans for America."

I realized then that the walk here had been a dress rehearsal. So I dutifully repeated what my father had said about my future, while my father drank his tea and nodded.

"I think," I said, "there are just too many European intellectuals in New York. So I've decided to go to North Carolina."

My father put down his teacup quickly so that the cup wobbled in the saucer. I saw the brown crescent of tea tremble. "Oh?" he said.

I continued to speak to Bob Hennessy. "I like writers from the American South, so it makes perfect sense that I would want to go there to continue my studies." I sounded like a right prig, but I believed the words as I said them.

And so, for most of the next year until they both were dead and I had left Ireland, this is how I spoke to my father about anything that was important to me: through the odd ventriloquism of Bob Hennessy's stroke, once a week, Sundays after Mass.

"Bob," my father said one afternoon, "remember when we used

to talk like young fools about who we write for? Oh, but you thought that was the most asinine question anybody could ask. But I convinced you to at least give it some thought. Well, you go first, Liam, you said, and so I said idiotic things like, Oh, of course, I write for myself, I write for the god Apollo, I write for eternity. I write for money, was what you said. And then you said the really…the best thing."

Here, my father laughed until he wept. After a time, he wiped his eyes and turned to me.

"Who do you write for, son? Tell, Bob."

"I have imagined a perfect reader—that's who."

"Ah, Bob, do you hear that? A perfect reader! But he's close, isn't he, Bob? He's in the neighborhood. Close to what you said. He's on the way, is he not?"

I waited to find out what I was on the way to.

"You said, Bob—well, really, we worked this out together over many a whiskey, did we not? You said to find somebody you love very deeply but can never have, and write for that person."

What happened to my dad in the end—that will have to be explained, though, truthfully, I want to know it too, because I wasn't there. I was at home, starting to apply for teaching work in America, changing my mind, starting again. And I was completely dumbstruck, like everyone I knew, that this charlatan, fraud, womanizer and rapist, had been elected President and was about to swear on a bible that he would uphold the law. That was why I wasn't paying attention. Also, I was thinking about Mam, who lived more and more in a twilit country where no one could reach her. Like Bob Hennessy's drawing room, only without doors or windows or tea or Nancy.

The short version is that Shamus and my father went out for a drink at Neary's, and then they quarreled. "He was raging," Shamus said, "at me, at you, at Mam, at God." Then he went bright red in the face, staggered out into the road, and collapsed. Gone before anyone could help. A week later, Shamus went swimming off the coast by Howth, alone. His body washed ashore just north of Dun Laoghaire.

The long version is years in the telling. It began when my father was born in 1947 and will end when I die in 2070 or thereabouts. It is a history, actually, for someone else to record.

But I go back to those afternoons in Bob Hennessey's guest bedroom when my father was showing immense kindness to his old friend and listening to his eldest son. His namesake. Who, admittedly, didn't have very much experience or knowledge with which to make scintillating conversation—even with someone who was grateful and could not reply.

"Tell Bob about your novel," my dad said on another Sunday afternoon, quite suddenly as I recall. He was standing at one of the tall windows looking out into the garden. Bob looked too, as if my father would describe what he saw. We had been talking about that, my father and I, through the conduit of Bob Hennessy's silence, about the loveliness and order of Nancy's garden, while Mam's had fallen into weeds and briars, but how when she rallied in the spring, she would literally claw it back to green. We believed she would rally in the spring. We believed in many impossibilities. Which is probably what drew my father's attention to my writing.

"There's not much to tell yet," I said.

"But a character. Sure, you've got that."

"I don't think you, Bob" (here I turned, pushed the plate of cookies a bit in his direction) "would find it very interesting."

"Do you find it interesting?" my father asked.

The truth was, I didn't. Or was afraid no one else would. Which amounts to the same thing.

"A young Irishman goes—"

"Oh, dear god," my father said. "Liam, you must spare us that all over again."

"I know."

We sat still in that moment, I'm not sure how long. It seemed an age. Some blooming plant outside the window caught the light and threw it into the room as a kind of garish violet washing the side of Bob Hennessy's face. I thought he looked like a Francis Bacon painting. Somehow, I knew he would not stay alive much longer. His gaze moved away from the window and my father's form—a dark pillar blocking half the light, a plinth—and fixed on me. If only he could say the thing he was thinking.

"At least make it about a woman," my father said. "I don't think the world cares much for young men these days. Young men have not given the world much reason to care about them, am I right?"

"There's bound to be a woman in there somewhere," I said feebly.

"Now you sound like Shamus." He turned away from the window, and we laughed. Bob Hennessy's eyes roved back and forth, reading us.

"I'm serious, though. And I'm sure Bob would agree. In fact, Bob, you've always said this very thing to me. Find a woman with a good story and a terrible secret. These are two different things. But find her, and win her over, and she'll give you your novel."

The University put out an alert on the morning of 7 October, and then the Chancellor sent a message over email, which was how everyone heard the news. I felt, as the Americans say, an extreme disconnect. Djuna Malik's collection of bluebooks clipped together was in the pile on my kitchen table. I could see it as I glanced from the Chancellor's email to the stack of notebooks and back again to the computer screen, waiting there on the bottom, saved for last because—well, why does anybody save a thing for last? Because it's the hardest or the easiest or because it's the best. In this case, all three. Hardest because she was so good, easiest and best for the same reason.

And I'll readily admit there was a good deal what's called magical thinking going on. If I could see her journal, Djuna Malik couldn't possibly be dead.

On Monday, I arrived early, to be able to get over the shock of the empty desk beneath the window. The sun seemed to be lighting its flat work surface with a particular glare. I knew how the students would look. Shell-shocked and afraid, trying to hide the frazzled agony of grave injury nearby. Survivor's guilt—or something like that. Pity and fear. But no catharsis. I was trying to remember what I'd heard schoolteachers did after 9/11. We can talk about it. I think all the teachers said that. Do you want to talk about it? But the students didn't. They wanted to *stop* talking about it. They wanted to curl up in their beds. They wanted their mums.

And that was in fact the scene in the room as Djuna's classmates began to appear. The empty desk. The girl called Taylor put a bouquet of flowers and a small teddy bear on Djuna's desk. I left them there all week, until the flowers began to look dead, and that seemed awful: how could we let the flowers die as well? So I brought in a carrier bag and folded the brittle stems into it and took them home and threw the flowers into my overgrown back garden.

The teddy bear stayed for three days longer, until one of the students sent me an email asking if I would take it away. The next morning, I tucked it into my backpack and carried it back to the rented house in Rosemary Street, where I set it in a corner of my sofa.

Hurricane Ismene closed the campus, though we had only a bit of windiness. Fitting, I thought, Djuna Malik whirling out of this world in flood and fury. Truthfully, I didn't think it. I *felt* it, as if the storm were under my ribs, shaking there.

When classes resumed, no one had the heart for the book club, including myself. When you're looking at such trouble, and it's looking back at you, the last thing you want to do is read about it. So I taught the usual, the required. Or I did some bad imitation of teaching. I stayed true to my word and did not assign a research paper.

Twice before the end of October, I walked to the entrance of counseling services, but I could not make myself step inside.

I gave their journals back. The semester got busy, the breathless hurtling toward final exams and the holidays, and we didn't have time for so much in-class writing. I didn't collect the journals again. I couldn't bear the missing one.

Which was technically not missing at all. Missing is a funny word in this context. I read every word Djuna had written, slowly since there was now no deadline, and carefully. She was a beautiful writer. In so many ways, her gift was like my brother's. Or my mother's, before she gave it up. Clear, patient attention to detail, observation. Raw anger. Directness. Like she was talking to me. And only me. The sort of attention that's almost impossible to get in real life.

There's a book out about that now: the rage and desire dead girls inspire in popular culture. *Twin Peaks, The Girl On The Train.* I'm thinking of something different here. I can see all the feminist scholars rolling their eyes.

Or maybe not—I'm still talking about criminal acts. Murder. Yes, there was a murder. Djuna and her housemates were murdered. But I mean another kind of crime. Stealing of a certain shade. Plagiarism in a sidelong sort of way. But something else too. Six weeks' worth of an eighteen-year-old's free writing couldn't possibly give me a novel, or could it? And would this not also be honoring the dead? Keeping Djuna Malik alive in a way? What's that bit Shakespeare says in the sonnets about immortality? *So long as men can breathe or eyes can see, So long lives this, and this gives life to thee.*

So maybe it's true about the dead girl: the man's identity becomes organized around hers—with none of her personality or perspective to get in the way. Except no. It's all her personality and perspective. It's all Djuna Malik. I'm the blank thing, the empty vessel that she fills up.

This is not my story to tell.

And yet.

That's how it works, is it not? The white men control the story. Jane Eyre's story is about Rochester. Elizabeth Bennett's is completely dependent upon Mr. Darcy. Middlemarch wouldn't exist without Casaubon and Will Ladislaw.

Emma Bovary seems in thrall to nobody, and look what happens to her.

The third week of October, I made a telephone call.

"May I speak to Nisha Malik?"

She would be thinking: Irish accent. A man. The steps of Wilson Library. I wondered if she would remember. So much putting together of pieces. I could hear Nisha's mind whirring and then sputtering out.

"Speaking."

"Oh." I coughed and cleared my throat.

From her: a long sigh that was as impossible to read as it was unbearable to hear.

"This is Liam McFadden. Djuna's literature teacher."

"Yes," Nisha said. "We met. Labor Day weekend."

"I wanted to say…. I'm very sorry."

I didn't say the rest. *For your loss.* That was the part I myself always hated. Nisha Malik was, I think, waiting for me to say it. I could hear wind and water in the background, waves coming into shore. Then she whispered, "Thank you." I don't think she meant to whisper, but it was all the she could do.

We listened to each other breathe.

"I'm calling because—I mean to offer my condolences of course. But also…the Department Chair suggested I get in touch."

"Thank you," Nisha said again. "All of Djuna's professors have been so kind."

"I apologize for going this long without…"

"I understand it's a busy time."

"It is."

"The hurricane," she said. "Everything."

"Yes. How did you come through? We heard it was quite bad where you are."

"It was for most people, but I was alright."

"I'm very glad to hear that."

Another sigh.

"I have something."

"Oh no," she said. She coughed. She sounded ill.

"Of Djuna's," I continued. "Her journal from my class." I heard her halfway gasp, then try to take it back. "I thought you might like to see it."

"Oh," Nisha said. "I'm very sorry. I'm…. The wind. Let me get back in the car."

"Of course." I waited.

"All right," Nisha said. "I'm all right now."

"I thought you would like to see this journal."

"Yes. Yes of course."

"We can meet on campus. Or another place. I don't have a car…."

"Campus is fine. Just tell me where."

"Would you like to see the classroom?"

Nisha said she would very much like to see the classroom. She told me what days she was free, thinking through her work schedule, driving time, the weather. We made a plan.

The classroom in Bingham was in shadow at this hour of the day, early afternoon. It was a cave, almost as if there were no windows, as if the space had suddenly remembered it was a basement. I wondered why I had thought to meet Nisha Malik here and why she had wanted to see this place.

Other classes on the hallway had settled in, and so I knew the footsteps I heard must be hers. I stood and waited. My hands shook, which half-surprised me, but I was after all a thief about to confess to his crime.

I was not prepared for her to look so much like her sister. This was foolish of course. We shook hands.

"Professor McFadden," she said.

"Please call me Liam."

We stood for a moment, frozen. I tried not to stare. Her eyes were very black, with deep shadows beneath them. She glanced at the bluebooks on Djuna's desk and sat down in the next desk over.

"That one was Djuna's," I said, pointing to the empty desk. "I didn't know if you'd want to…."

"I do, actually." She stood, changed seats, placed her hands on her sister's journals. I worked hard to keep myself from snatching them away.

"What shall I call you?"

"Nisha would be fine."

I sat beside her and pointed to the bluebooks. "These are the prompts Djuna responded to in class and also the homework assignments. I asked them to explore…their ideas about themselves and the world. Their families. What it was like to have come here. All that sort of thing."

"That's a lot," Nisha Malik said. She gazed at me as if she were having some other thoughts, as if she were seeing me and also not seeing. "It's everything."

"For some of them, it was too much. But not for your sister."

She touched the fingers of her left hand to the large format blue-book, Carolina blue.

"Sometimes this color hurts me," she said. "The sky in the fall."

"I think I know what you mean." She had not yet opened the bluebook. "Do you want me to stay? I can step outside."

"Oh no," she said. "Please stay. You might need to explain something." She met my eyes and did not look away. "I mean, if you have time."

"I'm free for the rest of the day."

She laid both her hands flat on the desk, breathed deeply, in and out, a couple of times. "Now that I'm here, I'm not sure I can…"

"I understand. Maybe we can start by talking."

"All right."

"Your sister is a very good writer, and I…" I couldn't go on.

"I'm glad you used the present tense. About Djuna."

"It's a habit I have. My father's dead, and I still say *Dad is*."

"Djuna is."

"I'm not sure when they become was."

"Or if."

We were not looking at each other, each speaking into some beyond, maybe occupied by Djuna. By my father. Shamus, too. And my mother. I wondered, somewhere outside this room and this moment, if I might ever talk to Nisha Malik about Shamus. I let my hand rest next to hers on the bluebook.

"What do you miss most? What do you miss least?"

Nisha Malik blinked quite rapidly.

"Sorry. Those were the first three prompts."

"Oh," she said. "Oh, I thought…."

"Sometimes context doesn't matter."

"What was the third one?"

"What puzzles you?"

"That one must be interesting to read."

"Fascinating. Sometimes I get an absolute laundry list. Those usually turn out to be the best writers."

"Djuna?"

"It's about five pages long. I think she was still writing when class ended."

"Oh," Nisha's voice broke.

She read through the three prompts quickly, quietly, as if a clock were running, I felt.

What do I miss most? My sister.

What do I miss least? Waiting for things to begin. Because now they have.

Nisha Malik closed the bluebook. "I think this might be too hard," she said. "Do you know we referred to UNC as her safety school?"

"Oh god," I said. "It's alright if you want to stop."

"I think I'll just have to go slow, that's all."

What puzzles me? Air (which is a secret way of saying everything. I just want to mention here that I like you already—don't tell the others. You seem cool. Like you're not trying too hard.)

Space travel. Why anyone would want to do it.

The way I feel about Kasim, my housemate, maybe my boyfriend. His brown-ness, which makes him almost too familiar to be a boyfriend if that makes any sense.

People's choice in artwork to hang on their walls.

My sister's past. Something that happened to her that she doesn't talk about.

I knew when she'd read that one: a tiny raise of her eyebrows.

My parents' death. How anyone could do that to another person. Make them beg for their life and then take it away.

How people discovered cooking made things taste better. I wish I had been there when the guy bumped the guy next to him, and that guy's piece of woolly mammoth or saber-toothed tiger fell into the fire and he was hungry enough or stupid enough to reach in and get it. Or maybe it wasn't a guy, maybe it was a woman, and she was alone, and she kept it a secret for days, just because she wanted to have this one thing that was totally hers and no one else's.

The way it feels to come home, right before I walk in the door. Sad and happy at the same time.

Plastic (or silk) indoor plants. How can you want them? Who (sorry, whom) do you think you're fooling?

Everyone else in this room right now.

The color lavender which is so beautiful that it's painful (see previous about coming home).

How our high school teachers love us and then forget us.

Dining halls.

Why Americans think all curry is yellow.

The color yellow.

My brother in law.

My sister's marriage.

That one, too. I could tell when she'd got there from the clench of her jaw.

Marriage.

Heaven.

Here, Nisha Malik looked up, shook her head to indicate, I guess, marvel, speechlessness, extreme grief revisited upon her. She inhaled as if she might scream. After a pause, she said it comforted her some to think of Djuna sitting in this classroom writing responses to these prompts. Then we listened to it: quiet, the hum from some piece of electrical equipment outside, unintelligible talk beyond the hallway, in a classroom, a professor maybe, then a student walking by, explaining something into her cell phone, planning for the weekend. Djuna in the air around us, inside a bubble of language, not knowing anything about what would happen that weekend, surrounded by other students wrapped in that same unknowing. All of them waiting for their lives to begin in some way, a trip home, a lonely stint in the library, a fraternity party, a first date or a second.

"Can you tell me anything about how she was in class? When she was writing?"

I thought for a bit, fixed a picture of her in my mind.

"Asleep," I said. "I mean, not literally. But that's how they all look when they're writing. Eyes cast down on the page. I always think how their mums would be jealous, how their mums miss seeing them like that, in peaceful slumber."

Nisha Malik didn't say anything. I thought she must have been thinking about her own mother, as I was of mine.

"Are you ready to go on?"

"I think so. I'll have to see."

An event that is interesting, humorous or embarrassing:

Too many to choose, Djuna wrote.

Something you found or find especially interesting and challenging:

Ditto.

"I'm sorry she didn't answer these," Nisha Malik said. "Your prompts are interesting. Where do they come from?"

"Out of my head."

The origins of an attitude or belief that you hold:

I believe my sister thinks of me more as her child than as her sister. She told me once that she had a miscarriage in college, just as her freshman year began. I believe she thinks of me as that lost child.

"It seems," Nisha Malik said, "that you may know quite a bit about me."

I didn't answer. Right then, I should have offered to let her take the journal away, but I couldn't. I was ready to tell her a fantastic lie, that the journal was school property, the Dean had told me the contents might be necessary evidence in the murder investigation. I had convinced myself that these things might actually be true.

"Is there more like this?" she asked. "I'd just like to be prepared."

"There's a bit."

A memory from your childhood that remains vivid:

My parents died in the Taj Hotel attacks in Mumbai in 2008. I still see my aunt coming across the room to tell me, how slowly she walked, how she cried so much that my uncle had to actually say the words.

When Nisha looked up from the page, there were tears in her eyes. "This," she began. "This is the sort of thing I want—I mean I've always wondered about that time for her. She was so young, and I was on the other side of the world. Now, especially, I feel I have to understand."

"I think reading her journal will help then. It may give you exactly what you're talking about."

"She wrote *journal* on the cover. It makes me feel like I shouldn't have even opened it."

"I tried to avoid that term in class because it seemed too personal. But really, the prompts got them there anyway." I pointed to the next one.

A family story that revealed something to you:

My sister and Michael talking about their college days together. So it's more than one story. He was dating her roommate and she dumped him. Her name was Sonia. My sister once went to a party dressed as Emily Dickinson and Michael's sister was there dressed as

Mother Teresa, and she got really drunk and my sister took care of her.
Michael becomes more human when he tells that story.

"Michael is my husband," Nisha Malik said.

"I gathered."

"Is there more about him?"

"Some."

Nisha Malik looked at her watch. "I have to get going," she said. "I'm on a meter." She slipped her bag over one shoulder, then stood. "I'll come back though. I will. I didn't know how it would feel to read what she wrote. Or this—" She swept her hand to the side, like brushing something away. She meant, I think, the classroom. "But I think it will be okay. Maybe even good."

She smiled a little, uncertain. I believed she had not done very much smiling lately.

Nisha Malik telephoned the next morning. After that, we began to speak regularly by phone, like people from the previous century. She wanted to say thanks, then to arrange another meeting, then to cancel. This went on for a couple of days. I didn't mind. I had heaps of time. And I confess some ambivalence. I was afraid if she returned, she would take the journal away.

At last she did not cancel, and we met again in the classroom, in the afternoon. We started as we had two days before, in our assigned seats, with the next prompt.

A place that struck you as unlike any other you'd ever seen:

"These are such good ideas," she said. Then she bent over the page.

Lucky Street Tattoos, on Highway 70, close enough to the airport that a person could walk. That seems like an interesting possibility: what to do if you have a long layover, since the tiny New Bern airport doesn't have a real restaurant. Inside there's an Asian theme going on, mostly Japanese, Samurai warriors, dragons, masks of mythological beasts with long, curved tusks. An orange sofa that looked comfortable, despite its awful color. On the far wall a slow-moving video of a fantastically and completely tattooed woman who was modeling for a male painter. He seemed to be drawing not her, but the designs on her body.

There was nothing for me to do but watch her read. I wasn't the least bit put out or bored. She was a character study: the many ways in which she didn't allow me to see her. She stopped reading after a few seconds to shrug off her coat. She curled her body away to catch the light from the window above us, she bent her head so that her black hair fell forward, hiding most of her face. She dug at the cuticle of her right index finger with a thumbnail. When she'd come to the end of the prompt, she looked up, but not at me.

"The tattooist thought I was Djuna's mom," Nisha said finally. "There was something about that… really about him…he was so young. His name was Troy. I loved it, being thought of as her mom."

I asked her why that was.

"I think because she was starting to feel gone. Isn't that horrible? Gone to college, I mean, grown up. Wise. Like she was seeing the three of us from a distance already."

"The family?"

"Yes. Like she was seeing us. Disintegrate."

I thought I'd best change the subject.

"I noticed the tattoo. One day, before class. And she saw me noticing and explained the meaning of it."

"She didn't make you guess?"

I thought that was a joke, but Nisha frowned and shook her head.

"She showed us the design and asked us to guess what it meant, the girl curled up that way. And we were so dense. We just couldn't get it. I remember she asked me, What would you be you feeling if you sit like that? Now I get it, that pain. Some days, I go over to that house and climb into Djuna's old bed and sit exactly like that."

I wondered about her saying *to that house.* I didn't know if I should ask a question. Really, I had already puzzled out the answer.

She turned to the next page.

An opinion that's changed in the last few months:

She followed the lines with her index finger, sometimes whispering a phrase, a single word.

White people: I didn't used to think about them much. I didn't really have to before the age of 8. My brother in law (my sister's husband) is white and I've pretty much grown up in their house, as much as I did in India—so there was a white guy around a lot of the time.

Nisha Malik stopped, looked up. We sat quietly for a time. I saw she was trying very hard not to cry. I felt my entire physical body and all my senses tensed toward her, waiting. And then, as if my attention had pushed her to do it, weep she did.

"What if I read it to you?" I said.

She seemed to consider that for a few seconds, and then she nodded.

A white guy eating Indian food, a white guy with Buddhist prayer flags hanging in his yard. He hung them as a defense against hurricanes—isn't that weirdly white? Like Blackly-white. Like old Black lady superstitious white. I'm not sure how I know what old Black ladies would do.

I glanced up at Nisha. She was smiling. "Your accent," she said. "It's good."

"Good?"

"It puts the words a bit at a distance. But it also makes them—I don't know how to say this—it's like you're reading from a novel, a published work."

Oh my, I thought. The irony.

But now there's this current horror of a president—a really white white guy—and most of my professors—white guys—you're a white guy—and some of my neighbors and some of the boys in my classes—white guys. Who don't eat Indian food or even know what a prayer flag looks like and seem so obviously white—like glow in the dark white.

Our neighbor, Felicity, who's white and I think may be pro-Brexit British but cooks better Indian food than my sister (but not as good as my mother). Felicity's son, Devin, who lives down the street from us in Carrboro, and is a strange angry white guy. He reminds me of Nick Rippons in Home Fires. *Like he can't help his own need to ruin something.*

I held the journal so she could see it, the bit Djuna wrote next. I couldn't read it out loud.

I'm not really afraid of him.

Nisha Malik put her head down on the desk. Something larger, unseen, come in through the wall and made itself felt.

"I wish…" she said, finally. "God. I wish she had been afraid. It's awful to wish that, but I do."

"I know."

At last, she raised her head.

"Is that all?" she said. "Can we end someplace happier?"

"There's a little bit."

Djuna went on: *So the opinion that's changed is about white people, specifically white men. I don't really like them very much, as a group. There are individuals of course (you, but of course, I don't know you very well and you might just turn out to be one of them). But now that I've written that, I can't think of any examples. Maybe my Chem professor—he's sort of sweet and goofy when he talks about his work on catalyst systems or about his partner. One of our neighbors, who dressed up on Halloween as The Wizard of the Neuse River and convinced me that I was the Keeper of the River. This was when I first came to live with my sister and he knew I needed something, some place of my own in the world, a way to belong. He brought me bags of shells and sea glass, "mermaid treasure," and notes from the mermaids in the river, written on scrunched up paper bags, with carrot tops attached to look like seaweed. The notes said the mermaids would only sing to me.*

Nisha shook her head. She said she was tired. I gave her my copy of *Home Fires*, and then she left.

Four days passed before I heard again from Nisha Malik. I wanted to phone her, but I knew that was not the way. And if she did call—I wondered during those four days—might it be only to ask for the journal? When her number finally appeared on my mobile screen. I answered after the second chime. I still did not know what to call her. "Nisha" seemed brazen.

"I liked the book," she said. "Thank you for loaning it to me."

I waited, not wanting to sound eager.

"I was thinking," she said, "that maybe I should take Djuna's journal. That way, I wouldn't—you could get on with your own work."

"It's no trouble, really," I said. My work? What on earth was my work? This office with its white walls, blank. The obvious lack of imagination. Beyond, the noisy life of the University—I could see it all from the windows here—liked I was locked in, myself in here, clutching the key.

"Are you sure?" Nisha said.

"Totally."

"All right."

I thought she sounded relieved—or I made her to sound so in my head.

"I read them an essay by David Sedaris. He's trying to learn conversational French. It's a great laugh. Then I asked them to write about their most memorable experience of trying to learn a foreign language. I asked them to think hard about the word *foreign*."

Nisha over the next pages. "It looks like Djuna wrote her usual laundry list."

"She did."

The language of orphan.

The language of missing mother.

The language of North Carolina. Bless Your Heart is not a blessing.

The language of Michael.

I stopped here in case Nisha did not want me to continue. Her eyes were closed.

My most memorable experience of trying to learn the language of Michael happened almost every day. It's a little like American sign language. Some of the gestures make perfect sense, but many of them seem random, like tics or palsy or flailing. It was like Michael was trying to learn the language of Michael. Like he'd been faking it every day for 36 years, every hour of every day scared that he might come up against a word or phrase he really didn't know. And all speakers of all languages were the enemy. My sister was the enemy; I was the enemy; the renters next door were the enemy. Dogs too. Money was okay. And fish were okay. Because when they opened their mouths, they were choking, dying, bleeding from the gills. And then he could eat them.

Nisha still did not open her eyes.

"Should I go on?"

"Yes."

That's all you need to know about the language of Michael.

Again, I waited in case she might need—I didn't know what she might need. After a few seconds, she opened her eyes and looked at me. "What's next?" she said.

"A dramatic event. It was a lesson about *in medias res*. I told them to start during."

Hurricane Bill, Djuna wrote. *My first hurricane. I'd been living with my sister less than a year.*

I pointed to the page. "Look here." Two lines blank.

"You can almost hear her thinking," Nisha said.

The empty lines are every bit as painful, but I wouldn't say that out loud.

Our neighbors in the big house invited us to stay there for the night. Their house had three floors, so we could all sleep above whatever water came up over the riverbank and the bulkheads. By "we all," I mean my sister and Michael and me, plus the renters in what we called the little house. She was a high school English teacher and her fiancé taught science. Their names were Ronald and Sarah. My sister really liked Sarah. They're still in touch, all these years later.

Our neighbors said we would have a hurricane party. We had never heard of that before, but we decided it must be something people did to use up all the food that would spoil when the storm knocked out the electricity, but also to calm themselves, find safety in numbers. Hurricanes were a fact of life, but people didn't used to worry about them so much. That's what my sister discovered.

Oh, but you said start during.

Ronald wore a suit and Sarah wore a velvet dress and heels, picking her way carefully across the wet lawn. Almost as soon as they were inside the power went out.

A lot of candles. Our neighbor had cooked a roast. I remember the house warmed up slowly and you could almost see it, the heat rising. We all went to bed.

Then it was dawn, the sun was coming up but still overcast, foggy. There seemed to be water in places where water had not been before. I wondered if the house had been cut off from the other four

on our road. Maybe we were an island now. Maybe we were float-
ing away, down the river toward the Pamlico Sound. My sister and I
would have to become mermaids. I really thought that then.

Two more blank lines.

But that's after. You said DURING.

Back to dinner: Ronald said the next weekend he was going to
meet his father for the first time. He said his father had left—run off
—before he was born. Something had happened to get them back in
touch. The hurricane party started to seem like an innocent version
of truth or dare. I worried that my sister would have to confess some-
thing, and I would have to hear it. I worried that she might be about to
say our parents weren't our parents. Or they were her parents but not
mine. I'd been keeping track of how many times she refilled her wine
glass, and it was a lot. She might say anything now, and I wouldn't be
able to stop her.

Three blank lines this time. Nisha and I looked at each other for
what felt like ages.

Later, the adults went out to walk in the storm. I was afraid to go
with them, but also afraid for them to go, afraid for Sarah in her velvet
dress and high heels, afraid that something would happen to Ronald
and he wouldn't get to meet his father. All six of them wore identical
yellow rain slickers ("foul weather gear" our neighbor called it). I
could tell my sister and Sarah because they were smaller than the
others, but then the perspective from the high window and the blowing
rain erased that distinction, and I couldn't tell who was who, and this
scared me even more—adults I depended on becoming aliens. They
walked south, facing away from me, their flashlights shining on each
other's backs, on displaced rocks, on sideways needles of rain. When
two of them clutched on to each other for support, I couldn't tell which
two they were or if they were the two that were supposed to go to-
gether. Our neighbor and his wife, my sister and Michael, Sarah and

Ronald. What if they weren't the right pairs? What would that mean? After a few minutes, they were so far away that all I could see were the flashlight beams, which seemed hysterical, sort of flailing, wildly out of control. The way I felt. I must have fallen asleep then or passed out from fear because I don't remember anything after that.

When the sun was fully up, Michael went next door to check on our house. He came back after ten minutes. He was crying. "It's dry," he sobbed. "It's totally dry."

My own voice caught in my throat. For a flash, I felt like I was Michael.

"I feel like I knew her," I said. "And you too, in a way."

"You did know her," Nisha said.

"Did she like college?"

"I think so," Nisha said. "She was figuring it out, how to navigate. She stayed up all night writing a paper on fake news and the protests in Charlottesville. She texted at 2:30 something like *This is college!* I coached her through the early hours of the morning, and then later convinced her to go to her 8 a.m. class. She sent me the paper afterwards, and it was a train wreck. She prided herself on functioning well on deadline. I thought about how to tell her there was a difference between *deadline* and *last minute*. But I decided she had to learn for herself. Now—I don't know how to think about even having had such a thought."

"I can't imagine."

Nisha said she had often found herself musing on the future. Would she and Djuna ever live very far from one another? Would a week go by when they didn't communicate? They would grow older together. She would stay healthy and not become a burden.

Now there was a hole in her brain, she said, where those ideas had been. Cold air whistled in and out. She pictured rock formations in the American west. One called The Needle: cold stone, desert wind rushing through, rushing from one nowhere to another.

One nowhere to another, we were. Two stone needles.

The next meeting was set for Thursday, at the very end of October, again in late afternoon, the first day you felt the chill of fall going to winter, the world tipping over the edge of dying into dead. The last of the sun played in and out of skeins of clouds.

"A traumatic moment."

"This one is hard, isn't it?" Nisha said. "I can tell from the look on your face."

"Aren't they all hard?"

"This one is worse then."

"It is."

I'm told that my mother died in the kitchen of the Taj Hotel, in the arms of a dishwasher who had tried to shield her with his body. He died too. Someone told me their faces were pressed together as if they were lovers trying to kiss, their bloody clothing fused as if they were joined at the heart. Which of course they were in the most horrible way.

I don't know what I mean by "of course."

Nisha had fallen into her usual stillness, eyes closed. She was wearing a lavender sweater, a sweet color against her skin, the shades of cloth and skin softening each other, almost moving, back and forth, alternating beams of light and shadow.

"Then I told them to go a little deeper."

The deepest I can go is that I hate the waiter. I hate him with a passion that makes me feel hot and furious. I hate his failure. He was a fucking failure. He got this one chance to do good in the world and he screwed it up. He didn't protect my mother. He didn't save her life. I hate him. I could write that sentence a billion times, and it wouldn't be enough. I hate him. And I hate him even more for being the last person to feel my mother's breath on his cheek, and her heart beat against his scrawny, useless chest. Why should he have that privilege? Why him and not me?

Suddenly, there was no more light in the basement classroom. Nisha reached blindly for my hand—I didn't know what it meant, but her grip was so tight that it left a bruise on my wrist, though I felt as if I must be hurting her.

"I don't think I want to be in this room anymore," she said.

"I know. I understand. There are other places on campus. The library."

"I don't really want to see any students. Or be near them."

"I rent a house on the road behind Franklin Street. It's very quiet."

The classroom was too dark for me to make out the expression on her face when she said, Yes, please.

The rental agent had called this little blue house a bungalow, because of the wide porch and the attic dormers. It gave me a start, *The Bungalow* being the title of my father's last novel. The agent had said it was odd for this house not to be rented, with its large back garden and fishpond, and my appearance that day must have been fate. The bungalow in Rosemary Street. Rosemary was—is?—my mother's name. Of course I was meant to live there.

"I don't know how you can leave here every day," Nisha said after I showed her through the rooms, a quick tour indeed, and out to the garden. "It's so calm. And the pond. I'd like that nearby. I'd sit out here all the time. The sound of water can be so soothing." We looked back toward the house. "The blue is different." She meant, I think, not Carolina blue, that powdery, airy shade. "Greener."

"Sometimes I do have a hard time getting myself out the door." I offered tea or coffee, but she refused. "Sit anyplace you like. There are a lot of options."

This was the main oddity of the house. In so small a space, so much furniture: two sofas, larger and small, two boxy armchairs pushed snugly together, a rocking chair, another quite lovely dark wood chair in the California Mission style (so the rental agent had explained, looking pleased with himself). I wondered where Nisha would settle.

Oh, but the teddy bear. She stared at it for a moment, then picked it up, smoothed the red bow around its neck.

"These come with flower arrangements," she said. "For sick children."

I explained that it had been in the classroom and why it was here now. Without comment, she set it back on the sofa.

She chose one of the paired armchairs, maybe thinking best to resume our side-by-side reading of Djuna's journal. She had carried the journal all the way from the classroom. Just past South Hall, I thought she might walk off into the evening with Djuna's journal, and I might never see either of them again.

Now I eased into the chair beside her—it was a bit too small— and she opened the journal. I saw she had been marking the page with her index finger. She placed the journal between us where the arms of the chairs made a wee table.

"This is a good one to end on," I said. "I know it's getting late."
Nisha nodded.

"Lighter, her writing I mean. Sweet, even a bit of a laugh. I asked them to write about their superpowers."

I can fly, so I always have to wear trousers.

I can see through walls. Not through. Into. So I know a great deal about electrical wiring. The room on the other side is usually empty, and not worth looking into. Sometimes a man or a woman passes through to get to a farther room.

I can change the past, but I don't. I let it be. I don't have any clue about what should have happened. That's not true, of course, Mr. McFadden. I can't change the past, and so it just sucks. But sometimes I change it in my imagination and that feels like a superpower.

Nisha put her hand on my arm. "Stop for a minute," she said. "This is just…this is a part of her I didn't know."

We sat in the blue stillness of the bungalow in Rosemary Street. I think Nisha whispered the word *magic*, but I've never been sure. Around my house, the late autumn night was perfectly quiet. The world had gone far away to get its dinner.

"Read that again, please, Liam."

I did.

"There's more." She tapped her finger on the page.

I knew Nisha was smiling. Because I was. I felt rather than saw it.

I can cause men to fall madly in love with me, and so I join a convent. But there is a gardener, a man.

I can cause great riches to come my way, so I must separate from my family because they will ask for money and I will give it to them, and they will ruin their lives.

I can write brilliant poems, and so I do, except for every eighth poem, which is a bad rhyming poem using moon and June and swoon, so that no one will suspect. The others I leave in libraries where clever, oversexed scholars will find them.

"Oversexed?" Nisha said. She tried to laugh, but the sound of it was awful to hear. Not a laugh, choking more like. So I reached for her. We looked at each other for a long time.

"Sure, no one has used that word in fifty years," I said. "How did she even know it?"

"More and more, I'm amazed by what she knew. But I think I ought to be getting back now."

"Are you sure you won't have a coffee? It's a long drive."

"Well," she said. "If you don't mind."

I struggled out of the chair and went into the kitchen. Would Nisha follow, I thought, but best not. What might she think of me with my French press and Peets coffee.

"It's so kind of you to do this for me." Somehow, Nisha had come into the kitchen without my being aware. "All of this."

"It's good of you to keep making the journey." I thought then the whole house of cards might collapse—she would ask to take the journal, and I would be helpless to refuse. I spilled ground coffee on the counter.

"It's good for me to get away," she said.

"That's a bit of why I'm here." I heard myself say the words as if from the other side of the world.

She didn't ask any questions, and I was grateful. I went about finishing the coffee and pouring it into mugs. I took the carton of milk from the fridge, put out sugar and a teaspoon.

We seemed to have run out of things to say to each other—or maybe there was too much to say. She drank her coffee quickly and was gone.

Without discussion, we began to meet at my house in Rosemary Street. We sat in our same chairs, every meeting, as my students do, as if they'd been assigned.

"I asked them to tell a myth with themselves in the starring role."

Can I correct the myth? Djuna wrote. *Of course I can. That's the only way to make this prompt interesting (sorry). I mean, think about it. Who would want to be in the starring role of most myths? Sisyphus? No, thank you. Leda and the Swan? Europa? Um, no. I wouldn't want to be frozen or drowned or turned into a tree.*

Djuna left two lines blank to do her thinking.

I'm fairly sure you mean western mythology. Eastern gods and goddesses behave differently. Still, the western myth I think about all the time is Icarus. He was so close. Not just to the sun—but to making it work. I would fly a little lower. Under the radar.

But if I were to do the assignment as you wrote it, I'd assume the role of Durga Puja. In Bengali myth, she defeated the evil, egotistical buffalo demon Marisashura, who is basically an early incarnation of our current president. One way she did it was by using her ten arms, but what really worked for her was a prophecy that the demon would be killed by a woman. So of course Marisashura assumed that meant he was immortal.

Ten arms. You know what that is? It's SOP. Standard Operating Procedure. All women have ten arms—maybe more. Ten arms. Code for multi-tasking. SLEIGHT OF HAND.

I showed Nisha her sister had written all in caps.

Great pun, isn't it, Mr. McFadden?

"She was so adept at language," Nisha said.

"Did she get that from your parents?"

"From our mother mostly. She was a great reader."

"And you too?"

"Not really. My head is for numbers. I work in a pharmacy."

"That's about to come up."

Outside, there was a clap of thunder, like a pronouncement, a warning. Raindrops spattered against the window. We turned back to the journal.

"I asked them to recall their childhood selves and was there something they said or believed that they now know to be a bit mad."

When I was little, I believed my sister was a drug dealer.

Nisha laughed out loud.

I didn't have any real concept of "pharmacist." She was far away, in America. I heard my parents talking about her graduate study. Why would she want to do that? my father asked my mother. And my mother had answered, Because it's the opposite of what you do. The most unlike thing imaginable. My father was a diplomat. He worked for the Indian government. What, I wondered, was the farthest thing from that? In my child mind, my sister's work was something like the dark arts, all that was shady, illegal, anti-government. I knew drugs were involved. I knew she was in New York studying how to make drugs. She was enrolled in courses like Medicinal Chemistry, Biochemistry, Compounding. My parents seemed frightened for her, maybe even frightened of her. During her one visit to Mumbai, she asked all the relatives what medicines they took.

"So I did," Nisha said.

I knew there was a drug problem in Mumbai. Our teachers talked about it at school. It's the Americans, they said. The tourists are bringing drugs into the country. Now I know that's not true. But every day, every hour, of the two weeks my sister was with us, I believed she was selling drugs to people in the streets. I also believed that she would be caught and killed by the police. So when she flew back to America, I was relieved. But because I loved her very much, I was also terribly sad. I thought I would probably never see her again. The drug dogs at the airport would sniff her out, and that would be the end.

But she called and seemed fine. Still I was afraid to talk to her. It was as if I knew this terrible secret about her that no one else knew, and she didn't suspect me.

I let go of this idea slowly, over the next two years or so. And now it is somewhat ironic, given the drug problems in this county. Last year, two people in my school died from drug overdoses. Pain pills. They seem easy to get. My best friend smokes a lot of pot, and I'm afraid she's headed for worse.

"This friend, do you know her?" I said.

"She's talking about Jamie," Nisha said. "I worry about her too.

I imagine she's having a really hard time with this."

For a time, we were quiet, watching the rain fall.

"How does it feel," she began, "to be the keeper of all these secrets for all these… children?"

"If I'm totally honest," I said. "I hope it's useful."

"In what way?"

I remembered the conversation with my father, before I even set foot in North Carolina.

"To get the big picture. Think about what's happened to them. The unexamined life, it's not worth living, is it?"

"Don't you hear that in Djuna's journal?" Nisha asked. "I'm aware of it on almost every page, in her voice. Sometimes even in the skipped lines. She's examining."

"But I can't do anything with what they tell me. I can't help them if they're in distress—"

"Yes, you can. Of *course* you can. Suggest they see a counselor. Alert the Dean of Students. He seems like such a nice man."

"I did that early in the semester. I asked a student about one of his journal entries. And he looked at me like I was completely mad *and* a monster. He said it was none of my business. He must have thought I wasn't actually reading what they wrote."

"Probably no one ever did before." Nisha shook her head as if to clear it. "But I don't know about the others or what's in their journals. I know my sister's, though. It's like—I can't explain it exactly. Like you gave her space to sort of expand."

"For Djuna yes. About the rest, who knows?"

"Do they ever inspire you?"

"Djuna did."

"Ironic, then, isn't it?"

"Sometimes, I think I might want to write *about* her."

"I know what you mean. A way to keep her around. Sort of get her back. I've thought of that too often."

"You have?" I couldn't help sounding horrified, maybe a bit angry.

Nisha didn't say anything. I felt her shrink away from me a little, fold back into herself.

"Construct an argument between three people. Djuna has notes here, titled *living off campus*."

"I don't need to read that one," Nisha said. "I know how it went. I said maybe next year. Michael said no. Djuna argued us into submission."

At certain points, she said, the argument became ethnic and religious, so Michael was locked out by virtue (or the lack of it) of his being white and male and Christian, and everybody had their feelings hurt in one way or another.

"It's the moment I wish I could have back," Nisha said. "Or when our neighbor said *I have a son in Chapel Hill*. Sometimes I picture those seven words like barbed wire. They're stretched across the air. And then I feel like I'm taking hold of the words, and the pain. I feel the shock of it in my hands."

"He's the one shot them."

"Yes. Devin."

I could see it too, could see exactly what she meant, the hammer claw I, the top of the first h, the slicing curve of the uppercase C and the two-pronged uppercase H. If you pictured the words like that you would know what they were: a death sentence. Literally.

We stared a bit then, there in my living room. I believed I knew what would happen, though I didn't know when.

"Shall we keep going?"

"Sometimes this feels like I'm in a speeding car, rushing downhill with no brakes. I can't stop, and the end is just…the end."

"Yes."

"So let's just keep going."

"Someone asked you to weigh the benefits of college. That's the next one."

Sometimes when I heard my sister and Michael talk about their college days, I felt like I didn't want to have anything to do with college. For instance: they took a course on rationalist philosophy together. I mean really, who has time for shit like that? There was something about a glass breaking because it knows it's hit the ground. Look at the president! I want to say to them. Everything in America is broken. Who cares about a stupid glass?

What color should be added to the Crayola 64 box? One caveat: the box cannot accommodate any more than 64 crayons. What color do you take out?

Add: immigrant brown

Remove: white. It doesn't show up anyway.

Nisha did not say anything, and wasn't that the perfect reply, the response I wanted, to disappear under her sister's words, to write myself out of the story, or rather to write it so tightly around myself that I disappeared inside of it. And became something else entirely. Like a metamorphosis. Or maybe we could do that together somehow, Nisha and I, write the story and wrap it around ourselves like a duvet.

The sweetest, most embarrassing thing an adult ever did in your presence.

Djuna wrote: *My sister and me and the Taylor Swift song Love Story on the dance floor at a wedding reception. My sister acted out the song. Most of the guests had just arrived from India, and they were exhausted from traveling. The reception reminded me of a fairy tale, everyone asleep at the tables, in armchairs, in the Century Club library. Like in Sleeping Beauty, after she pricks her finger on a thorn. By the way I know it's a spindle, but I don't like that version. What would she be doing spinning anyway?*

"Oh Djuna," Nisha said. "This happened before our parents died." She shifted in her chair to face me, which she had not done before. "They brought Djuna to the States with them, to a cousin's wedding in New York. It was a great party, in Manhattan, at the Century Club. But Djuna and I—I was so happy to see her. The joy of it kept her awake."

"The joy of it kept her awake."

"That's what I said."

"That's brilliant. Poetic."

She looked both pleased with herself and embarrassed to have been caught so completely inside this memory.

"Sorry to interrupt. Go on."

"We wandered around the Century Club, mostly quiet, giggling at all the conked-out relatives. The servers had stopped bothering to pass trays, just left them on the tables, so we grazed here and there, circling back to the dance floor, where the bride and groom were."

"Everyone can't have been asleep."

"I know that. I know it in my rational mind, but I like this version better."

"You're doing what Djuna did."

"Am I?" Nisha turned again, more—the word I thought later was *decisively*—toward me.

"Please go on."

"I seem to remember that the DJ or whoever it was played only quiet songs that wouldn't wake anybody. No 'She's a Brick House'— crazy. I know. I discovered this about fifteen years ago. That song is an American wedding thing. I don't really understand it. I don't remember the name of the band. Is the *she* supposed to be the bride? Anyway, Djuna and I started dancing. Then that Taylor Swift song started. 'Love Story' I think it's called. Maybe you don't know that one either. I don't know what came over me, but at the lines 'he knelt to the ground and pulled out a ring,' I did that, as if I were asking Djuna to marry me—or not marry me, but you know—just acting out the song. That part of the song."

Nisha stared off into the distance. "And the next lines are 'Marry me, Juliet, you never have to be alone.' I promised her that. And now she is alone."

I wanted to say, No she's not. I wanted to say, She's with your parents. Just like Shamus was with our parents.

"I can't get away from my memory," Nisha said. "It's not good for anything. It's not going to bring her back."

"In almost every prompt, I think, I asked the students to remember something. Even when I asked them to invent a thing, didn't they just go on remembering."

"Your accent," Nisha said. "It's like some magical language that runs parallel to English. Torn for thorn, tink for think, ting for thing."

"Magical?"

"It takes me out of this world, away from this life. A little bit."

"And that's good."

"Yes.

"Then I'm glad. Though I worry that all this is too much for you."

"It is, but we can't really stop now."

What she meant by that I didn't know, nor did I know how to ask.

"It's time to go," Nisha said. "I have to work tomorrow, but I'll be back Friday." She said she planned to check into a hotel, see some friends, eat in a nice restaurant, see a film. All those exotic things, she said. I wondered if this was a kind of invitation. Once again, I didn't know how to ask.

I had warned the class there would be poetry in the Troubles

Book Club. Here's some great trouble, I said. "The Waste Land." Was it also a political poem? Could a political poem ever be any good? The students had thought about this as much as they had thought about breakfast, which is to say hardly ever. This was near the end of September. The discussions took fire. "The Love Song of J. Alfred Prufrock," a funny poem they said, but also sad. Do I dare to eat a peach? Come on, they said. The guy can't even decide that much? Really?

The students loved "Howl," its bawdy anger, the raging at universities so close to what they felt right now. I showed them the footnote, with its fifteen "Holy!s" in the first line. The bum is holy, the nose is holy. At last we came to the hard question: could the politics ever be wrong?

I wanted them to write an imagist poem. I read them the famous one about the metro station in Paris, by the famously wrong-headed Ezra Pound.

"Do you know it?" I asked Nisha. She didn't, so I recited it. "I told them to look at what was in the room, on their desks. Djuna didn't know what to do, so she raised her hand and asked the question everyone was thinking: What do you want from us? I thought that was very brave of her. I don't remember what I said in response, only that it didn't seem to be very helpful."

"I don't think there's ever a right answer to that question."

"This is what she wrote."

Black Lives Matter water bottle stands alone
A brown scowl, an open mouth, a cry.

"The inside of a ping pong ball, I said. Describe it. Start with *it's like.*"

Djuna wrote

It's like the moon turned inside out
Jack cheese not Swiss

Peppered with pocks
You don't so much want to eat it as lick it
Like icing
Or it's like a snow cave, iced sides silent.
You shouldn't go in there, but you want to.

"She actually texted me this one," Nisha said. "I wondered what it meant. I texted her back and asked if she was okay. If she was getting along with her housemates."

"Was she?"

"She said things were great in the house. She said they were still trying to work out on a rotation for cooking meals. She said sometimes she liked eating by herself, but she wasn't sure if she could say that."

Nisha began to cry, and I put my arms around her, and then she was kissing me. Or, to be fair, I was kissing her. I'm not exactly sure how it happened, who kissed whom first. The scent of her: floral and sweet. I think it was only minutes before we were on the green carpet, our clothes in disarray. I knew I was in strange and dangerous territory, and also that I did not care. I don't know if Nisha felt the same. I wondered abstractly if I had locked the front door—sometimes the landlord dropped by unannounced to see what I was doing. I don't think he liked my accent. Then I didn't think anymore, though I was aware of what our bodies were doing, as watching from above or beside or both at once. Like dreaming, it was. How can someone be tender and ferocious at the same time? I am not just talking about myself now.

We half-pushed, half-dragged each other into the bedroom. She asked if the bed was mine, and I told her not a thing in the house belonged to me.

"You're right about that," was what she said.

There is some rule in the civilized world about this sort of encounter, perhaps more than one rule. A married woman. A grieving woman. Thou shalt not. A rule made of fragments, of broken ideas, verbs without objects. No way to exit gracefully. I understand why film directors give a couple the stage business of smoking cigarettes afterwards. So they can't speak. So that they will worry not about what's just happened but that they may inadvertently set themselves on fire. A bit of a problem, then, if neither one smokes.

"I'm sorry," Nisha said.

"Please don't be. I'm not."

She didn't say anything else for a few minutes. I was glad Djuna's journal was in the other room, a bit more magical thinking on my part, that what she'd written there was a kind of still-active consciousness, a way of knowing and sensing. Djuna might have been able to see us.

"You'd probably like for me to go."

I had in mind to say something like *if I did, I would say so*, but caught myself in time. What an ugly sentence, really a dismissal of the most callous sort. Who on earth gives voice to that kind of thing?

So I said nothing and we lay there, arms barely touching, for twenty minutes or so. Then Nisha rose from the bed and walked in the living room, I thought to gather her clothes. She came back with her sister's journal, handed it to me, and pulled the duvet over herself.

"What's next?" she asked.

"Are you sure?"

"I am."

I opened the journal. "A poem about an historical figure. You can see she made her usual list."

Indira Gandhi
Benazir Bhutto
Hillary Clinton
Parvati

"I don't know who that last one is," I said. "I should have looked it up, but I never did."

"Parvati is her second namesake."

"Who's her first?"

"Djuna Barnes."

"Ah, yes. She writes about that later."

"Our parents had some funny ideas."

"I think you should recite this one."

Nisha read through the poem silently, then looked at me with this completely lovely mixture of embarrassment and admiration. Not for me. For the poem and the poet.

When we made love, he held my arms
Over my head. All of them. So it was a busy night.
I hated him. He made me put my weapons
On the floor. No carpet so
The clanking was a din,
Except for the rope. My last left hand
Reached for it. 3 a.m. Can you tie me
To the headboard, my wrists.
Was there enough rope, he asked.
Never, I said.

The effect was frightening, exhilarating. It was as if they were all there in the room, Nisha, Djuna, and the goddess herself.

"I don't know how she knew to write a poem like this," Nisha said.

I lifted my finger from the page and drew it over the curve of her lips.

Nisha said she imagined that somewhere Djuna was leading the life of this second namesake. Not leading the life. Leading the death? She didn't know how to phrase it. Something about the next world. In the next world, she was Parvati, absorbed by Parvati. Merged. Language was so useless, she said, and I agreed. Language was sickly. Nisha wanted to rage against it. Djuna was *elsewhere*, she said, just in the next county from home, astride her tiger on Atlantic Beach. Dawon is the tiger's name. A gift from her father, the living version of the tiger necklace he presented her on her 7th birthday. Oh no, Djuna had said when she opened the package and clasped the necklace around her throat. Now the tiger is riding me. They had a cake every year, with candles, the western way.

"Every year, our mother said, make a wish that you will practice humility, and then she laughed. I remember Daddy took her hand across the space between their chairs. 'You go first,' he said. Mommy laughed even louder. 'It's my New Year's resolution,' she said. 'Every year. And Lent too. Which I don't really believe in.'"

"Lent?" I asked.

"They celebrated all the holidays. I remember New Year's Eve as one of the happiest times," Nisha said. "I wondered if Djuna remembered it the same way, but I was afraid to make her sad by asking. And now it's too late."

But the *elsewhere*, Nisha said, Djuna elsewhere. If only she could invent that geography and keep the thought alive in her mind, make the imagining a habit, like tooth-brushing. Not an idea that swims into consciousness and away again, a mermaid of a notion. Djuna on a tiger, but with fewer arms. Eight was too many, too crowded. Also, this Djuna didn't need so many weapons. Five was plenty. The discus was useful—maybe it could be more like a ninja star—what kind of weapon was a discus anyway? The trident too, that strange intersection of Greek and Hindu myth, obviously, for fishing in the Neuse River or the Atlantic Ocean, during peaceful times. The conch shell for making oneself heard. And the bell, for announcement. For warning. The mace could probably be put away. But the noose. Necessary in North

Carolina.

"Djuna could shout at the white men in white sheets," Nisha said. "Look y'all. I have one of those too!"

She didn't need the bow and arrow. She didn't need the scimitar. In the afterlife, she would have no need for a shield.

"In Hindi, the words are *chakra, shankha, gada, trishula, ghanta, phanda*," Nisha said.

A poem, I thought. That's what it sounds like. That's how Djuna Malik could write such poems.

At some point, Djuna would drop all these weapons and embrace Nisha with her many arms.

But now Djuna couldn't do that.

But I could.

She carried a particular scent, I noticed. Always the same, mixed in the same proportion. Roses and vanilla.

"This hurts so much," Nisha said after a while. "Not this." She touched my shoulder. "Not you, but everything else. For a few days, I could scream. I did scream. In the hospital. After. Sometimes now, I have to stop walking and bend over or crouch down because of the pain. In the park by the river. In the cereal aisle at the grocery store."

Every inch of her body burning with electric horror. Alive with absence. Hollowed out. A giant knife had carved out her insides, from her neck to her ankles, and then filled this space with pain. She was a human-shaped tube frozen full of agony in the midst of the living world. She didn't care who saw. She had no room for shame. She said that to me as she kissed me. *I have no more room for shame.*

Sometimes, Nisha wanted to read aloud from her sister's journal, read my words in the form of the prompts and then read her sister's back to me. I loved her voice, which was pitched at mezzo and a bit scratchy around the edges. I could listen to that voice, whispering in my ear, forever.

"'Write about a food that has some special meaning,'" she read. "'I want to smell this food, see it, taste it. Feel the burn.' Were you feeling hungry that day?"

"Likely so," I said. "There was a place in Dublin, not a great restaurant, but good enough, catered a bit to the tourist trade, called Sheerson's, where I used to go just for the shepherd's pie. I was missing that, I think."

Nisha was not surprised that Djuna had written about tikka masala, that her mother's had been better than Nisha's, but the neighbor, Felicity, hers was better than her mother's.

When she first brought it, she was embarrassed, and her shame had made it difficult for her to speak. Which was a puzzle when the object of the visit is to meet the neighbors.

Felicity's masala carried
Along the bulkhead
Close to the edge in case
She fell in, or to make that falling
Easier. You could catch the scent approaching
The ginger mostly. Ginger and marine,
Needle and metal.

"Oh my," Nisha said.

"She had some talent."

"Has," Nisha said, "I want to use the present tense."

I said I would do whatever she wanted. I meant it in every sense.

"Djuna said she loved it when you read to them."

"What would you like me to read?"

She said, Something you love, something you can't ever forget.

I knew some parts of it by heart. I could recite these parts on command, like Americans do their pledge of allegiance in school.

She was fast asleep. Gabriel, leaning on his elbow, looked for a few moments unresentfully on her tangled hair and half open mouth, listening to her deep-drawn breath. So she had had that romance in her life: a man had died for her sake. It hardly pained him now to think how poor a part he, her husband, had played in her life. He watched her while she slept, as though he and she had never lived together as man and wife.

I stopped here, moved on to a particular line I wanted to say to Nisha.

Perhaps she had not told him all the story.

A few light taps upon the pane made him turn to the window. It had begun to snow again. He watched sleepily the flakes, silver and dark, falling obliquely against the lamplight. The time had come for him to set out on his journey westward. Yes, the newspapers were right: snow was general all over Ireland. It was falling on every part of the dark central plain, on the treeless hills, falling softly upon the Bog of Allen and, farther westward, softly falling into the dark mutinous Shannon waves. It was falling, too, upon every part of the lonely churchyard on the hill where Michael Furey lay buried. It lay thickly drifted on the crooked crosses and headstones, on the spears of the little gate, on the barren thorns. His soul swooned slowly as he heard the snow falling faintly through the universe and faintly falling, like the descent of their last end, upon all the living and the dead.

"You should read this one." I didn't tell say its name. I couldn't. I had it in several versions, in my office and here in the bungalow, anthologized and also published with the rest of the stories. I knew its exact location among my books, always, everywhere I had ever lived. A lucky alphabetical happenstance, Joyce was always in the middle of things.

But at that moment, I was already late for my office hours. I could hardly believe my own cheekiness suggesting she stay and read the whole story, and then we could talk about it when I got back.

"Yes," Nisha said. "I'd like that."

The sensation of locking the door to the bungalow in Rosemary Street with Nisha Malik safe inside. The *sensation.* Wonder and joy. And fear, too. I imagined her moving through the rooms, touching the clothes in my wardrobe, the papers on my desk. I had nothing to hide from her. She could steal whatever she wanted. I felt then that I would give it all, willingly, down to the last crumb, teacup, postage stamp. She had a strange power over me. If she knew this, she would probably have hated to use it.

The campus on Friday mornings always had a wrecked, abandoned look about it (I still didn't understand the American college student practice of beginning the weekend on Thursday night). You had the sense that anybody moving about the buildings and grounds on Fridays was probably not very much fun. Myself included, I thought, quite suddenly. Inside the bungalow, with Nisha, I was a fascinating, somewhat exotic personage, with original ideas and the ability to turn a shapely phrase. Out here, I was exposed as a bore, a stodgy grownup whose life was already half over.

I stayed in my office for the required two hours. There were many good reasons to do so, the fulfillment of my contract chief among them. And I wanted to give Nisha time to finish the story, to think about it, to miss me, to perhaps imagine me as Michael Furey, though not all the way to the bitter end. Of course, I also had essays to read, class preparations for the next week, though I must say my heart was not in any of it, had scarcely been for weeks. Most of that time in my office, I listened: to the hum of the empty building, birdsong, odd, lonely-sounding student voices echoing between stone and brick, Greenlaw and Lenoir dining hall. The daylight, the sky, was full of sound too, the clouds seeming to emit a faint whistle as they moved past my window. Also an electricity inside my head that I recognized as a story taking shape, gears grinding, parts locking into place. I hardly dared move in case I should disturb this careful assembling, which seemed to be taking place quite outside my control.

In the last quarter-hour, I heard footsteps, not purposeful, and I wondered would I be in for it—conversation that would drag on in the usual way, the administration, the state government, the president. Never about books, which completely surprised me at first, but I was becoming accustomed to the rhythms and omissions which must, I felt, be endured.

The Associate Department Chair leaned in from the hallway, carefully, as if crossing the threshold would be harmful to his health.

"Liam," he said. "Really. On a Friday."

"But aren't you as well?" I sounded cheerful, optimistic, almost glad for the company. A great bit of acting, wasn't it.

"Good quiet time. I bet you're getting writing done. Sorry to disturb."

But he didn't withdraw or otherwise indicate departure. I opened my hands over the desk. "Marking essays," I said. "Endless."

"Right," he said, moving a step to the right so he was fully framed in the doorway. "I wonder if you've heard that Roger's retiring next year."

"I've heard whispers."

"So we'll need to replace him."

"I don't think Roger could ever be replaced."

"And if you had a book contract by then, which no doubt you will…. I understand the students really like you already."

I didn't know what to say. Contract. You will. *Really like*. It seemed this encounter had turned into a sort of nightmare job interview.

"But you know," he went on, lowering his voice, "a certain faction will want to hire a woman. A woman *of color*." He rolled his eyes, and then actually winked, this man with whom I had had exactly zero social interaction, as if we were drinking mates. "Too bad *you* didn't write *The Widening Sky*."

Nisha had fallen asleep on the sofa, the duvet from my bed pulled to her chin, the book closed over the fingers of her right hand. She had made herself a cup of tea. I didn't want to wake her, bring her back to the consciousness of all that we were doing. Maybe she could forget in sleep all her dead, and I could forget mine. I moved quietly into the kitchen, and set up my folder of papers at the high counter, positioning myself where I could watch her sleep, relieved to be once again, the fascinating, accomplished personage. Writing excruciatingly earnest notes in the margins of my students' papers, explaining them to themselves—the arrogance! Really, I was explaining myself to myself, trying to conclude, to write my way out, to make a tidy summary, an epiphany, an *apology*.

"Does everyone think this story is about them?" Nisha was awake, looking at me. "I mean one way or another. Either the lost love or finally understanding that you never knew this important thing about someone."

I had never thought of it like that.

"And," she continued, "there's always a party. And everyone is supposed to be happy, and really everyone is, until some sort of balance tips…"

I was afraid to speak. She had not asked me to say anything.

She went on. "It doesn't make sense, does it? Who lives and who doesn't get to live?"

I half expected to hear the tap of snowfall against the kitchen window, but instead there was only the purr of cars moving along Rosemary Street, the agitation of the neighbor's wind chime, a bell ringing somewhere far away.

It seemed a kind of magic that the next prompt was this one.

"It's write about home, and –"

"She wrote about Mumbai."

"She didn't."

An ordinary person, Djuna wrote, *would have trouble finding Mariana on a map. The GPS auto-corrects to* marina, *and then you're sunk.*

"That was Djuna's joke, one of her all-time best," Nisha said. "She was very good at puns."

"The highest form of humor."

Driving toward town from the north on the main highway, you had to pass a sunken boat, half submerged and rolled to starboard. The name was only half visible, L-a-y- but people might guess, Layla, *like the Eric Clapton song. The* Layla *had been waterlogged there at least ten years, and still as far as Nisha knew, no one claimed or removed her. Hurricanes did not harm* Layla, *which looked to have been a trawler with an enclosed cockpit. She rose with the storm waters, caught between marsh grasses and a ruined dock. Thus, that section of the highway has an abandon hope all you who enter look to it, which no one in Mariana ever talked about, except, in town lore, a visiting priest who was never invited back.*

Visitors to Mariana came away with two statistics: Mariana had more registered sailboats than residents and the lowest crime rate per capita in the state. You couldn't find a restaurant open after 9 p.m. on a Saturday night. The health club parking lot was full by 6:30 a.m., and late-comers had to find space beside the boarded-up grocery store and walk across an empty lot in between. A Walmart came to town, ran the grocery store out of business and closed inside of a year, leaving the town with no grocery until the Piggly Wiggly, 20 miles away, opened an outpost, affectionately known as The Piglet.

The Piglet did not sell pork rinds, but you could find bleu cheese stuffed olives, Seven kinds of IPA, and gelato.

Mariana had a music society, a film society, a women's club, two veterinarians and five churches. The bank president was also the mayor, which seems like a weird conflict of interest. She drove a red corvette in the parades, of which there were two: Christmas and Fourth of July. Afterwards, crushed candy shone along the parade route, as if Broad and Hodges Streets were bordered with rubies. Like those Russian pictures of holy people or The Peacock Throne.

"I remember she wrote that in her college essay." Nisha said. "I thought it was so beautiful, but not like anything else she'd ever written. I wondered if she read it somewhere. How did you think of that? I asked her. She said she was just driving around and the streetlights caught the wrappers and it was so strange and exotic."

I was a flower girl in the town's park soon after I came to live with Nisha and Michael. The bride's grown daughter sang a Hawaiian love song, and I had to keep myself from crying because I might ruin my new dress, embarrass the bride, but it was very hard because my own parents, who had been married for a very long time, had just died in Mumbai. I was a flower girl in three weddings in Mariana, all at the river's edge. It seems like important parts of a life take place on an edge and are in fact an edge, not an ending or a beginning as everyone seems to think.

"I asked her how she got so wise," Nisha said, "but she just shrugged and said sometimes she felt really old. Sometimes I wonder if that's the way to think about what happened. She was older than her years, and so…."

"That isn't any help, is it?"

"No. None at all."

Mariana was home to a foundation that made its money from timber sales and mostly funded college scholarships, including mine.

The foundation also owned four attached cottages a block back from the river, reserved for 'ladies of limited means.' There were never vacancies for more than a week. In the late spring and summer, the ladies sat on their porches or wheeled their walkers down to the park. On Halloween, they received trick or treaters. For Christmas, the Methodist Church sent carolers.

I hate writing about this because it makes me so sad. Twice sad, because my mother will never live there, and even if she could, it would be because my father was dead. Which he is. Which they are.

I walk past those places. And I wave to the ladies and admire the seasonal decorations on their porches, their patio tomatoes and basil in the summer, pots of yellow and burnt red mums, pumpkins carved and not, lights blinking red and green at Christmas, heart-shaped wreaths, impatiens, lobelia, nasturtiums in spring. It feels like visiting my mother's grave. If she had a grave. If I could visit it.

"Sometimes," Nisha said, "I think I see my mother. Across the river—like she's standing on the far shore. Sometimes floating in the air. When I walk by the river, I always take binoculars. So I can look across and be sure."

"Sure of which? That she is or that she isn't?"

"Just sure."

"And maybe spot a mermaid?"

"There's that too."

"The next prompt…I should warn you. Gun violence. Her first sentence was one hundred percent correct."

I predict you will get the same response from everyone in the class. I'm scared shitless. I don't have a gun. I don't know how to fire a gun. I know I will never learn. My brother-in-law has guns. They are downstairs in our house. I went looking for them a couple of days before I came to college. I had planned to drag them out of wherever they were and throw them in the river, where the mermaids would make them into something else, something useful, like a table leg. I didn't even worry very much about what he might say—I thought it was likely he would think my sister had done it, taken them, hid them, whatever. I don't think he would have considered that they had gone swimming forever. Maybe my sister would have gotten in trouble. I can't believe I just wrote it that way, like a little child—gotten in trouble! In any case, it was all moot because I couldn't find them. I didn't even know where to look. They might have been in plain sight for all I know.

And so why did I suddenly get this wild hair about my brother in law's guns? You guessed it! Yes, it was about the shooting in Las Vegas and the one in Texas and the one in the movie theater at the showing of Batman and the thousands since Columbine. But here's something no one knows: my brother in law gets drunk sometimes and sits with his guns and cries. And so I worry about him. I worried that once I'd gone to college, he'd get braver and he'd take the guns upstairs and hurt my sister.

Nisha didn't say anything.

"Is that why you moved out?" I said.

"Maybe. Partly. So many things. Some of them you know now."

I didn't want to ask this next question for a great many reasons, most of them selfish, but in the end, I had to know. "Do you think you'll ever go back?"

She gazed at me, then, or maybe through me, Nisha did. I knew, somehow, I was seeing the girl she'd been, half her life ago, when she was her sister's age, about to go off to college, brave and vulnerable and terrified. I felt in that moment that she trusted me, and I was honored by that, and chastened. Humbled.

"Not back all the way."

I had to stand, turn from her, walk toward the kitchen so that she might think I was after making more coffee and tea, getting us a bite

90

to eat, something, anything, to hide my pathetic happiness.

I could hear her ruffling through the pages of the journal. "There can't be much left," she said.

I tried to hear disappointment in her voice, but she sounded relieved.

"A handful, I think."

I asked the class to think about the person sitting next to them and imagine what was in that person's backpack. Mostly, they wrote about what was in their own backpacks. I could tell. Always toward the end of the exercise, when they ran out of imagining or got bored, the list would get a bit loony. Djuna's list was like that from the start.

Things I WISH were in my backpack. A tiny Mommy and a tiny Daddy. An MRE of curry, a Butterfinger bar, one of the really big ones they don't make any more in the interest of saving Americans from themselves. A fifth of vodka. A Phillips screwdriver. A cloak of invisibility, shrink wrapped. A rain poncho, which might or might not be the same thing. An inflatable skateboard. A round-trip ticket to Paris, dates open. No. Two tickets. No name on the second one.

"Then I asked them to write me a letter about what they imagined doing the rest of their day. Begin, I said, *By the time you read this.* I haven't a clue what that exercise was trying to do. Maybe make them think ahead. Maybe cause them or me to see what was really going on. I'm not sure. Djuna's is awfully hard to read now."

By the time you read this, I will have packed up my backpack (containing all those impossible items!) and left the classroom. I will have ignored the snarky things people say about you outside the room because they don't like to write or read or think so much.

Nisha looked up at me.

"No secret to me they get snarky."

However, I will not have defended you, and I'll feel bad about that for a certain period of time, maybe as long as it takes me to get out of the building. By the time you read this, I will have crossed The Pit to Lenoir and then freaked out about how loud and crowded it is in there, and how the various and global and locally sourced food smells merge into a fog of grease and sadness and decided I wasn't all that hungry. By the time you read this, I will have thought about my mother at least twice an hour and wondered what she would make of me in my head scarf and American clothes disappearing inside a sea of people in American clothes. She would not have been able to find me! So we would have been separated anyway. I will be frustrated by the time you read this, and sad. By the time you read this, I will have gone to and departed from my MEJO class, which I love because it affirms what I already know about myself as a writer. I will have gone to and departed from my American literature class, where I spent the hour thinking about ways to dramatize the ending of "A Good Man Is Hard to Find," in which I will be playing the Grandmother, so I will be the last to die. I will have ridden the bus home thinking about that, being the last to die and forgiving my killer. Recognizing him in that crazy way the Grandmother does.

Nisha covered her eyes with her left hand as if the page were too bright.

By the time you read this I will have slept and awoken, maybe several times, since you're not the fastest grader I've known in all these years of having to be graded.

"A character you have in your heads, I said. Imagine that the character breaks something on purpose, breaks something by accident, falls asleep and has a dream, then wakes up and makes a decision."

"And what does that teach them?" Nisha said.

"It's sort of about the subconscious," I said. "Causality. I'm not sure it teaches them anything."

Djuna wrote:

Djuna broke Michael's pocketknife.

"She wrote about herself in the third person."

"She was the only one in the class who did that."

She jammed the blade as hard as she could against the rocks below the bulkhead. She did this so hard and so fast that she wondered for a split second if she was really trying to commit suicide. It didn't take long for the blade to break off and fall in the river. What she had left in her hand was even more dangerous than the original knife had been. She marveled at that.

Djuna broke the last sailboat Christmas ornament. Nisha bought them—originally a set of four—mail order from Pottery Barn. Djuna knew she'd bought them for Michael, Nisha had, because Christmas and ornaments in their house had become so Hindu and so girly, so about Victorian shoes and ballerinas of all things and elephants and magic flying carpets and Taj Mahals.

Djuna was trying to be careful because she knew it was the last one. She unwrapped the sailboat ornament from the blue (not red, not green, or white, or pink) tissue paper, and then her phone buzzed and she looked away, and her hands stopped communicating with one another. The ornament fell through her fingers and smashed to bits on the hardwood floor. The sailboat, a three-masted schooner from another era, foundered against the Christmas tree skirt.

Djuna dreamed that she was walking across the United States, and she'd come to a sheer rock face. She started to climb, but there were no handholds, and her shoes were slippery. A man appeared beside her and agreed it was an impossible climb. He said he would go in search of another route and disappeared into the forest.

Djuna woke feeling relieved, becalmed somehow. She decided she would forgive Michael for everything.

"Oh, oh," Nisha said.

"Turn the page," I said.

It's hard to think about these parts of my life. The third person makes it easier, but I wish someone else could do the thinking for me.

"There's one prompt more."

Nisha wanted to light a candle. I had two that came with the bungalow: a large glass jar that was filled with wax that called itself pine-scented, and a votive in a frosted glass cup. I'd never put a match to them because I was afraid of starting a fire. So much tinder: books and papers and magazines…all wanting, so I imagined, to do something dramatic, make a scene.

I found a box of safety matches in the kitchen drawer. Then I thought Nisha might want to end by burning the journal. I placed my hand over the matchbox and thought about saying that I didn't have any, and so we couldn't light a candle. Then, still standing there, gazing into the open drawer, I felt a kind of letting go.

I brought out the matches, and she chose the votive, as I expected she would. When the wick caught with a tiny hiss, I felt it like a fuse line running in my chest.

"I asked them to write the story of their name."

Djuna, Djuna wrote. *Why should there be a D?*

It's complicated and ridiculous. My mother liked this American writer named Djuna Barnes. She liked a novel called Nightwood. *She said she liked it because she knew she had been too young to understand it and was saving it to read again. My father liked the character of Prince Djalma, an Indian, in an opera called* The Butterfly, *which he would recite continuously as if it were the* Vedas *or the* Mahābhārata. *They compromised, meaning my mother got her way.*

Now the ridiculous: Prince Djalma in an obscure French novel is killed by his own passion for his lover. I learned this later. It's a kind of Romeo and Juliet story. Prince Djalma takes poison, but he takes it so slowly that his lover has plenty of time to find out what he's done and take poison too. I imagine that my father didn't like that part of the story, but he liked the passion part and the Indian part.

"He did," Nisha said. "He was really such a romantic. Beautiful things made him cry."

I wasn't sure if I could read the next, the final part. But I knew I had to make the last push through. Somehow, we had to end this.

My mother had heard that Djuna Barnes lived across the street from e. e. cummings in Greenwich Village, and he used to shout out the window, "Djuna are you dead yet?" and she would shout back, "not yet, Eddie. I'll let you know."

Then there was no more to read.

Nisha's cry, a sound of unfathomable pain—that these words were the last—must have carried through the walls of my little bungalow, setting fire to the dry resinous wood of Rosemary Street, the entire silent neighborhood, then become an exploding star through the Morehead Planetarium dome, over the commerce of Franklin Street and into the Chancellor's office. I like to think the storm of grief passed through the Chancellor too, and she knew her days were numbered in that job, and this comet of grief gave her the strength to do what she did with the unhallowed ground on which Silent Sam had been anything but silent.

Making love to Nisha Malik was a way to find and keep Shamus. I can't explain it any better than that. Not right now anyway. Perhaps later, at the end. Whatever that end will be.

Find someone you can't have and write for her. That's what my father said Bob Hennessy told him.

"Liam," she said to me from her cover of darkness. "Can I tell you a secret?"

#3

Recall the most shameful moment of your life.

When I came to Boston from Mumbai, I had a baby. A baby that never was, that became decisively never the first week of college in a quiet spasm of pain and blood in the 4th floor bathroom of my dormitory. I showered, and then when my roommate had gone off to class, I made a phone call and an appointment and walked all the way to the women's clinic near M.I.T., and sure enough, I wasn't pregnant anymore. To the nurse I told one outrageous lie, the same one I told my roommate: that I'd left my boyfriend back home, an American called Stephen, that we still loved each other, but he didn't know. And then I told another lie: a week into my freshman year, I was about to sleep with someone new, and I walked out of the clinic with a packet of birth-control pills. The counselor said, *you ought to just slow down.*

All around me that fall, I detected in other girls the burden of virginity, and the race to lose it. Not a competition exactly, but rather three or four hundred private pursuits you could hear humming under the libraries, the dining hall, the Charles River in its private, quiet, somewhat lonely bed. Let somebody take this please, girls said to the chemistry textbook, the coin-operated dryer, the Canadian beer in its sweating bottle, we can't carry it anymore. It's too heavy. It's too useless, actually sort of embarrassing.

Mine was gone and I didn't miss it. But my roommate Sonia, who was a chummy and forward, seemed to think I needed an encumbrance too, a problem.

"You should tell him," Sonia said. "Stephen should know."

"And why is that?" I answered. "What difference would it make now? It's like nothing happened."

"Is that how you feel? That nothing happened?"

"No."

"Well then. Two people in love should be honest with each other."

I watched her turn away, hand in hand with Michael, the boy who in the coming weeks might or might not help her lose her virginity. Sonia wasn't sure, and I didn't understand her hesitation. Michael was charming and sensitive, a bit of a loner, I could tell. His mother was a social worker in Cambridge. His father, a professor of Economics, had died suddenly the year before. He'd practically grown up on the campus. His hair fell to his shoulders in golden ringlets, his mournful expression reminded you of one of a Burne-Jones or Rossetti angel. I was, at that very moment, wearing Michael's denim shirt. All Sonia's friends wanted to wear this shirt, and Michael let them. Everyone looked good in that color, blue like water in a child's painting, girls' faces brightened and calmed by the shirt's history of use, frayed cuffs and collar, girls finally at peace.

Stop being such a virgin, I wanted to shout after Sonia.

The sky was often a harder blue, and terribly close, as if it might fall down and smother everyone. This was a sensation I had not had back home, in any of the cities I'd lived in, where I hardly ever thought about the sky, only about the street, the path in front of me, which would lead to university on another continent, America, far away. I badly wanted to leave Mumbai. Many people think it is a dream city, but I hated every square mile of it. And solitude, I never considered that in Mumbai, in a city of 20 million people packed tightly together. But here, in America, there was so much solitude, even in the crowded dining hall, the dormitory, the entire campus, the greater Boston area. This kind of isolation captured me, drew me into its desire for distance: I opened a bank account over in Central Square, which I also hoped would keep me from making frequent or whimsical withdrawals. But it turned out I walked alone to the bank several times a week with no intention of using the ATM or going inside to cash a check. It was as if I had to keep moving, as if I needed to be lonely.

I enrolled in a philosophy course called Introduction to Rationalism. The section leader was a graduate student in his late 20's. The other students were Sonia's Michael and fourteen sophomore boys, all waifish, thin and whip-smart. Michael called them the Rat Pack. I understood almost none of the reading. But I was learning a great deal: I started to see the difference between an idea that needed to be understood and one that needed to be memorized. It was a part of that prayer, the one a lot of girls hung in their dorm rooms, about things you can and cannot change. The wisdom is in knowing the difference.

"The problem of morality," the section leader told us one day in late September, "is that God doesn't really care what you do." He had invited some of the class for a drink at a bar where the beers were served in a cross between a beaker and a Pyrex measuring cup. I thought that was perfect: experiment and control, in the same glass.

"How do you know this?" I asked.

"God's got bigger fish to fry," one of the Rat Pack boys said.

"God *is* a bigger fish," another said.

"Sort of," Michael said. "Orderly and harmonious. Order and harmony. That's God. And you think you're free, but you're totally guided by economics."

"I don't think I'm ever going to understand this," I said.

"I'll give you points for trying," the section leader said. He patted my forearm.

"Can you do that? Can you actually give me points for trying?"

"Not really," he said. "I can mention it to the professor."

"Please don't make me sound stupid. I understand some of it. The Leibniz thing about pre-established harmony."

"I don't even get that," the section leader said.

"It's completely daft," I said. "The glass shattering because it knows it's hit the ground, and not because of impact. Why would I understand that when you don't?"

But I knew the answer. Damage is a fine teacher.

"Michael, isn't that your shirt Nisha's wearing?" This was Sam, the most appealing of the philosophy boys. "It looks good on you." He was from Alabama. To most English words he either added a syllable or left one out. I could listen to him talk all day. The waitress brought the check, and Sam leaned in closer. "Can you loan me twenty bucks, honey? I'll pay you right back."

Honey. I said okay.

"Why did you sign up for this class anyway?" he asked as we were leaving. He winked. "To meet guys?"

Without waiting for my answer, Sam headed off toward the river houses, and I crossed Mass Ave, wondering at the cheekiness of his question. Why *had* I signed up for Introduction to Rationalism and Introduction to Biology and Math 1065 and French Novels in Translation? To meet guys? Because someone told me to? To find order and harmony, to undo my damage, to erase the baby that never was? I stopped in front of University Hall, which was of course, dark, locked up for the night. Outside, John Harvard's statue sat like a sentry. The man depicted struck me as sublimely handsome, with a scholar's long nose and sullen gaze. There was a story that a man younger and more attractive than the real John Harvard had posed for the sculptor. Sometimes drunk girls climbed up onto the statue and sat in John Harvard's lap, whispered their problems, and asked for his advice on matters of the heart.

"Should I tell anyone?" I asked John Harvard, who seemed at first unsure, then completely paralyzed with indecision. He was looking past me, I realized, at something going on in one of the dorms across the Yard. My question didn't interest him. Don't bother me, brown woman in your borrowed finery, he seemed to be saying. Do your homework. Go read a book. You don't have anything I want.

By the middle of October, I was walking to Central Square nearly every day after class, not to withdraw money from my account, just
to keep moving, stay outside. I took the long back way, past Ellery
Street and the Broadway Market, past Cambridge Rindge and Latin,
just when school was letting out. After a week, I came to recognize
some of the children, the groups, and their particular ways of bursting
out into the weak afternoon sunshine. Sometimes I stood in the cluster
of parents, mostly mothers, waiting for their children. No one spoke to
me, but no one seemed to mind that I was there.

I found that I was more interested in the children who walked
away without a mother or father, who had no one waiting for them. I
tried to read their expressions as their eyes flickered over the crowd
of parents, and then away into the distance. I thought I understood
the look and the feeling: *Maybe Mommy is here today. She just might
be. She might have been let off early from work or called in sick this
morning.* My attention soon distilled toward a pair of boys, Indian or
Pakistani, but more than that it was hard to tell. I decided they were
brothers. One was surely in 12th grade—I felt I knew this by the way
he carried himself—and the other was a bit taller, but so slight and
childlike, gangly like a colt. This younger one was quicker to laugh,
and joke with his classmates. The elder brother seemed serious, sad,
and spoke to the younger brother quietly, and led him away when, it
appeared, he could no longer tolerate the banter. Soon I was able to
see it coming. The elder brother would roll his eyes, look pointedly
at his watch, and then with surprising tenderness, slide his arm up
around his brother's shoulders. The younger brother always turned to
him, surprised, startled as if he had awakened from a shallow sleep, a
fragment of dream.

On the Friday before the Thanksgiving holiday, Sonia's Michael
followed me out of the section meeting. "Hey," he said. "Do you want

to study together?" It was instantly clear, as if he'd said so out loud, that the section leader had told him to ask. This was an obvious sensory truth—as we had learned from the Rationalists, explicated by the Rat Pack and the section leader—quickly observed, immediately understood, Michael's oblique eagerness, that he wanted to do whatever he was asked, thinking it might somehow affect his grade. I liked that about him. His attention, bestowed this way, filled me with an odd confidence.

"All right," I said. "But I have to go somewhere first."

I pointed toward Broadway, and he looked down Quincy Street as if it were an expanse of desert or frozen tundra, someplace he'd been and didn't want to traverse again. "I've got to go to the bank," I said. "In Central Square. But I like this route, even though it's longer."

"Okay," Michael said, as if he weren't actually agreeing with me. "We'll pass right by my house."

That happy confidence bloomed again in my veins. I thought taking drugs must feel like this if you don't lose consciousness. I had observed this sudden power and assurance in some of my high school classmates, actually, the ones who bought pot from the American backpackers. "Sometimes I walk by the high school," I said. "You went here, right?"

"I haven't gone very far away," he said. "Not like you."

So when we came upon the throng of parents at the school, Michael knew most of them, including his mother, who was here to collect Michael's sister. I had seen his mother, of course, stood very close to her a couple of times. I could tell Michael's mother was about to mention this but then changed her mind. Her face was very expressive. I wondered if this made her more or less of a help to her social work clients.

Michael's sister was a 10th grader, called Amy. When she saw me with Michael, she looked puzzled. "Where's Sonia?" she said.

"This is Sonia's roommate," Michael said as if it were an answer to the question his sister had asked. "Nisha Malik."

What I heard in Michael's reply I would think about later, after Sonia had broken up with him, and even years after that, how I was defined by Sonia, maybe a way to get back at Sonia. Get back with Sonia.

When the two brothers emerged from the building, I pulled on the sleeve of Michael's jacket and pointed. "Who are they?"

His face settled into the Burne-Jones gaze. "Your countrymen," he said. "I'll introduce you."

Their names were Ravi and Birju Harischandra. Ravi was a 12th grader and Birju was in 10th grade and was both childlike in his manner and very tall for his age. Their parents lived in Varanasi, but their father's brother had risen out of poverty and become educated and now taught in the Department of Religious Studies at Harvard, so they had been sent to Cambridge for schooling. Ravi's uncle was pressing him to study Engineering at M.I.T., but he wanted to study literature. But really, he wanted to go home. He said he missed his mother and his sisters. When he said this, Birju suddenly became very angry. He stopped walking beside us and curled his hands into fists. Tears stood in his eyes. "I *hate* you," he called to Ravi.

"He can forget for a while," Ravi told us, "but then I cause him to remember. He's just a child. They never should have sent him away. But we had nothing there."

"And your uncle had all this." I gestured toward the shadow of Harvard.

Ravi nodded. "It's lonely here. People leave you alone. Maybe that's the same thing."

"Only if you want it to be," Michael said.

All three of them, Ravi, Birju and I looked at him, but Michael stared back at them and did not explain.

On Monday, I met Ravi and Birju after school, as if I was their parent, as if it had been arranged—they did not seem at all surprised to see me. We walked four blocks to Ivy Street, where their uncle lived in a small, neat house. The neighbors were also Harvard professors—Drs. Preminger and Castellini from Economics and Biology. This was a bright day, though very cold, the sky that same color blue that had so pained me in September. Their Uncle Raj was at home, a prim, quiet man I had once exchanged a vague greeting with when we passed on Kirkland Street. At home, he was cordial, offering to take our coats, unaffectedly kind to the boys, particularly gentle with Birju, who, despite his height, seemed much younger, childlike, I thought. Uncle Raj asked about homework and sports and the progress of something that sounded like a holiday pageant. Birju, I understood, would be playing the parts of four different Christmas personalities.

"He loves a costume," Uncle Raj said proudly.

"It's not anything weird," Birju told me.

"It is a little bit weird," Ravi said.

"Birju's a dreamer," their uncle said. He curled his right hand into a fist and knocked softly on Birju's skull. "A fine imagination in here. A flower ready to burst forth."

Uncle Raj led us into the kitchen, where there was a stone fireplace, and in it, a jolly, crackling fire. He busied himself making hot chocolate, the European way, he explained, melting a bar of Scharffen Berger and serving us in tiny yellow porcelain cups.

"I can't cook," he said. "Ravi does that. This I can do though."

"Your chocolate is the best," Birju said.

"How are your classes?" Uncle Raj asked me. I told him about the Rationalism course. Descartes, Leibniz and Spinoza. "That's quite the trio," he said. "Did you know none of the three ever married? But so interesting. Descartes had a daughter with a servant girl, Spinoza was an expert lens-grinder, and I forget what it was about Leibniz. But still, never married, none of them."

"He was an alchemist," I said. "Leibniz was. That was his first paying job."

"Yes," Uncle Raj said. "That's it. Imagine. Someday I would like to speak with you further about your reading." Then he excused himself to pack. He would be leaving the next day for Vermont, to spend the Thanksgiving holiday with a friend.

"He met her on the Internet," Ravi whispered after his uncle had disappeared up the stairs. "I showed him how to do it. Match Dot Com. He's very excited. He says he believes he's found his soulmate. Which seems neither religious or philosophical. As you can see, he is a little obsessed with marriage."

Then came the moment the world changed. I could track every single thing that happened later from that pause, in which Ravi looked at me pointedly, silently, but also like an animal, or some creature that does not feel the world as the rest of us do.

"We'll be by ourselves here," was all he said.

And so we were, the way people are alone in their dreams, even in a frenzy of activity, among a cast of thousands, there is still that feeling of isolation, an inability to connect. In my dreams, anyway. My parents believed I was going to Sonia's house in Brooklyn. Sonia herself would be staying with Michael's family, and so I felt I had not told a complete lie since I would be only a few streets away.

From the moment we entered the house Wednesday afternoon, Ravi and Birju and I became three different people, a family in exile, from our country and from our worldly selves.

Ravi took my bag and led me upstairs to his uncle's small bedroom, dropping the bag at the foot of the bed. "I share the bigger room with Birju," he said. "It has its own bathroom. Yours is here. I'll show you." Across the hall, he opened a door and turned on a light. "All the comforts of home," he said. "And no roommate." I thought this was odd. Ravi and Birju would be my roommates. Perhaps he meant no one in the same room. This must be what he meant, though I wondered if even *that* would be true.

In the third room, the small study, Birju was watching an Indian film on a large desktop computer. He looked up, dipped his head toward me in deferential greeting. It was almost unbearable to me, how young he seemed right then. He said something in Hindi quickly, as if he did not want me to understand. "No," Ravi said. "We'll call Mum later," and then added, "in English."

"That's okay," I said. "I get tired of English too. Thinking that way all the time."

"So do I," Ravi said, first in Hindi and then in English. "The language makes no sense. I get so aggravated." He led me away from Birju to the other end of the hall and down the back stairs. "Sometimes I'm very angry. But I still want my English to be perfect. Just to show them."

The kitchen smelled of yesterday's fire. I went to stand by the fireplace and could feel warmth radiating from it. "Uncle Raj builds a fire every afternoon," Ravi said, "but I'm not very good at it." He knelt at the hearth, took up a pile of newspapers, paused and read the headlines, as if he'd forgotten what he'd started to do.

"Let me," I said, and I told him about the years my father worked for the Indian ambassador in Stockholm, and how drafty the house was, and how my mother and I spent all day building and then tending a fire. Ravi's uncle kept three neat stacks: one of newspapers, another of small branches and the third of logs, cut into two-foot lengths. I showed Ravi how to lay a lattice of kindling across the andirons, with the larger logs on top, roll newspaper into tubes to fit under the kindling, then fill any empty spaces with blooms of paper. I reached for the box of safety matches, but Ravi dug into this pants pocket and drew out a blue disposable lighter.

"I can handle this part," he said.

We stood side by side and watched the paper take fire, hungrily at first, then more slowly, almost invisibly, as the flames entered the paper tubes. I was thinking about the house in Stockholm and how my mother described that year as living among the pale, still, undemanding dead. So I was startled to feel Ravi's arm circle my waist and then move slowly up my back. He took hold of my left shoulder and pulled me closer. He spoke into my hair.

"What happened to you? When you got here. Michael said his girlfriend told him—"

"*Garbhapata*," I said.

"Which sort?"

"Miscarriage."

I could feel him nodding.

"Are you sorry?"

"No."

"Well, that's good then."

"Yes."

"Did you tell him? The boy?"

Before I could say anything, we heard Birju's step in the hall above, his feet pattering on the stairs. We stepped apart, and I thought of my parents, whom I often glimpsed moving the same way when I entered the room.

Birju appeared, wearing a shiny silver jacket and trousers. He'd combed his hair so that it parted in the middle and hung unevenly around his face. He'd dipped the jagged ends in some kind of wet glitter.

"Oh my God," Ravi said.

"No," Birju told him, shuffling in a kind of sideways moonwalk.

"But close."

"Usually he's some sports hero," Ravi said. "He loves basketball."

"This is not basketball," I said. I touched the sticky points of his hair. "You're a star."

Birju closed his eyes. He heaved a theatrical sigh of pleasure. "Exactly," he said.

"How did you get that?" Ravi asked me.

"Well, she's amazing," Birju said. "It's *obvious*. She's brilliant. Let's keep her. Let's keep her *forever*."

This is what really happened.

My school in Mumbai was the American School of Bombay, the rather stuffy institution where diplomats sent their children. In my last years, I was actually one of the few Indians here, one of only four in the Sixth Form. The local parents had formed their own separate association and then came to a sudden conclusion, awakened from the colonial nightmare, as one of my departing friends put it. These parents withdrew their children from the school, sent them to schools in Fort or to Bombay International School. My parents, however, slept deep inside the colonial dream and all its capitalism—my mother was an accountant with Air India, and my father was currently commerce assistant to the Swedish ambassador. And, truthfully, I didn't want to move, not yet. My parents had made it clear I would be going to college in the U.S., and I planned to give my full attention to that change.

Escape, really, was how I thought of it. I knew once I came to America, I would never—or rarely—go back to India.

In the late winter of that year, a group of American boys seemed to spring up out of nowhere, like a gigantic and cynical mushroom. Seven boys who had never particularly liked one another, played different sports—one played no sport, except for video games—locked into place like a jigsaw puzzle, and suddenly you could see the whole hideous picture. I thought I might have heard the click of their machinery, which was one big voracious jaw, moving all the time, either in jeering speech or consumption. They wanted everything, either to control or destroy. Games, dances, teachers, especially female teachers, and girls, particularly brown girls. I tried to stay out of their way, and I managed it, all through that long spring, through endless review and A-levels and college acceptances, never mentioning my own acceptance, moving in fact to the back row in classrooms, through the summer and working—I finally convinced my parents to let my get a job—at the British Embassy, up to the third week in August when the office staff took me out for a drink at the Taj Hotel. And here, in the Starboard Bar, was one of the seven, Stephen Balfour, bored and angry about something and already drunk. He moved to my table, and when the last of the staff, who all had husbands or wives and children, stood to leave, he convinced me to stay for another round. "I never really got to know you at school," he said. "This is my chance."

I was flattered, I would admit that later, and I hated myself for it. Or maybe I was bewitched, in that old twist of history, by this young American Puritan man who turned me into some devil of his own desiring and then passed judgment. When we left the bar and met some others of his set just coming into the hotel, I understood dimly that this was no coincidence, that they'd been summoned, either by telephone or by the scent of a weak and fearful creature. I recalled thinking that nothing bad could happen because we were in a public place. We walked to someone's house where there was a party. The other guests were mostly older people I didn't know. Talk swirled around me, delicious gossip about American colleges in large, glittering American cities, New York, Chicago, San Francisco. Stephen was going to school in Boston, on a basketball scholarship. We must, he said, be sure to get together in September.

I remembered most of what happened after, saying no, and then saying nothing. I felt some pain, a long way off, it seemed. And then he took me home. When I woke up, in my own bedroom, my parents were standing beside the bed, and the knife of a headache had started digging behind my eyes. My parents did not speak. Their expressions were impossible to read—I had never seen anything resembling the masks they appeared to be wearing—they may as well have been featureless, blank ovals of flesh above their necks. I went back to sleep, and when I woke again, I was alone, and the day had escaped. I felt no pain, none at all. My head seemed light on the pillow. My senses were terrifically acute: the leaves on the rain tree outside my window rustled inside my ears. The shadows in the room had heft and breath. My mother was cooking the evening meal: ginger and cardamom tingled on my lips. I lay still under waves of these sensations, waiting for their accumulation, and then I felt another, lower and deeper. I can only describe it as knowledge. An image came into my head, quite unaccountably, of a man in a fishing boat on the Arabian Sea, ruining the emptiness of my view, and then he turned the boat north and disappeared, leaving only agitated, disturbed water, that brokenness called wake.

Preparations for my departure and the trip to Boston consumed the next few weeks. My parents were tender, but resigned, not emotional. They seemed to be looking over my head, at the rooms of the house without me in them. I was—I understood this finally—already gone from them. They spoke to me as people do to the dead. Many of my father's sentences began with the words "You won't want…" or "You won't be needing…." I did not think it at the time, about how bereft they would be, their only child flown away.

The night before I was to leave, my parents invited the whole family for a farewell meal. We had not seen any relatives for weeks, though I did not notice this until they were present again. I had always loved my uncles and aunts and cousins deeply, and this affection came back to me that night as if I had somehow forgotten it. And though some light of happiness seemed to glow around them, I realized I was changed. I could see I was not myself. I was the glass that knew it had hit the ground.

At dusk, I sat outside with my favorite cousin, Meera, who was looking forward to the prospect of visiting Boston, as soon as she could convince her own parents to let her go. We were sharing a can of Coca-Cola into which Meera had poured rum from a small flask. "You're getting away," she said. "I almost can't believe you did it without.... I thought at any minute—" The blankness on my face must have stopped her.

"Any minute what?" I said.

"He's talked about it," Meera began. "Stephen...."

"What?"

Meera looked off at the sunset. "What you did," she said quietly.

"Who knows?"

"Everyone."

As I spoke, Ravi sat down at the kitchen table. "But you came here anyway," he said after I'd stopped talking. "To the homeland of that pig. I could kill him."

"He's here."

Ravi raised his head, glanced quickly through the living room to the front door and half rose out of the chair—as if I had meant here in the house. I tried not to say more but, in the end, it was like drunkenness again, and I could not stop myself.

"At Boston College. He has a scholarship to play basketball."

"So he was untouchable," Ravi said. "We'll see about that."

"You can't."

"Can't what?"

"Whatever you're thinking."

"Who's going to stop me? Are you going to stop me?"

I sat down at the table beside him. The salt and pepper shakers appeared to me, motionless here on a lace doily, as a sort of couple. Uncle Raj used a pink-colored salt in a Lucite grinder: the female. The pepper grinder was slightly taller, made of what looked like teak: the male. The female could be seen through, the flesh of her, the depth of her, exposed. The male was impenetrable, closed up.

"Of course I'm going to stop you," I said.

We were the same age, nineteen. Ravi had been kept back a year in primary school. This allowed me to be older, even though I was not, and Ravi, I could tell, was ashamed. The head of school had counseled Ravi's parents to have him repeat his second-grade year, and then this man had tormented him, calling him *deri* and *badir ganva*, the village idiot. The truth was, Ravi said, he loved his mother and couldn't bear to be parted from her. We told each other such things Thanksgiving night, as a persistent snow fell, after we had stuffed Birju with the foods he loved, American turkey sandwiches and Ruffles potato chips, canned cranberry jelly, chocolate pudding in plastic cups, and let him watch as much television as he wanted, mostly American sit-coms. Then Ravi and I sang him to sleep. As if we were his parents, and he our child, we seated ourselves on either side of his bed. He wanted to sing Christmas carols, he said, now that it was the official beginning of the holiday season. When his voice dropped out of the end of "Silent Night," Ravi and I sang in a whisper to the end.

"He likes you," Ravi said. "You make him so much happier."

"He wants to keep me forever."

Later that night, after I'd gone to bed in his uncle's room, Ravi knocked on the door, and I invited him in. He wore blue and white striped pajamas. I could smell toothpaste and cologne. For an instant,

I saw myself thirty years older, in a marriage of my parents' arranging, and I shut my eyes against that vision.

"Sorry," Ravi said. "Does that mean no? Or does it mean yes?" When I didn't reply, he sat down on the bed.

"It's okay," I said, opening my eyes. "It's just…the last time… the first time. I don't even remember it."

Ravi reached to turn off the lamp beside the bed. He lay down. The darkness was complete, but for the red eye of the smoke detector. "Well," he said, "I don't know anything at all about it."

"You have to know *some*thing."

"Just the obvious."

Why didn't it matter, I wondered later, that we knew so little about each other? I believed there would be time to discover more. And really, Ravi was in possession of my deepest secret. It could be like alchemy, making something base into something precious.

On Black Friday, we scoffed at American consumerism and went instead to basketball practice at Boston College.

At first, I had resisted, but Ravi promised he only wanted to observe and would not say a word. He convinced me that I would feel better if I saw this boy—he would cease to be a ghost haunting me. I said okay, that Ravi was probably right. And anyway, Ravi had said, he's just a first-year. Maybe he's not on the varsity team. Maybe he went home for the break. Some small part of me wanted to see him. I couldn't have said why back then, but later I realized it was the lost baby, the loss, the damage.

We sat high in the stands on the west end of Conte Forum. Ravi had been there for hockey games and believed we would not be noticed. Birju was excited to get out of the house and watch live basketball, and so he paid no attention to our conversation.

"Which one?" Ravi asked.

I scanned the players out on the court and shook my head. "I don't see anyone who looks like him."

"He's just a first year. Look at the bench."

I did this and spotted him immediately, Stephen Balfour, seated next to a coach who was speaking to him and gesturing toward the court. Stephen listened intently, with his whole body. I could not so much see this as I could remember it. From school, I recalled the same lean of the shoulder and cock of the head, how he had positioned himself this way in those too-small desks, especially in subjects he wasn't good at or taught by female teachers. And in the bar that night back home, how he asked about my parents and my plans for college, bending toward me with that same attention, which was really born out of superiority and selfishness.

"The one in the gray t-shirt," I said.

Ravi pointed across the arena, then moved his index finger to the right, like a child pretending to shoot at a row of targets.

"No!" I yelled the word and grabbed his hand. Birju jolted from his daydream of sports glory. The players on the bench glanced up at us. I dropped my head to hide my face.

"Stop it!" Ravi whispered fiercely. "There are at least eight of them there in gray t-shirts. I was pointing that out to you."

"I thought...."

"I know what you thought."

Another coach called to him from the court, Stephen sprung off the bench, cat-like, the ball almost already in his hands. Right away, Stephen Balfour was in charge, as he had been in school. Calling the shots, that was the phrase, and here it was literally true. I had tried not to think of him or any of them for three months, but now he had suddenly come to occupy every corner of my mind, every fold of my brain. I knew Ravi was staring at me. I was beginning to understand that men sense this, that they have a kind of radar for a woman's attraction to other men. And sometimes observing that attraction makes them angry.

"Stop it," Ravi said again, his voice like a blade.

I tried to stop, the feeling of being consumed, swallowed whole, but I couldn't. "I hate him," I said, but I didn't mean it. Didn't mean it enough. "That one," I said. "The one who seems...."

"Aggressive."

We watched the team practice for another half hour and did not speak. Stephen Balfour loped up and down the court, almost always handling the ball, though he seldom took a shot, and when he did, he missed.

"He's like a sheepdog," Ravi said. "He moves them around, and they all just follow." He shook his head, made a dismissive sound, a sort of hiss. "Let's go," he said. His face was suddenly very close to mine, his lips pressed to my ear. "I have an idea," he said.

Again, Ravi woke Birju from some glorious fantasy—I could tell by the slow back and forth of his head, the sadness in his eyes. "No, please," he said to us. "This is the *greatest*."

Ravi smoothed his brother's hair. "Time to go."

We walked to the top of the stands and out through the portal. Evening had fallen. This surprised me, that the world could be this dark just after you turned away from so much brightness.

Outside, a man, maybe in his thirties, seemed to have been waiting for us. He began to walk in our direction. "Hey," he said, in a voice that sounded neither friendly nor hostile. As we came into the glow of the parking lot lights, he stopped, thrust his hands into his coat pockets. "You're just kids, aren't you? All right. But practices are closed. Security." His eyes fell on my scarf. "And we don't want any spies from Cambridge."

Ravi made a scoffing *pffft* sound. "She doesn't know the first thing about basketball. She kept asking where the goalie was."

"Right," the man said, rolling his eyes. "I gotcha."

Ravi put his index finger to the side of his head, moved it in a slow circle. Again, I thought of a child with a pistol. Birju, who stood just beside me, reached for my hand and held it tightly. I did not know what this gesture meant, but I would remember how warm his hand felt, as if we were in another place, a different season, back home.

We walked almost all the way back to Cambridge. At Memorial Drive, the path opened onto a field of perfect snow, completely un-touched, no footprints or sled tracks, nothing.

"It looks like a cloud," Birju said. "Like a cloud fell down to earth. Sometimes when I'm in an airplane, the clouds seem....I don't know. I'm surprised that they're empty."

"Empty?" I said.

"Yeah. Nobody's sitting on them."

"Like heaven?"

"Sort of. Like it's a waste of space. Or nobody's thought of it yet."

"You did," I said.

"Yeah, but I'm just a kid."

We stood gazing at this miraculous white, and then Birju broke away from us and walked out into the field. He lay down, and then he began to move his arms and legs, up and down, apart and together.

"A snow angel," Ravi said. "Uncle Raj taught us to make them."

Birju went still, and then very carefully got to his feet. He walked back toward the road, placing his feet inside the first footprints, and turning after every step to cover the print with snow. He was quite good at this, very thorough. When he reached the sidewalk, the illu-sion was complete: the snow angel had descended from the sky, made its mark, then heaved itself upward again. A clean getaway.

My parents came to Boston for the winter holiday, with the astonishing news that my mother was going to have a baby, a girl. They stayed in a fancy hotel on Copley Square, one of those connecting to a central web of shops and restaurants, so that tourists could have their rest and relaxation without ever having to go outdoors. This was in fact exactly what my mother wanted. She had all the outdoor city life she desired back home; now she needed to rest. She wanted to buy American baby clothes, sit for a manicure and a pedicure, have her hair cut and colored, and sleep. For these two weeks she would have nothing to do with Air India, with the ethereal realm of numbers, sales, profits, losses. She wanted the pleasures of earth, she wanted to sink into this earthly and bodily surprise of motherhood.

My father, who was never really on vacation, liked to walk, to take in a city a quadrant at a time, on foot. After breakfast in the hotel dining room, my father and I would watch my mother disappear into the tangle of shoppers, and then we would venture forth, toward the Boston Harbor or Faneuil Square, the North End or Beacon Hill. My father's destination would be a late lunch at a restaurant he'd already chosen, called ahead to reserve a table. After lunch, we would visit precisely one tourist attraction, and then walk back, or take a cab if we felt like it. Sometimes he would have to stop to take a phone call from the Embassy, but this was rare; because of the time difference, he did most of his work at night (I didn't, honestly, know when he slept during those weeks). Along the way, we would talk about politics or my studies or his work. Sometimes, as if temporarily released from the present, he would tell me charming stories about his childhood in London, his college years at Oxford, where he'd met my mother.

I wanted to be able to imagine my parents back then like Ravi and myself were now, strangers in a strange land, but I couldn't quite do it. My parents were so happy, and the promise of a new baby seemed to make them more content. Standing outside Faneuil Hall, I was struck by the most unusual desire, extraordinary for a person my age: I wanted to be more like my parents. And in the same instant, my vision already blurred by sudden tears, I saw him, twenty meters away, Stephen Balfour, laughing, arm in arm with a young woman, then bending low to kiss the top of her head. She wore a blue and green pashmina over her coat, and he gathered handfuls of it, then reached to wrap it tighter around her shoulders. She was blonde-haired and white, probably American, and I noticed for the first time how few people around us looked like my father and myself. I stopped walking and turned away. If I waited, they would move farther ahead and out of sight.

"What is it, sweetheart?" my father said.

"It's nothing." I tried to think of what might keep my father beside me. "Sometimes there's this dizziness. I probably need glasses. I just have to be still for a minute." By this time, I could do nothing to hide my tears.

My father took my arm and led my back the way we had come. "Do you want to sit down?" he said. "Are you hungry?"

"Maybe." I looked up, across the street and saw a restaurant placard: The Golden Bowl. "Let's go in here," I said. "Is that all right?"

"Of course," he said. "Anywhere you like."

Inside the restaurant, my father asked for a quiet table at the back. This made me wonder if he'd seen Stephen Balfour or guessed—though I told myself that would have been impossible. My father seated me so that I faced neither the door nor the window. All this time, his eyes searched mine, even as he ordered a beer for himself and a glass of wine for me. The waiter hesitated for a moment, calculating my age. Then he said, "As you wish."

For some minutes after the waiter brought our drinks, my father maintained this concerned silence. My impulse was to fill it up, to chatter about school, maybe go so far as to introduce the names of my new friends, Ravi and Birju. But a profound fear had settled inside me, a kind of vision. The whole world was made of shining glass—I was staring now at the golden bowl logo on the restaurant menu—the empty bowl balanced on a star or on the head of a pin, something sharp and brittle and small. And if I were to say the wrong words, the bowl would topple and shatter. The waiter returned and I tapped my finger over the words for soup, for salad. "Very good," he said. He listened to my father's order, then disappeared.

"Your mother and I," my father began. "We think.... We thought.... Well, you seem to be doing all right here."

"I am," I said. I could express this much at least.

"You wrote that the Philosophy was difficult."

I told my father I'd never studied so hard for anything as I had for that exam. I wanted him to be proud. I wanted right then to hear him say those words. The sight of Stephen Balfour, so close, in regular clothes, with a girl, a woman, had brought back all the shame I'd felt after I heard how my parents found out about that night in August. Somehow, I'd managed to leave that shame in Mumbai, but now it was as if my father and Stephen Balfour had unknowingly conspired to bring it to me. *Here*, their voices whispered just below the soft music playing from the speakers overhead. *Look what you forgot.*

"Are you glad about the new baby?" I asked.

"We were shocked at first," my father said. "But that didn't last for long really. Late pregnancy is concerning." My father looked as if he would cry, but then he brightened. "Your mother is in very good health. We always wanted you to have a sibling. After we're gone...."

"Please," I said. "Let's not talk about that."

"All right. Let's talk about dessert instead."

As my father ordered coffee and a slice of chocolate cake, snow began to fall. With great intent, it appeared: no first, tentative spit, but rather a sudden, blizzardy curtain of big, wet flakes.

"We'll have a white Christmas!" he said and, in celebration of the weather, ordered a brandy to go with the coffee. "This is wonderful." He and my mother loved Christmas, the English sort, with fog and snow, roast beef and plum pudding. He had in fact arranged for such a meal the next day in the restaurant at the Liberty Hotel. He held my hand across the table. "This must be your present to us."

We finished lunch and my father settled the bill. The maître d' called a taxi, then held a large gold umbrella over us as we got in. My father directed the driver to the hotel, then sat back and closed his eyes. The reason we had hurried into The Golden Bowl was forgotten, his worry momentarily erased by weather. I vowed I would not upset him again. The snow poured down and whitened the world but did not clean it.

#4

Most things will never happen; this one will.

When Ravi and Birju returned in January, they seemed changed, Ravi especially. First of all, there was less of him. This I could feel through his shirt when I put my arms around him, just outside the arrivals hall at Logan Airport. And I could see it that afternoon in my dorm room. We were alone—after my parents' visit, I had stayed on for Winter Session, but Sonia had not—and shyly welcoming each other back, remembering things about each other that we had really not known very well before.

"Didn't your mother feed you?" I asked when I regained the power of speech. We lay side by side on my narrow bed.

"I hardly saw my mother," Ravi said.

I wasn't sure what to make of this statement from the boy who had once loved his mother so fiercely he couldn't leave her to go to school.

"Was she ill?"

He looked as if I'd said something preposterous. "No. Why?"

"Well," I began. "If you hardly saw her…."

"A friend took me to the mountains."

"A friend?"

"His name is Azmi."

"Birju too?"

"Yes," Ravi said. "Birju went with me."

This talk felt like an interrogation. I noticed suddenly that the room had turned cold: these venerable old buildings with their ill-fitting window glass.

"What did you do there?"

"We skied. We built men out of snow." As he spoke, Ravi stared into the air.

"Did you miss being here?" I was going to say *miss me,* but saved myself at the last minute.

"I felt very far away," he said. "I felt very high up. In the mountains, I mean. The air is so thin. And we were at about 5000 meters. Looking down. I couldn't stop staring at it. The little world below. It's so small and insignificant."

There was something cold and dismissive in Ravi's voice, drifting off into breath as he fell asleep. *We built men out of snow.* I touched his shoulder, half-expecting to feel ice. He woke and stared at me, momentarily confused, his eyes black pits I might fall into. Then he got out of bed and dressed, turned, covered me with the blanket and the comforter. He left without saying a word.

Ten days earlier, I had been walking with my father in Boston when Stephen Balfour had appeared and vanished. I felt an echo of that same sadness now. And shame. Had Ravi really ever been here, beside me, that close, really that *same* close if you thought about it? How could something so physical, so bodily also be an apparition? What did any of it mean, such intimacies between two people? These questions came at me in waves, like waves, a sickening pause between them, a moment without gravity, and then the blunt force of another inquiry. I thought I might drown right there, in that narrow bed.

In the course of the next few weeks, Ravi seemed to shut down. We hardly saw each other unless I waited after school, and then Ravi took Birju by the arm and rushed past me without speaking. Twice Birju came on his own to my dorm. He was lonely, he said. Uncle Raj had a new teaching schedule that kept him late. If he was home, he was talking to the Match Dot Com woman from Vermont. "He's *besotted*!" Birju proclaimed. "He actually *giggles* on the phone with her." And Ravi had taken over the small study. "He closes the door and locks it," Birju said. "He locks me *out*."

I tried to believe that Ravi's distance and distraction had to do with college admissions, and I left him alone. He had dutifully applied to Harvard and M.I.T., Birju said, and, in the spirit of too-little-too-late rebellion, to Berkeley. He laughed about this in a way I later found chilling. "That's Ravi being radical," he said. "But really, he wants to go home, or maybe to Karachi. He says he doesn't belong here. He says he can't fit in." The only person he ever seemed to talk to was Azmi, his friend from the mountain camp.

I hardly knew how to respond. I wanted to reassure Birju, but my own discontents were growing. I, too, worried about fitting in. Sonia had found groups of friends from—well, I wasn't sure exactly where these other women had come from. One was the daughter of a famous movie director, another two years ahead of us and captain of the women's sailing team, and both were stunning, beautiful, American in ways I knew I could never be. Another had the same last name as the Anthropology library. Sonia made weekend trips to someone's ski cabin in the Berkshires and to a beach house on Cape Cod. She fell in love with the son of a Congressman from Connecticut.

After that, I spent a lot of time talking to Michael, who was surprised, blind-sided, he said, and very sad. "Do you think she'll come back?" he asked. "Do you think she'll get tired of all the...." He shaped an explosion in the air, both fists clenched and then opened suddenly.

"Excitement?" I said.

"I guess I'm not very exciting. But I really thought I was important to her."

"I thought I was too."

"We're a pair, then," Michael said, and I was surprised by how happy those words made me feel.

Together, we registered for a class we believed would be the antidote to Rationalist Philosophy. Swedenborg, Blake, and Coleridge. No Rats, we called it. As in the previous semester, I found a lot of the reading impossible to understand, until the section leader, a different graduate student, not very friendly and not interested in drinking with undergraduates, said, "Just pretend these writers are children." It was as if someone had led me out of Plato's cave. I thought of Birju and the snow angels, his sports gods, his clear vision of heaven, his dreaminess. He had stopped dropping by the dorm after school, and I missed him, acutely, sorely, as if he were my own child. I realized I had not seen Ravi for a month, since the start of the semester. I called, but he did not answer the phone.

In the second week of February, Birju left a message saying his uncle was going back to Vermont for Valentine's Day, that the Match Dot Com woman seemed to be a real romance. So, Birju was planning a party. Just a few people. Not going to wreck the house. They were thinking of a costume party. The Famous Unloved. Bachelors and Spinsters.

I asked Michael, but he didn't want to go. He'd started hanging out with a group of boys, men—I didn't know what to call them—older than he was, from the business school. He said shocking things, like he was going to change his major to Economics. He didn't get the point of the humanities.

"I think," I said, "you mean you don't get the point of happiness."

"But don't you have the same problem?" Michael shot back.

We were sitting on the steps of my dorm, both waiting, I realized, for someone who would very likely not appear.

"I like for other people to be happy."

"Sonia's happy," Michael said.

"Point taken."

"Point taken like a knife straight to the heart."

"Oh, Michael," I said. I leaned closer and reached my arms around him. Michael sighed, then hugged me too.

"You smell like…humanities," he said.

"Well, you smell like money."

"Even though you know that's ridiculous. Money doesn't have a scent."

"Some people think it smells like happiness. You'll let me know, OK?"

We let go, then waited, for Sonia, for Ravi, a little longer, until Michael said he was meeting his sister after school. He asked me if I wanted to come along, but I didn't.

I went to the party as Emily Dickinson, in a puffy, frothy white dress borrowed from Sonia. My plan was to rush into the house and go straight to the downstairs bathroom and close the door. It was going to be very funny. But when I got here, the bathroom was occupied, so I stood outside, a nervous girl in a white dress. I looked like an emergency.

A boy wearing a false beard and a ragtag suit stared at me as if I were a confection and he was starving. "We should have been a couple," he said.

"Do I know you?"

"Henry David Thoreau."

"Perfect. But what's your real name?"

"We're not supposed to tell."

"Who says?"

He pointed across the room at Ravi, who was deep in conversation with someone who might have been dressed as Jesus. "Leibniz," he said

"I love it."

"You love me?" He sounded afraid.

"Henry," I said. "Can I have something to drink?"

In the kitchen, kids crowded around a keg or sat on the counters. I was certain that not a single one of them could drink legally. It was only a matter of time before the police arrived. I stepped in line behind

Mother Teresa, who gripped a red plastic cup in each hand. I could see that she was already quite drunk, and this set alight a terrible anxiety, the depth of fear I remembered from Christmas, outside The Golden Bowl.

"You should stop," I said. Mother Teresa turned, her mouth open in too-theatrical surprise. She frowned then, and somehow that gesture enabled me to recognize Michael's sister, Amy.

"I will," she said. "In a little while."

I filled my cup halfway and went to look for Ravi. I found him still talking to Jesus. When he saw me, Ravi raised his cup, waved me over. "We were just talking about alchemy," Ravi said. "Me and Jesus. He's big on that too."

The way Ravi spoke was very strange, detached almost, as if he were thinking of something else, a place very far away.

"Are you worried about all these kids?" I said. "Drinking underage."

"You're underage," he said.

"I know. That's why I'm going to finish this and then take off. You probably want me to go."

"If I did, I would say so."

Ravi reached for my arm, which caused Jesus to shake his head. "No couples," he said and turned away.

"There's a girl in here who's really drunk," I said. "Michael's sister."

"Michael was invited too," Ravi said. "Birju invited him."

"Is he here?"

"I don't know. Why do you care?" He gripped my arm harder.

"His sister—" I began.

"You and the American boys," Ravi said. "You just can't get enough of them, can you?"

I waited for Michael on the front porch. Emily Dickinson in a blue parka, red mittens, a beret, a Harvard scarf. I looked like a girl who had gone out just before bed to walk my dog and locked the door by mistake. And the dog had wandered off. I was joined briefly by Helen Keller and Oprah Winfrey, who stayed only as long as it took to smoke a cigarette. They didn't ask about my costume. Helen Keller didn't laugh when she tripped up the steps and said, "I can't see a thing in these stupid glasses." I thought about what Ravi had said, about American boys, and wondered at the truth of it. I had no idea who I was or what I wanted or why I was here, on this porch, at this university, in this country.

Birju appeared from around the side of the house. He looked years older in a navy-blue suit and lavender dress shirt open at the neck. He'd slicked his hair in the manner of certain Indian actors.

"You look…" I said, "like yourself."

"Well, I'm not *myself*. I'm Virgate Kohli."

"Ah. Not exactly unloved, is he? But does anyone here even follow cricket?"

"Are you joking? This is *America*."

"Right. For a second, I forgot."

We looked at each other, shivering under the porch light. Strangers in a strange land. Of course it was impossible to forget, even for a second.

"What are you doing out here anyway?"

"I'm waiting for Michael. His sister is really drunk. I thought he should take her home."

"Yeah, he probably should. She's passed out in Ravi's room."

"*Ravi's* room?"

Birju tried to laugh. It was the first time I had ever seen him seem sad. "You sound like me," he said. "Anyway, nobody can get in. He's guarding the door."

"So he's still in the study? It's tiny."

"He doesn't mind. He calls it his *cell*. Before tonight, he only came out to go to school and eat. Not even always to eat. I think he was hoping you'd be here."

"I don't know about that."

Michael arrived then, dressed in black, darkness emerging from darkness except for the gold of his hair. I almost asked him who he was supposed to be, but then I decided this was probably his way of observing Valentine's Day: mourning. He eyed my costume suspiciously but did not comment. He turned to Birju.

"Mr. Bollywood," he said. "Where is she?"

"She's okay," Birju said. "Upstairs, sleeping it off. Nobody's bothering her."

"That's good," Michael said. "Thanks."

"She wasn't really that bad off. No puking."

"Let's see if we can wake her up."

Inside, the party was winding down. A dozen or so people lay sprawled around the living room. A boy in an indeterminate costume sat by himself in the kitchen, staring into the empty fireplace, sipping from a pink plastic cup. "Ran out of the red ones," he said as we passed through. A boy and a girl were kissing in the hallway.

"Hey," Birju said. "We won't be having any of that. It's not one of *those* parties."

The study, I remembered, was the middle room at the top of the stairs. The door was closed, Ravi nowhere in sight. Birju tried the handle, then, smiling devilishly at me, drew a key fob from his pocket and unlocked the dead bolt. He stepped back and waited to see what Michael would do. I imagined we were thinking the same thing: It's his sister. He gets to decide. He gets to open the door and see whatever sight there was to behold.

Michael leaned into the door, listening. The woman kissing

in the hall sighed, a tiny moan, and Michael's eyes went wide. Birju cleared his throat and when Michael looked at him, he tilted his head toward the couple below. Michael rolled his eyes heavenward, grasped the doorknob, turned it, pulled the door open. From the drop of his shoulders, I could tell Amy was alone. He disappeared into the room, and I heard the wheeze of the mattress on Ravi's bed. Birju and I edged into the doorway.

Mother Teresa, young again, was sleeping. I believed Michael was so taken by the sight of her that he had to sit down. "Amy," he said. "Amy." He touched the blue band of her wimple. She didn't move, and so he leaned closer. "She's breathing," he whispered, "but she's really out." Then the three of us kept perfectly still. It was a kind of reverence, I thought. Because this bed occupied almost the entire room, it was as if we were seeing Mother Teresa lying in state, just as we had two years before. And there was something odd about this bed too—it took me a moment to realize it had been built to hold storage drawers below, but these drawers were missing. It was a platform, like a table. The corner of a sleeping bag stuck out from the space below. I turned to Birju.

"It's weird, I know," he said. "He likes to sleep on the floor."

I crouched and peered underneath: a sleeping bag, books, a silver goose-neck desk lamp, a blue spiral notebook, but no Ravi. "Why?" I said.

Birju shrugged. "Simplicity, he says. *Preparation*."

"For what?"

"The apocalypse? I don't know. He's got his reasons."

I did not want to see the books. I did not try to look at the spines, the titles. Instead, I gazed at the empty space, imagined Ravi lying here, sifting information, arriving at conclusions, taking notes, making plans. For what? The thing he would do. The thing I said I would stop him from doing. Michael's sister shifted and the platform creaked.

I stood. We looked at Amy for a little while longer, her miraculous calm. I realized the books beneath the bed, their size, arrangement and color were seared into my brain, ghostly, like the negative image in film photos. One book was a kind of manual, half under Ravi's sleeping bag, folded open to show instructions, an illustration of parts.

The mind is curious. Curious in all senses, unfathomable, and yet...what? Shallow. In certain places. Like a body of water. The tides make troughs, and sandbars too. The eye sees, and the mind knows what's been seen, and then the tide inside the head shifts, rises. The water is suddenly up to your neck. A cloud masks the sun. A moment ago, you could see all the way to the bottom, but suddenly your own hand, just inches below the surface of the water, is obscured. So too, your arms, legs, the feet you should use to get back to the shore. I was trying to explain it to myself, the refusal to understand, for so long, two months, what I knew Ravi was doing.

Michael's sister opened her eyes, turned her radiance upon us. "Give me ten more minutes," she said. Michael whispered, "You always say that," but the tone of his voice sounded as if he were telling her she was the most wonderful creature on earth. So we left her, trooped downstairs, finished what little beer was left in the keg, marveling at how orderly this party had been. A few red cups left here and there, empty crisp bags, pizza boxes. These were good children, obedient and tidy. Couples were messy, I decided. Single people were fastidious. Maybe because they had so little, they left nothing of themselves behind, not so much as a forgotten glove. Barely a whiff of cigarette smoke or perfume or spilled beer.

"Uncle Raj could come home right now," Birju said. "There's nothing to hide."

By 1 a.m., Amy was fully awake, and the three of us were waving goodbye to Birju. Under the porch light, he was breathtakingly handsome, the wealthy and generous heart throb at the door of his suburban estate.

We walked west on Broadway toward campus. Michael's sister would sleep in his dorm room since their parents were not expecting her home. Other people were walking back from parties, from Valentine's Day dates, couples arm in arm or knocking playfully into one another in the hopes of more touching later. No wind, so the cold was a fact you could almost forget, the stars a happy glitter overhead, as if to punctuate the laughter all around. Michael held his sister's hand. Very quietly, Amy sang a pop song from the radio. Christina Aguilera? Amanda Ayala? Paula Abdul? I couldn't tell one from the other, and this made me feel ancient, far removed from all hopeful falling in love, beyond it, in a mix of numbness and relief.

We stopped at University Hall, Michael and his sister crossing the Yard to Matthews South. It might as well have been early evening. Dorms were alight, voices called and sang, music thumped in the common rooms and lobbies. The glow from the Square was like sunrise from the wrong direction. Michael asked if I wanted to come in.

"No thanks, you two. I have to go write a few hundred cryptic poems."

"Okay, Emily," Michael said. "Thanks for the call tonight."

"No problem. You would have done the same for me."

"Sure," he said. "I would have. Maybe someday I will." I couldn't recall telling Michael I was going to have a sister. Maybe I had mentioned it to Sonia.

Ravi was waiting, outside Weld, half in shadow. I was about to call his name when he said my name. We stood quietly for a minute looking at each other. I wanted to kiss him because I wanted to be kissed. As if in response to this notion, a siren wailed on Mass Ave. Police going somewhere else, some other emergency.

"That was a great party, Ravi. Nice people."

He shrugged, looked away over my shoulder. "Birju's doing."

"But you—"

"I wasn't going to let that happen to Amy. What happened to you."

"It wouldn't have. Not those kids. They're all so sweet."

"Even sweet kids…. I'm sure some people think Stephen Balfour is a sweet kid."

A small light went on inside my head, a line of brightness along the bottom of a closed door. Wake up, it said. Wake up before it's too late. "Do you want to come up? Sonia's away for the weekend. I think she actually said *Hyannisport*." I put force into the name, as Birju would have done.

Ravi nodded, and I unlocked the front door. A few people I knew lolled on couches in the lobby, girls called Kate and Lisa, boys called David and Max, and Sam, the one I'd lent money last semester, which he had still not repaid. All five of them blonde, good-looking, American, probably a little drunk. Sam especially, caused that same fluttering inside me. He was a little cryptic poem in my head: You Owe me Money—Honey—But the Only Interest—is Mine. I wondered what Ravi and I looked like to them. A matched set, a pair, an absence of light, and therefore nearly invisible. Acknowledgment was only the briefest flicker of their eyelids.

"Are you in costume?" Sam said to me.

"Emily Dickinson." I linked arms with Ravi. "This is Leibniz."

They all laughed, suddenly and happily, as if this was the best joke they'd heard in years.

"Together at last," Sam said. "Perfect."

We had started up the stairs toward my room, but I couldn't help glancing back over my shoulder at Sam. He was giving me the thumbs-up, and the look on his face—a pout, an invitation—was something I both memorized *and* understood.

I didn't know if it was that last glance from Sam or the certainty that Sonia wouldn't disturb us or the idea of floozy Emily Dickinson or all three, but something new happened that night, something that could never be denied or undone, some raw, naked, powerful, lustful phenomenon. The glass knowing it was about to break. I had not ever felt this great hunger—my own—for our bodies to be entwined, limb over limb, almost confused in that way. Was that my leg or Ravi's? His breath or mine? Our ribs, shoulder blades, hips, knee bones, all suddenly sharp, about to pierce the skin as if they were broken.

"Roses and vanilla," Ravi whispered. "I would know you any-where."

"Your new room is very unusual," I said later, toward dawn. The Yard seemed to have finally fallen asleep. I had the sense that for miles around I was the only person speaking.

"You were there?" His grip on my shoulder tightened and then released.

"When we went in to wake Amy."

"Who's we?"

"Michael, Birju and I."

"Michael?"

"I called him. I was worried about her."

"I locked the door."

"Birju had a key."

"That little shit."

"You left. Where did you go?"

"I had to meet some friends."

"Why?"

"I just did."

"Who?" Ravi didn't answer. "I saw the books under your bed. The manual."

Ravi rolled onto his side, then over me. "I have to tell you something." He whispered these words into my neck, his lips over the beating vein.

That was how I found out what he planned to do at Conte Forum on March 9 after half time, when Boston College played Syracuse, the backpack left under the home team's bench. It was a very simple conversation. Quiet. No shouting. Brief. I told him he couldn't do it. He asked if I intended to call the police. I said if he were doing this for me, for revenge, he didn't have to. He said it wasn't just for me, it was for the whole world. Fear is a weapon, he said. It's more powerful than guns and bombs. These were the words he said, but I knew they came from somewhere else, his new friends or the books underneath his bed. The sun rose, golden, balanced itself carefully on the window ledge. The light leapt off the snow and dazzled my bedroom.

Just slow down, the counselor at the women's clinic had said. I should have asked how to do that. What did *just slow down* mean? Don't fall in love? Maybe it meant don't talk too much. Don't tell anyone. Never, never, never tell anyone. Telling was always the problem. People should only know what they can see, without explanation, find truth in the orderly harmony of what exists. I would have to search out this orderly harmony. I tried. I studied my William Blake, who was ultimately no help: The bible fails to give us a motive for the creation. Shouldn't Adam and Eve come first, and then once they've wrecked the world, God could remake it? First, we have to wreck the world. In the beginning, things are wrecked, damaged beyond recognition. Only then could the world be made.

But then I found this: active evil is better than passive good. Did I want to be better than Ravi? I didn't. I wanted to be just like him. Why didn't I know this already? The truth of my desire came as a complete shock—it very nearly had a sound, a thunderclap, a blast. I'd spent my whole life with westernized parents, sometimes in different, western countries, then in a high school for expatriates, and now in the jewel of the west, America, and here in the gleaming eye of that jewel. And that life had all been comfortable, until six months ago and the relentlessness of shame. Shame that this thing had happened, shame fallen on my parents, but shame also that my body couldn't hold on to the little life forced upon it, shame that I felt relieved, shame that I had kept all this shame to myself. All of this shame—Ravi had shown my shame could be transformed into rage. All of it into rage, explosive, destructive, murderous and absolutely justified.

My parents wanted to fly me home for spring break, but I said no, dreading the long flights, the familiarity and scrutiny of home life, the sinking back into the ooze of shame. I thought I should buy a silver bikini and go to Florida with those people, the girls gone wild. Maybe I would find some friends among them. Maybe the counselor at the women's clinic was wrong, and what I really needed to do was *just speed up*. The way Birju would say it, in italics. Catch up with everyone else. I'd fancied myself far ahead, but here I was, fallen in love with a high school boy, going to parties with high school kids. Where was the rage in that?

So instead of haunting Cambridge Rindge and Latin, I took the red line out to Chestnut Hill and did my ghosting at Conte Forum. After almost an entire day of wandering around outside, finding and losing my nerve, I caught the train back to Kendall Square, walked the rest of the way to the dorm, did my homework, went to Passim's for dinner, sat at the smallest table by the walk-in fridge, rushed to my chem lab, had an hour of civilized, empty conversation with Sonia and fell into bed.

The next day, I went again to Chestnut Hill, but this time I found the right door and the real nerve, and got myself inside Conte, following the sounds. Several people asked if they could help me, and I said no. To the man who asked if I was crazy and told me I couldn't go in without a ticket, I said I had to, that it was *a matter of life and death.*

He let me go, and I wondered later if it was because I didn't look dangerous or because I did.

Inside, I was surprised to see so many people, paired men and women who appeared to be parents, maybe faculty, a great many students. I began to understand that this was some sort of exhibition or press event, a benefit game maybe, but all of that was outside of me, like voices in another room. I walked around the upper gallery to the home team side of the court and stood looking down. My entire consciousness was focused like a laser beam on the back of Stephen Balfour's skull. I descended the bleacher steps slowly but without looking down at them, sinking like a stone until I reached the row of seats right behind the bench. Only one of Stephen's teammates turned to watch. He had a nice smile, sweet like the kids at the Valentine's Day party. I thought, *too bad about you.*

"Stephen," I said. There was shouting from the stands, from the court. I called louder. "Stephen!"

He turned then. The bloom of recognition made me think of a human face rising through a body of water and breaking the surface, a distillation of features, sharpening, almost painful clarity. He turned back toward the game, but his shoulders trembled a little, or so I believed. I moved down the row of seats until I was directly behind him. "Stephen." For some reason, I was whispering. "I want to talk to you."

One of the coaches turned to stare, blinking as though his vision was fogged. "Miss," he said, "What are you doing? This is a game. He can't talk to you now."

"He can't?"

"No." He stabbed his index finger toward the court, the game in progress.

"Why not?"

"Are you fucking nuts?"

"No," I said. "It won't take long."

"It's okay," Stephen said to the coach. "She's okay. Can I have a minute? I know her."

The coach nodded and Stephen rose, stepped up onto the bench and swung himself over the railing. "Come on," he said to me. "Let's go up." He pointed to the top of the arena, the portal. I started ahead of him, stopping twice to make sure he was following.

I realized then that I didn't have a plan or a script. Or I had too many plans. But even so, I had no idea what I would say when we reached the top. I should have remembered that Stephen Balfour would of course speak first.

"You can't prove anything," he said.

"I was pregnant."

"What? I wasn't…" He caught himself. "You're insane."

"You people have to stop saying that. I'm one of the sanest people you'll ever know."

He seemed to consider the possible truth of this. "So what do you want from me?"

"Nothing." I told him there was no baby.

"Then why are you here?"

"I just want to warn you. You make people angry."

"I do?" He looked down at the crowd cheering. "How?"

"How do you think?"

He stood there for a moment, staring at me, utterly mystified. It was like the world stopped. I thought about that later: why should the whole world stop while Stephen Balfour considered his place in the scheme of things? Because it always did. Because the universe waited for people like Stephen Balfour, rich, white, American boys, and the universe always would cool its giant heels until the Stephen Balfours resolved it could start moving again.

"Look," he said finally. "I've got to go back to the game. Please don't do this anymore."

"Do what anymore?"

"Come here."

"It's a free country."

"Not really."

But I did go there again. On March 9th to watch Boston College play Syracuse. I bought the most inexpensive ticket and sat up high, opposite and as far as possible from the Eagles' bench. None of the players could possibly see who I was, but I could see them, see all the duffels, packs and ball bags stuffed under the chairs, a strange riot of color, confusing, all mixed up, as if their contents had already been blown out into the open. I watched Stephen Balfour handle the ball with his usual ease and grace. Even though I could not see his face clearly, I knew how beautiful he was. *Handsome* was probably the word he would have preferred, but it was not accurate, I thought then. Because there was now something vulnerable about him, his heart-breaking belief in immortality, his certainty that like other passionate, dogged young men who perpetrated great harm, his face would glow like the moon, that his body would emanate the scent of roses and he would live in paradise. His teammates, too, boys I didn't even know, but had come to recognize, all of them became gorgeous in their exposure to harm. Their large, strong, elaborately muscled bodies couldn't protect them from anything.

The game moved along sluggishly—out of bounds calls and fouls and free throws. The two teams were very well matched, it seemed, the score nearly always a tie. "Somebody's *got* to wear out," the man beside me muttered. At the end of the first quarter, I made my way down to the concession area, where the crowd was crushed together, loud, cheerful. I found a student who looked to be well into his third or fourth beer, stood right beside him, made a show of searching my purse, then asked to borrow his cell phone. I dialed 911, turned away from him, spoke quickly. I handed the phone back, joined a group of bored sorority girls leaving the Forum. "I'd rather just drink," one of them said. Good idea, American college girl. I almost invited myself along.

Play was halted immediately, Conte was cleared, though this took time and resulted in a small stampede at a few of the exits. I watched emergency crews attend to some of the injured, one of whom was a little boy. But better to be knocked down and bruised a little and be able to get up and go home. I waited at a distance, listening to the chatter around me, steeling myself for the explosion. Most people assumed this was the work of an angry sports fan, an attempt to break the concentration of one team or the other. "Some kids in high school did this," a woman said, and I turned toward her, open-mouthed in shock, until the woman added, "to get out of taking a test." I watched the police lead in the trained dogs and the deactivation squad's arrival, in their specialized clothes clutching their sensitive equipment. I stood in the waning afternoon light, into the evening, shivering, hungry. After a while I realized I was waiting for Ravi to appear, to thank me, to hate me, to acknowledge somehow that we were now in fact just alike. A few minutes after 9 pm, the announcement rang over the PA system: no bomb was found. Play resumed and continued far into the night. It was close, but Boston College won.

The bomb detonated instead on Ivy Street, inside Uncle Raj's house, upstairs, in the middle of the hallway, Ravi's room. You could see this if you walked by on the opposite side of the street, if you knew what to look for, if you stood clutching the police tape. Like I did in the days afterward, trying to get a sense of the damage, of who had done what to whom. Here it was, the whole place, laid open like a doll's house, the front room, the kitchen half burned, a fragment of staircase, the charred mattress on Uncle Raj's bed. I wanted to cover it up, come back in the night with some colossal blanket and find a way to drape it from the chimney to the front lawn. I hoped the fire department or the city or the University might bring over those blue tarpaulins, if only to keep people like me away. But no such shroud appeared. Someone wanted us to look, I decided. Someone wanted us to see the house in which Birju and Ravi were together in the small bedroom. The police put it together quite easily, what happened next. One of the boys called out to his uncle, who was on his way to bed, just saying goodnight to the Match Dot Com woman in Vermont. Uncle Raj walked out into the hallway, the phone still pressed to his ear. Don't touch that, he said. His last words. The blast opened the house, tore away the façade. Those were the words in the newspaper, as if I had written the article myself.

The Religious Studies Department expressed its utter shock, its deep dismay. No one had suspected. Dr. Harischandra had never seemed…. Words failed. When had he been radicalized? He had not left the U.S. for years. His students adored him. His sister had trusted him with the care of her sons, whom he loved as if they were his own children. The woman in Vermont turned out to be a nurse, originally from Texas, a widow. Feels like twice, she told the journalists. He was pretty quiet about his life, she said. I had no idea. Not a clue.

As other news buried this news, as spring came into the Yard, and the world greened and trees opened their leaves, slowly, slowly, an idea began to open in my mind. I was the only person who knew what had really happened in the house on Ivy Street. And no one thought to ask me about it, or, I was beginning to believe, ever would. Sometimes, Michael would notice that I'd gone quiet and ask what I was thinking. I couldn't say. I couldn't say, I am thinking of my missing friend Ravi.

I shook my head. "Nothing really," I said. "What are you thinking?"

"Well, I'll tell you," Michael said. He'd kissed me then, and I felt—I'm almost ashamed—relieved.

***

"So, Liam," Nisha said. "There you have it."

That she would trust me with all this—I didn't know what to say.

"What is it I could do for you now, Nisha?"

"Don't forget Djuna," she said. "It's like what she wrote herself: *I wish someone else could think about certain parts of my life.* Don't let me or anyone else forget her."

I said I wouldn't. I told myself *to just slow down.*

"I'd like to know the story of your name," I said. "I'm thinking it's either very simple or very, very complicated."

"Simple," Nisha said. "It means night."

Not simple. Not in the least.

"What about yours?"

"It means protector. Which I have failed to be every day of my life."

"Why do you say that?"

"My mam," I began, "was also a novelist. By her own account very minor. I would get after her about the *very*, how minor is minor, but look here, you're wrong anyway. When I was a lad, we used to go into bookshops and stand in front of the place where her books would be. Just the two of us. Her first novel was published when I was thirteen. My father was raging. For one whole day. And then he never said another word about it. Not that I heard anyway. But what did I do but nick his camera and walk into Hodges Figgis and take photos of my mam's book in its rightful spot. I took his books off the shelf, put them in another part of the alphabet. I shot the whole roll of film, from different angles and at different times of the day. I asked strangers to take up her book and read a page so I could take a photo. I explained why, and no one refused. I made a collage of the photographs and had it mounted behind glass and framed..."

I made myself stop. We both listened to the deep silence from Rosemary Street.

"Your mother must have really loved it. Beyond loved."

"She hung it upstairs in her room, so that she could always see it from her chair. Sometimes she would say, half to herself, 'I expect I'll have to read that novel one day,' and she'd give me a wink."

"'And write me another,' I would say. That was my part. I always said it right on cue. One day, she lowered her voice to a whisper, said maybe she *was* writing another, just possibly, but on the shtum, so no one would notice."

"Was she?" Nisha said.

"She was. She had. It was brilliant. As good as Maeve Binchy. Better."

"I wonder," Nisha said. "I don't know why I thought just now to ask this. Did your mother keep a journal?"

"She did. All four did. We kept ours hidden from my father, but I'm pretty sure I know where hers is. Someday I'll go back and find them."

"All four?"

"I had a brother."

I thought of my vow, taken when we spoke about writing her sister's life. Remember, I Liam, I said now, how it feels, the diminishment, when you tell a secret, a terrible, private thing, and the person you've told doesn't, somehow, do it justice. Remember how that feels.

"Had," Nisha said,

"He's dead. Drowned not long after my father died."

Nisha did the most astonishing thing then. She sat down at my feet, on the carpet, the green tendrils of synthetic material looking like grass, as if she were in a small field. I knew, though I'm not sure how, this was her way of paying respects.

"We're a pair," she said. "Why didn't you tell me?"

"This was for your sister."

"I don't think so," she said. "The world doesn't work like that."

"How does the world work?" I hadn't meant for the words to sound so much like bloody crying.

For a moment, Nisha didn't answer.

"I don't think *work* is the right word. In fact, it's the wrong word. The world just seems to lurch on, from one broken thing to the next."

"It does seem that way."

"So how do you think this particular lurch will end?" I said.

"What do you mean by *this*?"

I didn't know what I meant. We looked at each other for a long moment. I believed that I had not ever been in love with anyone before now. My mind would not let this thought go further. I remember the sensation of that, like an iron wall beyond, over, through which I could not see.

"It won't end," she said then, "as long as I have a piece of my sister I can keep. Some physical piece. Maybe that's crazy and morbid."

"Normal, I think. That's why people keep ashes. It's why people write books."

She said not ashes. She said, how would I know ashes are even hers? She said that was the wisdom of a funeral pyre. You see the body go in, you see what's left. I think this is what she said. It was hard to tell with a voice so broken. Then she leaned in and blew out the candle.

The night was mild and clear. She left the bedroom, moved through the kitchen and out the back door, into the wreck of a summer garden and the pond. The landlord said I could do what I wanted, plant the garden and fill the pond, or just leave it to go to weeds. At first, I spent Saturdays cleaning the overgrowth, running water into the pond, thinking to put in koi and waterlilies, but after Djuna Malik was killed, I threw the flower bouquet from the classroom into the weeds and never went near the pond. Now, I worried Nisha would find this bouquet, feel the dry stems with her feet and just know, and it would crush her to pieces.

I dragged the duvet off the bed and followed. I found her—her eyes glittered in the pitch black—in the middle of the waist-high weeds, and wrapped the duvet around us. I believed I felt the flower stems like spiny straws under my feet. All that ruin—a garden of waste and ruin, a stagnant pond. We dropped onto the overgrown earth. We did not make a sound, so frenzied and raving mad that we had run straight through all the noise of the world into silence.

A week after the murders, Nisha told me, the district attorney's office said it was all right for the victims' families to clear out the rented house in Carrboro. Kasim's parents, Gauri and Maninder, decided that meeting to do this was the logical way to proceed in the face of such illogic: divide the possessions, the linens, the furniture, the kitchen utensils their children would never need again, in this house or any other. At first Nisha wanted to tell them she couldn't get there, and so they could have everything, but slowly she came to the desire to see the place, stand in the spot where Djuna had been last. She felt like she was trying to find her way down a dark path in a black and frightening forest, and she wondered if the house in Carrboro could be the end of the path. Michael offered to go with her, but Nisha didn't want him. She wanted the house to herself as she had wanted Djuna's wrecked body to herself, to be unobserved in grief. Not to bother anyone else. It was a strange, illogical, backward indulgence, she knew that, but the knowing did not help.

She began to look for a way to be alone in the house: arrive early or say she had a change of plans and would go a different day, a few days later. She didn't think she could bear everyone else's devastation on top of her own. She would crumble. Or they all would. She pictured herself falling to her knees on the kitchen linoleum and staying there.

That morning, Gauri texted to say they would be late. It was nearly unbearable: their third child, Shameen, had fallen from her bicycle, suffered a concussion and was in hospital. She would be alright, but of course, plans had to be changed.

Someone, the rental agent perhaps or the police crew, had cleaned up the blood. Nisha now knew that Kasim had been shot just inside the front door and his sister in her bedroom. Djuna had been in the kitchen. Nisha went there first. She knew suddenly what she had wanted all along was not anything that belonged to Djuna, but to see where she fell and—this shocked her most of all—find evidence. A bullet hole, a broken chair, a nick in the linoleum.

There was nothing. The kitchen looked as if the children had left for their classes and would return in a couple of hours. Three place mats and three napkins, the orange, green, and yellow stripes like kinte cloth, remained on the table around which chairs were neatly tucked in. Dishes, silverware and coffee cups rested in the drainer beside the sink. Djuna said they hardly ever used the dishwasher because everyone was so good about the washing up. One of the final sentences Nisha had said to Djuna: *That won't last.* But, in the worst way, it had lasted.

Nisha opened the refrigerator: yogurt, a Britta water carafe, a bag of apples, a loaf of rye bread, condiments. She would leave those for Kasim's mother. She shut the refrigerator door and turned away, vaguely disappointed. Nothing of Djuna's, at least not that she could tell.

The cabinets: boxes of coffee pods for the Keurig, a vacuum

sealed cardboard container of chicken broth, a box of microwave popcorn packets, an unopened bag of quinoa, dried cranberries, cans of tuna and diced tomatoes, a jar each of kalamata olives, salsa, harissa. Curry mix packets—Nisha wondered if she ought to hide these from Gauri. Chocolate chips, brown sugar, rice, oatmeal—steel-cut and regular—sun-dried tomatoes, soy sauce. A life in food. They had never got around to baking chocolate chip cookies. This thought stopped Nisha in her tracks. Djuna wouldn't ever again taste a cookie, a bit of chocolate.

And then she saw it, along the bottom of the stove, three splashes of blood, oxidized brown, each one the size and shape of a dried chickpea. She knelt and looked more closely. Djuna must have fallen right here. A kind of awe flooded her brain, as if she were suddenly in the presence of the living Djuna. This was better than ashes, whatever *better* now meant in the world. She stared, and then her mind began to revolve very slowly: how to keep this blood, how to take it off the metal of the stove and keep it with her. She ticked off possible methods, then rose from her knees and began slowly, carefully to open drawers, as if too much movement might crumble the blood to invisible dust, thinking through how she might do this, weighing the possibilities as she discovered what each drawer held. When she came to the dish towels, she knew. She'd bought these, white flour sack squares, the best, really, for drying pots and pans, dishes, glassware, and hands. She saw that most of the towels had never been used—there hadn't of course been time enough to go through the whole dozen.

She chose a towel from the bottom of the pile, wet it under the faucet, squeezed out the excess water. She folded the towel in half and in half again, until she was holding a damp bit the size of an envelope. She knelt again and very carefully pressed the towel against the spots of blood, then peeled it back. There was the likeness. A Catholic might be put in mind of the Shroud of Turin.

No, she thought, not a likeness. More. Better. The thing itself. She folded the towel.

Again, she opened drawers until she found a box of storage bags. She pulled one from the box and slipped the towel inside, ran her fingers along the seal, pressing hard.

There, she thought, there. I have you. The last living part of you. She felt almost as if she'd rescued her sister. For the first time in weeks, really since August, when they had first dropped Djuna here, she felt a tiny sliver of peace.

Not quite an hour later, Kasim's and Sariah's parents arrived. When Nisha heard them, she put down the clothes she was folding and walked out into the hallway. She realized she had not planned what to do—whether to embrace them and keep silent or deliver the stupid platitudes. As if by mutual agreement, they all three stood still, frozen, and stared at each other, as if waiting for an explanation. No rush to embrace or even to speak. Perhaps they could understand what had happened to the children just from looking. This, Nisha thought, is what people see when they look at me. They read my thoughts: *If only I could have looked at her longer.*

"How is Shameen?" she said finally.

"Shameen...." Gauri said.

"She's still sleeping," Maninder said.

"That's good," Nisha said. "I mean...I would think. Probably."

"Yes," he said. "We can't—the doctors thought an induced coma...."

Nisha realized she was blocking their way to the kitchen and the back bedroom. She stepped aside, into the doorway of Djuna's room so they could pass. Maninder shook her hand. Gauri carried empty boxes and did not pause.

"I'm afraid," he said quietly. "I'm afraid she won't wake up. I made Gauri leave the hospital. I should go back. They said they would

148

let us know, but I want to be there just in case."

"I understand," Nisha said. "It's just too much, isn't it? I'll pray for her."

"Thank you." Maninder walked back the way he had come. After a while, Nisha heard his car engine. He had forgotten to close the front door. Nisha hurried to do so, and then she turned the dead bolt.

She tried to think what Gauri would want—to be left alone or not. She moved back into Djuna's room, picked up and folded another t-shirt, the yellow poll monitor shirt from the 2015 primary election, when Djuna began to be interested in politics. Nisha had one of these shirts too.

From the back of the house came the flutter and bump of books falling, and then a shout. She thought Gauri had said *damn*. She lay the yellow shirt in the box on Djuna's bed and walked out into the hallway. She called to Gauri, but there was no answer.

Gauri was not in the kitchen. Nisha glanced into the room that had been Kasim's, but it was empty. Sariah's room, next door, also empty. Nisha listened carefully, heard what sounded panting from the other side of Sariah's bed.

Gauri was sitting on the floor, wedged between the bed and the wall, beside an open backpack, textbooks and papers spilled out. Gauri held a cell phone. She was texting. Tears ran down her cheeks.

"Oh, Gauri," Nisha began.

"I shouldn't be here," Gauri said. "I should be at the hospital. Maninder made me leave. I don't want to be in this house."

"I can drive you back if you want."

"I wouldn't ask you to do that. I know you don't want to go anywhere near that place."

"You're right," Nisha said. "I don't." All of a sudden, she felt as if her body had grown too heavy. Stars glittered at the top of her vision. She sat down on Sariah's bed.

"Don't," Gauri said.

Nisha leaned forward and stared at the carpet. "I'm sorry. I just need a minute."

"I know it doesn't make any sense," Gauri said. "But I don't want to be near so much death."

At first Nisha didn't understand, but then she saw them all in her mind's eye, huddled together.

"You mean my parents."

"Yes."

"I can't help it," Nisha said. "I didn't do anything."

"I know," Gauri said. "I'm sorry. I'll call Maninder to come and get me."

Nisha stood and made her way quickly through the house and into Djuna's bedroom. She lay down on the bed and closed her eyes. The roaring in her ears gradually drained away as if she had inserted earplugs. The silence was so complete that she touched her fingers to her ears to make certain. She wondered if she'd fallen unconscious, and during that time, Gauri had left. She thought of a poem from school, the one about the fine and quiet place, and struggled to remember all the words.

"But then it came to me," Nisha said. "And it was like I was back in school. I heard the swishing of girls' uniform skirts as you passed by them in the hallways, the slamming of lockers, the smell of the refectory. *The grave's a fine and quiet place/But none I fear do there embrace.*"

She seemed to be waiting for me to say something, but I couldn't.

"So now I do have some of her," Nisha said. "I thought that might be enough, but it isn't." She pressed her palms flat on the blue-books between us, as if she were holding down a great weight.

"I feel like I want to start over from the beginning and read all

150

the entries again. Start from the beginning and go all the way through, then start over again. I feel like it's the only thing I want to read ever, for the rest of my life. But, then, I don't know. I'm still on the outside, looking at her. Looking at a ghost. I want to be in it too. It sounds crazy, but I don't want her to be alone.

"We can do that," I said. "We can write you back in."

"I don't think I understand what you're talking about."

"I have to admit something to you. I wanted to keep your sister's journal, use it to write a novel, put my name on it."

"But why would you want to write that book?" Nisha said. "It has nothing to do with you."

"Not on the surface, but some parts of it, I…some parts feel so familiar."

"In what way?"

"I can't explain."

"Well, then, how long have you been thinking about this?"

"After the first few prompts if I'm being totally honest," I said. "More seriously since she was killed."

"Is that why you called me? Is that why—" Nisha flung her arm toward the bedroom. "Is that why you wanted to keep talking?"

"At first, when I first called, yes. But then as soon as I met you, I…"

"What if I'd asked to have her journal back? What if I'd walked in and held out my hand and said I'll just take it with me?"

"I would have given it to you, " I said. "But then I would have found some reason for you to stay."

"Why?"

"Because I realized how sad I was, and I could see you were too, and I just thought that we might…."

I thought she would take my hand then, but she didn't.

"I couldn't write a book from only Djuna's journal. There would be just the one character, and what kind of novel would that be? You should be in the book and Felicia and her masala, and Jamie, even Michael. Everything that led to Djuna's being here."

"So she's not alone?" Nisha said.

What was it she wrote? *I wish someone else could think about certain parts of my life.*

"I wonder what she really meant by that."

"See her life a different way? Put it all together in one piece?"

Nisha nodded.

"What if you granted her that wish?" I asked her.

"Where would I even start? I'm not a writer."

"I'll show you where. We can write it together."

II.

#5

Imagine a ghost. Start *during*.

"So, I'm figuring it out, this bless your heart thing," Djuna said. "It basically means fuck you."

Michael put down his spoon, folded his hands as if he were going to offer a prayer. "Not always, Djuna," he said. "Sometimes it means you're amazing."

"In a cynical way, though," Djuna said. "Like you're so fucking amazing you're pathetic."

Nisha listened to this exchange carefully, trying to appear as if she were not paying any attention at all. It wasn't a full-blown argument yet. Maybe it wouldn't get there.

"It's a form of southern hospitality," Michael said.

"I think," Djuna said slowly, "southern hospitality is basically bullshit."

"Nisha?" Michael said. "Does your sister have to use that kind of language when she talks to me?" He picked up his bowl and spoon and carried them to the sink.

"Oh, Michael," Nisha said. "She uses it when she talks to me too."

"Well," he said, "you're family."

"Aren't you?"

Michael slammed to spoon into the sink. "I don't know what I am around here anymore," he said. He leaned into the kitchen counter, hyper-extending his elbows, which made him seem larger, imminently explosive. His back was to them. Nisha could see his head shook slightly.

"This is kind of what I'm talking about," Djuna said quietly. "No one here really says what they mean."

"I'm not southern," Michael said. "Your sister's not southern."

"We're about to get a new neighbor who's not southern." Nisha wasn't sure why she said this—what point it proved, whose side she was on.

Djuna continued. "Somebody said to me in class the other day, Wow you must get really tan in the summer. When what she meant was, you're a brown freak."

"Maybe she didn't mean that," Nisha said. "Maybe she's one of those white girls who can't tan."

"Like me," Michael said. He turned, crossed his arms over his chest, cocked his hip. The air seemed to rush back into the room, into their lungs. Whoosh! Everyone could breathe again, laugh, maybe even float.

"I just wish," Djuna said, "there was one person here from India. Just one. Preferably a girl, but I could deal with a boy as long as his parents didn't try to make us get engaged."

"I remember wishing for that too," Nisha said.

Michael turned away again, stared out the kitchen window. His arms hung, relaxed at his sides. Nisha walked to the windows facing the river. The sun broke through the cloud and shone in a silver strip on the far shore so it appeared the tide had rolled out and left a beach. She thought she could make out a small figure standing there, on that shelf of light. Mommy, she thought, that's you, isn't it? You're so far away. How can you hear us from over there? Can't you come any closer?

"I'm going to call Amy," Michael said. "It's her birthday."

"Oh, sorry," Nisha said. "I forgot."

"She might not be home anyway." Michael picked up his cell phone, crossed the room to the door, let himself out onto the deck.

Nisha and Djuna watched him go. When he was settled into one of the deck chairs with his back to them, they exchanged a look, raised eyebrows.

"Where does Amy even live these days?" Djuna said.

"Honestly, I'm not sure. She's moved back and forth between

Ohio and Iowa so many times I've lost track. I'm still sort of amazed she ever left home."

"Home being her parents' house?"

"Right."

"She doesn't really like you, does she?"

"Not really."

"The whole lot of them. They think Michael married—"

"Djuna. Please. I don't want to talk about it."

"A black girl."

Nisha rose from the table and went to stand behind her sister's chair. She combed through Djuna's long hair with her fingers, dividing it into thirds, beginning a braid. She leaned down and kissed Djuna on the top of her head. "Well, bless your heart," she whispered.

"Very funny," Djuna said. Her shoulders relaxed. "That feels so nice."

"Mommy used to do this whenever I came home."

"Do you ever wonder," Djuna asked, "where home is?"

"I guess I don't think about it," Nisha said.

"You try not to."

Nisha felt a flash of anger, just a little, mostly because she knew Djuna was right.

She believed home was wherever she made it, wherever she was. She was home in and around Boston because she was in school there. Now she was home in eastern North Carolina because she just was. What would be more complicated was the homelessness she would feel when Djuna wasn't part of this physical home.

"My spirit sort of shrugs at the question," she told Djuna

For Djuna, home was India. And then it was nowhere. And now, on the way to college, it was literally nowhere, unknown.

"I think," Nisha said, "I felt very at home sometimes in Boston. I knew the neighborhoods. I knew Cambridge and the streets around

MIT. I knew Newberry Street where Mommy liked that one hotel. Everybody who looked like me was an outsider. At least you knew where you stood."

"What about here?" Djuna said.

"No."

"No, what?"

"Sometimes when no one understands much about you," Nisha said, "it can be a good thing."

"You feel kind of elevated. Misunderstood is special."

"No. Or sort of. It's like you have a third eye or an extra arm or you've been to outer space. You know something most people don't know. And when you find other people from India, you don't have to talk about it. You can just know."

"Well, that will be nice."

"In college," Nisha said. "You'll find them in college."

"I hope so. But I have to say, no matter where I end up, I'm worried. All the white people. All the white people who won't trust me. What if I'm packed into a dorm with them?" Djuna paused, took a deep breath. "Do you think I could look into living off campus?"

"Let me think about it," Nisha said.

Who had lived off campus in Cambridge? Vegetarians and pot-heads. And Michael. Before she ever walked to Porter Square, where Michael lived his second year, Nisha half-believed she would find cows and pigs and chickens roaming freely, unafraid of butchering, or stoned kids staring off into space. Michael thought this was very funny. She'd never felt comfortable in those houses, though. The shared kitchens, lines for the bathroom, people coming and going at all hours, half of whom didn't even live there. Her parents had wanted the safety and supervision of the dormitories for Nisha. Surely, they would want the same for their younger daughter.

How could they want anything now, Djuna would ask.

Who else lived off campus? Professors. The house on Ivy Street, the house she had last seen blown open, exposed. A house full of injury and death. Sometimes that house entered her dreams, even all these years later, appearing as a sentient being, bloodied, shaking in pain, howling wind giving the house a voice. A haunted house in the truest sense.

And yet. Uncle Raj's house had been a refuge for Nisha, an escape from the noise and frenzy of college. She had been happy there, before the awful end, with Ravi and Birju, the boys Michael had first described as "your countrymen." Maybe Djuna could find that too.

The new neighbor was called Felicity Graham.

"It's coals to Newcastle," Felicity Graham said. "Which I always thought was the same as a bus-man's holiday. Meaning you just get more of the same whether you want it or not."

"Thank you," Nisha said, taking the pot Felicity held out to her. It was barely warm. The scent of ginger—exact. She could close her eyes and open them and she'd be in her mother's kitchen in Mumbai.

"It's a sort of tikka masala, but really more like dal. It's what I cook best, so I thought it would be insulting not to bring it. To bring you my horrifying chicken divan or my lasagna with the half raw pasta."

Djuna was just coming in the door from school. She sniffed the air. "Did you cook?" she asked Nisha. "Really?"

"Your barmy new neighbor did," Felicity said. "Welcome to the neighborhood."

"We should be welcoming you," Nisha said.

"Seriously?" Djuna said. "You brought Indian food to the Indians?"

"This is Djuna," Nisha said to Felicity. "Djuna, be polite."

She set the pot on the counter. Djuna dropped her backpack by the door, crossed the kitchen, opened the silverware drawer, and took out a spoon.

"Will you have a seat?" Nisha asked Felicity.

"I'd better stand until there's a verdict," she said. She pointed to Djuna's spoon going into the pot.

"Oh my god," Djuna said. "Lamb? Where do you even get lamb around here? Unless you keep sheep. I know there are cows and pigs down the road." She brought the spoon to her lips.

"It's probably better warmed a bit more," Felicity said.

Djuna dipped in for another bite. "Wow," she said.

Felicity looked at Nisha. "Is *wow* good?"

"Wow is phenomenal," Djuna said. "This may be better than my mother's."

Felicity turned to Nisha. "I guess that's high praise. Yours must be pretty good."

"Hers is terrible," Djuna said. "The problem is she hates to cook."

"But you said—" Felicity began.

It was simple enough to explain but always seemed to suck the air out of the room. Nisha wished Djuna would say it, but now she'd grown quiet, turned away from them toward the sink, took a long time rinsing the spoon she'd just used. Outside, water slapped against the bulkhead. The windows were open, so they could hear it, a painfully human sound, an open hand against someone's cheek.

"We're sisters," Nisha said.

"Well, actually, that's something of a relief," Felicity said. "I was just trying to work out how old you must have been when you had her."

"I can imagine," Nisha said. In her mind, she juggled the rest of it, whether she needed to talk any more about her parents.

"Are you here for a visit, Djuna?" Felicity said.

Yes, it seemed she would have to.

Djuna turned towards them. She was smiling awkwardly as if she didn't know exactly how the mechanics of smiling worked. "Sometimes I wish," she said. "But no. Our parents are dead, and so…."

"I'm very sorry," Felicity said.

"Thank you," Nisha and Djuna said in unison.

Nisha turned to Djuna. "We're good at that, aren't we?" she said.

Djuna made a guttural sound—disgust mixed with horror and sadness. When you encounter something that's both pitiful and ugly. Like a harelip on a child. Nisha had no idea why that was the image that came to mind.

The three of them, Nisha noticed, stood still, facing in different directions, the afternoon light falling on different parts of their bodies. She could tell—or thought she could—Felicity wanted to say something about death and loss—or she thought she could tell. The realtor who handled the sale of Felicity's new house was a terrible gossip, and so Nisha knew that Felicity and her husband had retired from New York, that they bought a big house on Dolphin Point, that a month later, he was killed in a boating accident at their dock. Felicity didn't want to live in that house anymore.

Grief doesn't really translate, Nisha told herself. It's yours or it's someone else's, and that's that.

"Does anybody want tea?" Djuna said. "My sister's got me into this terribly civilized habit of tea with milk and honey after school."

"I'll have a cup," Nisha said, too quickly. "Felicity?"

"As the accent would suggest, I'm a fan of tea. But I'm trying to drink more coffee."

"We have coffee. Iced if you like."

"Yes, thanks. That would be lovely."

"My sister makes coffee ice cubes," Djuna said. "So it doesn't get watery. Which I thought was brilliant."

"Oh, it is!" Felicity said.

"We're all trying so very hard, aren't we?" Djuna said. "Actually, though, I'm sorry. We didn't get introduced."

"That's true," Felicity said. "I'm Felicity Graham. And yes, we are trying very hard. That seems to be what people do, though."

"I've seen you in town," Djuna said. "What do you do?"

"I've just begun delivering the mail." Felicity folded her hands in her lap. "So I'm here and there. I expect you've seen the flashing light on my car, which I dislike. It worries people. What do you do?" She pointed to the backpack. "I mean besides school."

Djuna glanced at Nisha. "Not much," she said. "I guess what I do now is wait. I wait for colleges to accept me. I wait for school to be over. I wait to graduate."

"She's already been accepted at Chapel Hill," Nisha said.

"But that's not where I want to go," Djuna said.

"It's a really good school," Nisha said.

"I have a son who works there," Felicity said. "He likes the town."

"How many times do I have to say it to you?" Djuna's voice was a low growl, like a trapped animal.

"I know," Nisha said lightly, quickly. "It's *here*."

"I have to get out of *here*."

Felicity, Nisha saw, was watching them for an opening. And then she found it.

"In the old days," she said, "I would fill you with terror. My very presence. Because I would bring the letters from the colleges."

"That's how I got mine," Nisha said. "We were the last ones, I think. Envelopes either thick or thin."

"I don't know how you stood it," Djuna said. "This way is so much better. An email."

"It's still waiting, though, isn't it?" Felicity said. "You'll get in lots of places, I bet. These days. You know—diversity and all that."

For a moment, no one spoke.

"I also throw pots," Felicity said.

Djuna understood before Nisha did. Nisha was thinking about the two glass walls in Felicity's new house.

"Do you have a kiln?" Djuna said.

"I have one on order. And then I'm going to build a studio."

"What kinds of things do you make?" Nisha said.

"The usual. Bowls, mugs. Vessels of all sorts."

"Things that hold and carry," Djuna said.

Felicity looked at her with what seemed to Nisha great tenderness. And curiosity. "What will you study at university, Djuna?"

"Um…." She was smiling, Nisha saw. "Literature. I like writing. I'm thinking I'd like to be a writer."

"Is that so?" Felicity said. "How very interesting. I hope you'll come down and see my things for carrying and holding."

"Of course," Nisha said. "I'd love to." She tried to put her arm around Djuna's shoulders. "We'd love to."

"My sister did pottery in college," Djuna said.

"I was terrible," Nisha said. "My prettiest piece was porcelain, meant to be a bowl, but it collapsed on the wheel to have this sort of ruffled edge. The glaze saved it from complete ugliness."

"Mommy loved it," Djuna said.

"The red. Like berries. She preferred all things red, even if they were ugly." She turned to Felicity. "Anyway, I'd love to see what you do."

"Super," Felicity said, setting down her glass. She'd held it the entire time, Nisha noticed. Her fingers had gone white from the cold. Short, bitten nails. Thick fingers, very strong. "I'd better get going. Leave you to dinner and homework and all that." She handed the glass to Nisha. "Thanks for the coffee. The ice cubes really are brilliant."

"Thanks," Nisha said. "See you again soon, I hope."

"Yes," Felicity said. "I'll make sure of it. Enjoy the tikka."

"We will," Djuna said. "Tonight."

Nisha had to resist the impulse to watch Felicity until she was out of sight, *wave you off*, they said to guests. Felicity might find it odd. Djuna came over to the window, watched until Felicity had disappeared into her house.

"She's funny," Djuna said. "'Diversity and all that.' I don't think she has a clue."

"Do you know her story?" She told Djuna what the real estate agent had said.

"She does have a sort of fragile look. When she said she was a potter, it made sense."

"Life imitates art."

"I think it's supposed to be the other way around. According to the art history textbook."

"As usual, I've got it all wrong," Nisha said.

"No. You're just being creative."

"Right. Anyway, she's apparently a good cook. Did you ever notice how artistic people tend to be good cooks?"

"Somehow, I think Van Gogh was a terrible cook."

"I know what you're thinking. Please don't say it."

"I won't." Djuna checked her phone, stood up, walked to the windows, stared out at the river. "All this stupid banter. I'm trying to stay calm."

"You're doing a good job at the moment."

"I'm kind of like a howling animal inside. Do you think they'll all come in on the same day?'

"It could happen like that."

"In a way that would be good."

A week later, when in fact all the other college decisions were released on the same day, it was the farthest thing from good. Nisha was at CVS when her cell rang, just leaving to meet Djuna at the high school so they could check emails together. Djuna was crying so hard she couldn't speak. Finally she managed to say that every single college had rejected her.

"Damn it, Mommy and Daddy," Nisha said aloud as soon as she was alone in the car. "You're supposed to have some power. You weren't supposed to let this happen." She wondered if she could say anything to make Djuna feel better. She didn't think so. She drove the two miles to the high school thinking somehow there had been a mistake and hoping that thinking could make it so. She found Djuna in the parking lot, sitting in her car. She pulled her car in beside Djuna's, got out, climbed into Djuna's passenger seat.

"It can't be right," Djuna said. "It can't be. I'm so embarrassed. But it can't be right." She refreshed the emails on her phone over and over. She sobbed. She pounded on the steering wheel. Nisha tried to hold her across the console between the seats, but Djuna pushed her away. Sun blazed in through the front windshield. Nisha had a sense of complete exposure, that there was nowhere to hide, even though the parking lot was completely empty except for them.

"At least it's over," Nisha said.

"No, no, no," Djuna wailed. "It's not over! It can't be over! I wanted to go away so bad. I have to go away. This can't be right. She punched letters on her phone. "Maybe I missed something. Here." She tossed the phone into Nisha's lap. "You check. Please tell me I'm reading them wrong."

Nisha opened the emails, one at a time. After each one, she had to return to Djuna's account and choose another admissions portal. It was slow going, excruciating. Rejection after rejection. Six. She looked up at Djuna and shook her head. Djuna gripped the steering wheel and lowered her forehead onto her hands.

"I must be just a piece of shit," she said. "No one wants me."

"Chapel Hill wants you."

"But I can't do that. I have to get out of here."

At that moment, the principal walked out of the building. He was a kind man, quite young for the job. He called everyone "friend" in a way that seemed entirely natural, appreciated by parents and students and teachers. But no, Nisha thought, not now. Go away, friend. He stood for a moment under the front portico, looking directly at them, considering maybe. And then something, some intuition, made him turn away, walk in the opposite direction, toward the baseball field.

"Let's go home, Djuna," Nisha said. "You can leave your car here, and I'll bring you to school tomorrow."

"I can't go to school tomorrow. I'm a fucking failure. Everyone will know."

"They won't know."

"They'll ask. The teachers will ask."

"You can say you don't know yet."

"Nisha, that's stupid. It's all over the Internet. Everybody knows."

They looked up at the school building, quiet, abandoned, now waiting to reanimate, fill with people and opinions and gossip.

Okay, okay, okay, Nisha thought. We can't solve this here. "Let's just go home and talk about it. I'll drive you. You can relax and check your phone. If you text people, then they'll know. I know you don't believe this, but by tomorrow, they will have moved on."

"No they won't."

Nisha can't remember how they got out of Djuna's car and into hers and back to the river. She thought maybe Djuna fell asleep. Nisha was glad for unconsciousness, even though she knew it wouldn't last, and the whole scene would replay itself for Michael, which it did. He tried to comfort Djuna, as Nisha had, until Djuna said the one awful, true thing: they would never be able to understand how she felt. They had both got into the college they wanted.

"That doesn't make me incapable of understanding," Michael said.

"I'm pretty sure it does," Djuna said. She went back to her computer.

"What are you doing there?" Michael said.

"I'm looking up directors of admissions. I'm going to write to them. I'm going to ask them to tell me why I wasn't accepted."

"Djuna," Michael said. "Why don't you step away from the computer for a little while? Give it a rest."

"Leave me alone."

"It's not going to change anything to write to them."

"Michael," Nisha said. "There's no harm. Just let her do it if she wants to." She put her hand on Michael's arm, but he shook it off.

"I should break her fucking computer."

Nisha could see Djuna had frozen. Slowly and carefully, she closed the laptop, slid off the sofa and disappeared into her room.

She saw it in her mind's eye as if he'd already done it: Michael breaking Djuna's computer. He took it off the sofa, pulled the computer out of its fabric sleeve and threw it against the wall in Djuna's bedroom. He noted the way the machine separated, screen from keyboard, frame from screen, housing from hard drive. He counted the letters that left the keyboard: F, J A, N. He wanted them to spell something. He wanted this whole exercise to be a way to get Djuna's attention back from wherever she was.

Nisha wanted to ask Michael why he would say such a thing. She wanted to pack a bag and pack another for Djuna. The two of them would leave this house and drive to Chapel Hill and wait for school to start. She could feel some electricity in her body hastening her toward the bedroom, her suitcases.

"The least we can do," she said instead, "is let her live off campus."

Michael didn't say anything.

Later, Djuna was lying on the couch with her back to them, earphones in. It was possible that she'd fallen asleep. The setting sun zoomed through the window over the kitchen sink, blinding if you looked west. Some mysterious refraction made a rainbow on the top of Djuna's head.

"I'm not sure what made you change your mind about the housing," Michael said.

"I think right now I'd do anything to make her happy."

Nisha discovered she had the same exercise schedule as Felicity Graham, who turned out to be the very best gym-mate: which was to say, not a mate at all: focused, intense, working too hard to converse, in and out in an hour. Afterwards, in the parking lot, they exchanged greetings, had a bit of a chat, town news. Nisha suggested they meet for a glass of wine and have a real conversation. Felicity said she had been thinking the same thing, so it was arranged. Nisha could tell that Felicity wanted to ask about Djuna's college applications but held herself back. And Nisha couldn't bring herself to offer the news—or couldn't see how, decide what tone to take. The hurt was still raw, though Djuna seemed to have got a little ways past it. She was awarded a grand scholarship. It was clear she would be either first or second in her class and would make a speech at graduation. A balm of happiness began to seep into place gouged out by pain and failure.

They met at a bar near the town dock, where they could sit on the porch and look out at the transient boats. They ordered glasses of wine, Nisha following Felicity's lead. People coming into the bar stopped at their table to say hello to Felicity, ask how she was doing.

The entire town seemed to know her, cherish her. They sipped at their wine between these interruptions.

"How did you end up here?"

"My husband was from Ceylon. Sri Lanka. I guess you and I are a kind of mirror image. He was in the import business in New York. Then he wanted warmer weather."

"You seem to have made a lot of friends very quickly."

"Yes, but it's taken a sort of turn now." Felicity was silent for a moment. "I expect you know how this feels," she said finally. "All these well-meaning condolences avoiding the word *dead*."

"I do," Nisha said. "Though my parents died a long time ago. I don't talk about it."

"Please don't tell me you never get over it."

"If I told you otherwise, I'd be lying. But I think everybody's grief is different. Separate. Personal."

"I don't believe that," Felicity said. "I don't believe grief is personal. I think it's got to be shared. It has to be. Nobody can do this alone."

"I think it's done alone here."

"Yes," Felicity said. "That's what they try but—I heard a writer say this just recently, on the radio. That whole American myth of rugged individualism falls apart when you're trying to grieve something profound on your own. It's just too much to lift. That's why, you know, in some cultures—yours, my husband's—the women practice ululation."

"I remember. And you can hear it from really far away."

"It's just chilling, isn't it? But what other noise would you make when you find death?"

It was hard to tell what confusion of feeling lay behind Felicity's expression.

"So," she said. "I really can't contain myself. About the college news. Is it going to be Harvard then?"

"No," Nisha said, and she told the story, just a couple of sentences. "She's made her peace with Chapel Hill."

"I'm shocked," Felicity said. "I thought surely…the demographics, as they say, the legacy—isn't that what they call it? Her race."

Nisha tried not to feel annoyed, insulted. "None of that made a difference. Obviously."

"How is she taking it?"

"As you might imagine. But she's thinking she might feel better living off campus, and I think we'll let her."

"Well, I'm still shocked. In this day and age."

"What this day and age is seems to be up for grabs. And also dangerous in *the demographic*, as you say."

"Do you feel afraid?"

"Sometimes. In Cambridge I probably wouldn't feel afraid. But maybe I'd be foolish not to."

"Do you ever think," Felicity said, "that in many places in the south, this would never happen? Us, together, having a drink." She extended her arm next to Nisha's on the table. "You make me look so much whiter."

"Wasn't that how it was to be with your husband?" Nisha said

"My family was horrified. They thought he was dirty." Felicity said this with a theatrical frown and shake of the head.

"And ate odd, smelly foods. Michael's family seems to feel the same way."

"You lot do eat odd, smelly foods, but my ancestors grew to like that sort of thing when you were cooking for us in Bombay."

"I wonder if there's a complex for that, when the captor begins to imitate the captive."

"If there were, no one would say so."

"Your husband wanted to come here. What did you want?"

"For him to be happy." Felicity scanned the boats in the anchorage beyond the town dock. "For him to live a long time."

"I'm sorry."

"Thank you. I'll ask you the same question, then. What did *you* want?"

"For him to be happy. And then my sister came to live with us."

Felicity tipped her chin up as if she'd got the scent of something. "A child complicated things," she said.

Nisha nodded. She wondered about Felicity's use of the past tense.

It seemed as though Felicity wanted to say more. She twisted the white cocktail napkin into the shape of a pointed finger.

"My husband wasn't a very good father. He was happiest when Devin wasn't there. I think now he was jealous." Here Felicity paused, smoothed the napkin back into a flat square. "He wanted a baby. But then it was hard for him to understand that I couldn't give him my full attention, that he had to share my attention with Devin."

"I think…" Nisha said carefully, "I believe I understand what you mean."

Felicity's house down the road seemed to be made of glass and light and water. The previous owners had renovated and then moved into town. Nisha had never been inside.

"It's a bit overdone," Felicity said. "And any other site would be too exposed, but here, with no close neighbors, but here, it's wondrous. All I see is sky and water. And boats. From any window."

They were standing in the kitchen. The kitchen window faced the edge of the property where Felicity had stored her husband's boats, five of them, a dinghy, a Carolina skiff and three sailboats, parked at odd angles to one another. It looked to Nisha as though they had been dropped there from the sky.

"What a perfect mess I've made," Felicity said. She dipped her head in the direction of the boats. "I could blame it on the transport company, but I won't."

"The longer I live here," Nisha said, "the better I understand that's just how boat people are. They have different ideas about space."

"From living on boats, you mean? We did that for a few months, but it wasn't my cup of tea. As it were."

"It wouldn't have been mine either. But I think when sailing people get on dry land, they feel...*expansive*."

"That's a funny theory."

"Probably wrong. And insulting. Don't tell anyone."

"I won't," Felicity said. She pointed to one of the sailboats, the most dilapidated. *Apsara* was painted across the transom in a font made of curves and scimitars. "The red one. Why he would buy a sailboat without a mast I haven't a clue. Except now it seems like a metaphor. I expect you know what the name means?"

"Good guess that I would know." Nisha nudged Felicity with her elbow.

"Not too terribly racist of me."

"Fairly racist. But I forgive you because you're a foreigner."

"Very funny. My husband bought it in D.C.," Felicity said. "Technically, Maryland. From a doctor who said a friend had asked him to keep it, and then the friend disappeared. She seems to have a long history of good intentions."

"How do you mean?"

"A boat's a she. You know that. You just forgot."

"No, I mean the long history of good intentions."

"Well, my husband intended to work on the boat, get her back in the water. The doctor intended the same. So did his disappeared friend. I'd say that amounts to a lot of bad karma." Felicity bowed her head, stared at her feet. "Sorry," she muttered.

Nisha reached over, grasped her forearm. "No," she said. "Don't worry. That wasn't completely offensive. Anyway, karma is neutral."

"Thank God," Felicity said.

"You're pretty funny, you know that?"

"I used to be funnier."

"The *apsara* I know is a water nymph," Nisha said. "It means going between the waters and the clouds. Perfect, actually, for a sailboat. If I had ever had a daughter, I might have named her Apsara."

Felicity sighed. "I'm sorry you didn't. But you've been so good to Djuna. I don't want you to think I don't like being a mother. Or being my son's mother."

"I think all parents must feel that way at some time. I'm sure my mother did."

"Which reminds me. The thing I wanted to tell you. My son lives in a nice neighborhood just beyond Carrboro. He says there are houses to rent all the time. Nice solid suburban brick houses."

"Doesn't that seem like—I don't know," Nisha said. "Suspicious? That much turn-over."

"I hadn't thought of that."

"Have you been there?"

Felicity turned away, busied herself at the sink. The chime of glasses and silverware seemed unnecessarily loud.

"I've seen pictures," she said. "It's simple, but there's a little fenced yard out back. He made a garden and grew some tomatoes last year."

"What does your son do?"

"I'm not sure now. A cable company, I think. He used to take care of some of the buildings on campus. He said he was in buildings and grounds. I always thought that sounded rather funny. A bit like a ghost."

"It does," Nisha said. "You should go up there sometime. The campus is beautiful."

"So I hear."

This was the moment, Nisha thought, when you either asked or you didn't. She wondered if there was some kind of a cheat, a half-way ask.

"Does he come home often?"

"We just don't see eye to eye on much of anything," Felicity said. "I try so hard sometimes, and a conversation will seem to be going along fine, and then I'll just ruin it."

Nisha went to the sink, put her hand on Felicity's back, between her shoulder blades. "I'm sure it's not just you. Conversation goes both ways."

"I wonder sometimes if deep down I really don't like my own child."

Nisha felt Felicity lean harder into the hand on her back.

"But returning to the subject of Chapel Hill," Felicity said briskly. "I can ask Devin if there are houses to rent in his neighborhood."

"Thank you. I think. I was never sold on Djuna living off campus, but I guess—" she nodded toward the wrecked boats—"that ship has sailed, as it were."

"Ships do that," Felicity said, "or else they knock you overboard at your own dock, and nobody's paying attention, and you drown."

"Oh Felicity," Nisha said. "I don't think you could have done anything."

"But I think I could have."

"Do you ever feel," Nisha asked Michael later, "that you could have done something to save your father? Could have prevented his death?"

"No," Michael said.

"Really?"

"I couldn't have stopped a heart attack."

"I keep thinking about my parents. I could have visited," Nisha said. "Remember how we talked about going to India for Thanksgiving that year?"

"We decided it would be too short a trip to go that far."

"But before that, we thought there was a way we could take off most of November."

"Realistically...."

"I know. But if we had been there...."

"We might have been out with them," Michael said.

"Sometimes I wonder if that would have been better."

"Then your sister wouldn't have any family."

"No. She would have been with us."

"So, we'd all be dead."

"Yes."

"So," Michael said, "you're blaming me for all of us not being dead."

"I'm not blaming you. There's nothing I said about you deciding not to go."

"It sure sounded like it."

They stopped talking for a while, watched the river go on its way.

Michael cleared his throat.

"Using your logic," he said, "tell me how I could have saved my father from having his heart explode in his chest?"

"I don't know."

"He was dead before he hit the ground."

"But don't you want to have done something?"

"There's no point in thinking like that."

"Really?"

"Really. No point. We don't have any superpowers."

"Remember," I said to Nisha, "how I asked them to write about that. Their superpowers."

She nodded. "So you suppose I have some too."

"Don't you want to have any?"

"All right," she said. She stood and walked to the front windows and waited there, her back turned toward me. "I can read minds, so I know that right now you are wishing you could be working on your novel."

"I am," I said.

"So you are. Right. Here's another, I can cause fire to spring out of nowhere, and so I keep my eyes closed most of the time, except at night, and then the bed always bursts into flame."

"You're frightening me."

"It was a metaphor."

"Like Felicity's boat without the mast," I said.

"That's how she saw it. I think she meant her husband. Or maybe her life now. I'm not sure."

"My mother's second novel was called *Apsara*."

"Amazing. Do you have a copy?"

"It was never published."

"Why not?"

"My father. And I think she lost interest in it. She was beginning to slip away from us then, though we didn't realize."

"You know what apsara means then?"

"You tell me."

"It's a kind of water nymph. They live with Indra in heaven, but regularly come to earth. They're the wives of the heavenly musicians, the Gandharvas. They're shape-shifters."

"Mam put some of it at the start of her book: one of their number, Ramdha, is said to have been produced at the churning of the ocean. A cross between a muse and a mermaid, they entertain gods and are caretakers of the brave dead."

"The brave dead. I wonder who's *not* the brave dead."

"I can't think of anyone right now."

"Could you have saved your brother?" Nisha asked. "Or your father? Or your mother?"

"Yes," I said. "Of course."

I knew better than to ask Nisha this question about her sister. I'd read it: the argument between three people. She said it happened a lot.

In early May, Michael and Djuna argued over something she had said to Nisha, something careless and untrue that hurt Nisha's feelings: *you never really wanted me to come live with you. I was always just a burden. A complication.* Nisha knew these remarks came from a deep well of fear—she remembered the feeling, though she had not said any of these things to their mother before leaving for college. But she knew other mothers and children fought bitterly, as if to ease the pain of imminent separation, as if to enable themselves to say *I'll be glad when you're gone. I'll be glad when I'm out of here*, though neither mother nor child probably ever uttered those particular words.

The argument escalated, and Nisha went outside to sit on the deck and then around to the other side of the house, crouching between the tomato plants, hurt and afraid.

Finally, there was louder shouting and heavy footsteps inside, causing the glass in the windows to shake. Nisha climbed the stairs and opened the door. Michael was standing at the sink. Djuna was huddled under a gray blanket on the sofa.

"He scares me," Djuna said.

"Come on," Nisha said. "What happened?"

Michael picked up his phone and left the house. Djuna threw off the blanket, stood up. Nisha could see she wasn't hurt.

"What happened, Djuna?"

"I don't want to talk about it. I don't want to talk to you."

Djuna went into her bedroom and then moved back and forth between the bathroom and her room. She was packing, Nisha believed. Tomorrow they would go to Chapel Hill for Admitted Students Day.

Nisha felt very tired. She had not been sleeping well. She went into the bedroom and lay down. She heard Michael come in, and then she must have fallen asleep. He was standing beside the bed, talking to her.

"Djuna left," he was saying.

"Really? Are you sure?"

Nisha got out of bed and texted *Djuna where are you?* and Djuna answered that she was sleeping at a friend's house tonight, Nisha could meet her tomorrow to go to Chapel Hill. She didn't feel safe there tonight. Michael was so angry. He threatened to throw her out of the house. Literally, pick her up and throw. Later, Nisha told Michael he couldn't do that, threaten a child with physical harm.

"I was defending you," Michael said. He got into bed and turned out the light.

Nisha finally convinced Djuna to come home, even though at one point Djuna texted *you act like he's the only problem. I don't want to be around either of you.* But later, she came back and apologized to Michael and demanded that Nisha hug her goodnight.

"Michael's fine now," Djuna said, whispering into Nisha's hair. "You're the one being a bitch."

Nisha hugged her anyway. Then she turned off all the lights, lay down on the sofa and wept.

In the morning, she poured Michael a cup of coffee as was their custom and made his lunch. When he left the house, she felt relieved. She thought they would probably never speak of this, but she did not know how she would get past the terrible hurt, pain running from her chest to her knees.

If you're raised with an angry man in your house, Felicity said when Nisha told her the story, there will always be an angry man in your house. You will find him even when he is not there.

"Do you think that could possibly explain Djuna?" Nisha asked me. "The angry man? Djuna and Devin? She found him even though he wasn't in the house?"

And who had been the angry man in my house? My father or Shamus? Or myself? Or all of us? And what did it mean, the angry man? And how did the angry man get into the house at all?

To answer this question, you had to go back ages, all the way to the beginning, and maybe past where it was you thought the trouble began.

"I think the angry man comes into the house," Nisha said, "because he has to explain something, and he can't find the right words."

"My mother used to tell us that the villains in fairy tales were cruel because they were lonely. The angry man must be lonely, and he doesn't know how to break the spell."

On the day of Djuna's graduation from high school, in the early morning after Michael had gone into town, Nisha made herself a second cup of tea and settled into her chair. Not the chair in her study, where she gazed at the river, wrote letters and kept her diary and her privacy, but the chair in the main room where she balanced her checkbook and read or watched television in the evenings. Time for reflection, she'd told herself, but from a different perspective, with a different view. She thought of this view as the public river, as opposed to the private body of water she saw from her study.

For ten years, she thought, I've raised this child and made us a family, kept this house, cooked dinners and breakfasts and packed lunches. I've done a good job. No one is dead or on drugs or in prison. Ten years is a long time.

Now she wanted to do something different, something else. She wanted to spend time alone. She wanted time by herself to recover from the brutalities of this year, this terrible year during which it seemed no one could agree on anything and now had endangered each other's lives.

Very soon, she would do this, find this time. She was waiting to hear about the possibility of an apartment in town. Five blocks from the river, true, but it was furnished, so she would not have to disrupt this house. In case Djuna wanted to come back here, everything would be as it was before. Nisha might take a print from the bedroom, the Georgia O'Keeffe, Santa Fe Chamber Music Festival Eighth Season. Nothing else. Clothes from the closet, the drawers. Nothing that Djuna would miss seeing.

Ten years. She had loved Michael, and she supposed she loved him now, in a way. But the feeling wasn't all there—the love felt like a shadow. Something like the outline of a piece of furniture when it's stayed in the same place for many years. When you finally move the chair or the table or the picture, you can see where it was because the floor or the walls have been bleached by sunlight or darkened by age above or around or below.

Tonight, Djuna would give a speech and collect her diploma, and Nisha's hands-on work would be done.

A flash then, about a hundred yards from shore. Dolphin feeding, which looked like play. Suddenly one of them leapt, a perfect curve, an arc out of the water and back in, that iconography of dolphin. Nisha rose from her chair and let herself out onto the deck. Dolphin again in the air, another perfect leap and splash. That's for Djuna, she thought. The creatures are coming to celebrate her.

Their neighbor next door was leaning on the deck rail, holding a mug of coffee, the same one always, sailboats racing madly. He seemed to be watching the dolphin too but did not speak or move. Nisha imagined his wife still asleep. She would hate to have missed the dolphin spectacle.

She walked back inside, warmed her tea. The neighbors had been married twenty years. They would stay married. They would have this view of dolphins for the rest of their lives. Nisha wondered why she couldn't find a way to be like them.

About a mile out on the river, a trawler loaded with crab pots, chugged past the house. No serious fisherman ever moved so slowly in that direction on a weekday morning in early summer. And there was something else that caught her attention: the man's hair, black and sleek and long, blown back in the small breeze created by the lazy pace of the boat. His skin dark too, neck and arms revealed by a billowing white shirt, so much material it might have been a kurta. She couldn't see below his waist—the stacks of crab pots were too high. She couldn't imagine this shirt would stay clean, though crabbing was the least messy sort of fishing you could do, which was why she liked it herself.

Something shook loose inside her—a stone falling from the top of her chest and nicking against her heart on the way down—she could almost hear the little tap of it. *Wake up.* She stood and crossed to the door, lifted a pair of binoculars from the bookshelf. And there he was. Ravi. She was sure she was mistaken, and then not sure, and then struck by a bolt of pure happiness. And then afraid. He was dead, had been dead for nearly twenty years.

Then she was ashamed. Of course, the man in the boat wasn't

Ravi. Why would she have wanted to conjure him?

"Turn around," she said out loud, fixing him in the binoculars, heavy and wavering in her left hand. She replaced the binoculars, eased into her chair. She felt old and estranged—no, kept at a distance—from her own life. It was like looking through a telescope at something both ancient and very far away. Binoculars, telescope, neither very useful these days.

"Turn around," she said again, to no one, to the air, to the years between Ravi and now.

Later, in New Bern, Nisha arranged for the catering of Djuna's graduation party—a collection of vaguely European and Middle Eastern sandwiches, fruit, an elaborate cake with the UNC logo. This seemed the way these parties were done. She was so pleased with her own efficiency, she thought she might give in and buy Djuna the $200 dress she wanted. Djuna was home, putting the finishing touches on her speech, and then she would drive to New Bern, and they would meet for lunch. She thought she might be named valedictorian, but the Principal had telephoned Nisha, calling her "friend" in that sweet, sad way and said Djuna was still second in the class. Nisha had an hour to spare, so she went into a restaurant downtown and sat at the bar and ordered a beer. She was happy. The next few days would be exciting and joyful. Then Djuna texted. She was lost, Nisha's directions were terrible. Why had Nisha done this to her? Why wouldn't she help now? Djuna phoned then, sobbing, asking for directions. It was impossible to understand what she was saying or where she was. Djuna hung up, texted again: Why are you being this way? Why are you such a bitch?

Five minutes later, she had found the restaurant, but was still sending fuming, cursing texts.

Come in with a smile and an apology, Nisha wrote back.

Djuna did come in, but with neither. Nisha fed her, and she

calmed down.

Ten years of *Nisha fed her and she calmed down*. It was someone else's turn. Or, rather, it was Djuna's turn to feed herself and calm herself down.

Ten years of feeding and calming.

Now, Djuna was asleep. Graduation had been accomplished. Her speech was brilliant, wise, far outshining the valedictorian, who was, to be fair, a mathematician and what the teachers called "a grinder." Djuna said of this girl: *she never takes the joyful classes.* She meant music and art. Tomorrow Djuna would begin her summer job, serving drinks and ice cream at the coffee shop in town.

The stranger in the fishing boat—something about him. It made no sense, what Nisha was imagining. His black hair had been a bold, angry blot on the canvas of the morning, like spilled ink.

He was looking for something. Suddenly she could see the relentlessness of time, how one gesture leads to the next, closer and closer to the radical act that turns out to be not one act but a ripple, driven by the force behind it. Like wake from a boat. And then, in a few minutes, there's nothing. The surface of the water calms itself, moves on, west to east toward the Sound.

"He was the angry man in your house, wasn't he?" I said to Nisha. "Ravi."

"He wasn't ever in my house."

"And never will."

"When I knew him," she said, "he was just a child, not a man." Nisha pushed herself out of the chair, wearily I thought. She started to put on her coat. "Let's go outside. This is a lovely house, but sometimes…"

"It can be a bit gloomy. Probably me, making the gloom."

We sat at the edge of the overgrown garden. I waited. I would wait for as long as she wanted.

"I see versions of Ravi all the time," she said. "Boys—and girls too—trying to figure things out. Confused, angry, looking for some peace. Djuna's friend Jamie. They want some relief. A little happiness. They don't know where it should come from."

At the pharmacy, the manager told Nisha that whenever she was filling a prescription for Oxycontin or any other strong painkiller, she should pay close attention but not appear to be doing so. Most of what she might need to know about the patient was already in the computer. Vicodin, same, she said. Pay attention only to that information regarding refills and quantity. Consult me or call the prescribing physician if you have questions. Don't be afraid to say no. I probably don't even need to be telling you this. Do you read the rap sheet in the free newspaper? Do you see what most folks get picked up for in the county? Possession, selling, using. And that really bad stuff, fentanyl, cut all through it. So kids are starting to be afraid of what they can get out there. They want what they can get from you. She gestured around the store. In here.

The hardest cases were the boys in their late teens or their 20's, sometimes it was impossible to tell exactly how old they were because they kept their heads down or turned half away from the window. Sometimes they said they were picking up the prescription for their mother or their father. Grandmother. She wanted to say, I know what's going on and I can help you.

But of course, she couldn't help at all. Mostly no one could. Maybe if the county police were involved. The sheriff and officers knew all the kids from duty at the high school, from breaking up fights and negotiating fender benders in the parking lot. Other kinds of benders after football games. They had attended the same high school themselves with these boys' parents and played football or fought with the fathers or been in love with the mothers. And so they would try to help the boys get into rehab or if that didn't work, they'd sit next to the mothers at the funerals and try to look stoic. And fail. Miserably.

"Djuna said that kids were using heroin, not so much pills. It was cheaper, the high was like a rocket, not like gentle numbness, and kids liked that better. It kept on getting cheaper. You could get a hit for five bucks. Cigarettes cost more than that. Lung cancer was going to be a thing of the past, a hazy memory, ancient history, they bragged. Kids felt as if they'd found a cure, all on their own, without scientists, without any adults at all."

One day, Djuna took Nisha to the road where kids she knew got high. Nisha wasn't sure why Djuna outed this spot. It seemed to be some sort of compact between them before Djuna went away to college, a gift. Or something else. As if she were saying, *All right, I'm leaving you to guard this place. To know where kids are if their mothers are distraught, beside themselves with worry. This can be your job now.* Nisha didn't want to ask too many questions.

The road ran east off the highway, just past a town called Alliance, which bleeds into the towns north and south, the only demarcation the brick box of a post office. After two curves and past a dozen squat red brick houses, the road runs straight east though fields that would be soybean or tobacco, perfectly straight and seemingly endless. Djuna showed Nisha where they parked their cars and lay down in the road and looked up at the stars.

"Why do you lie down in the road?"

"It was Jamie's idea. To see the whole sky, she said. And you can."

"Wouldn't the hood of the car be safer?"

"Maybe."

"Not being safe is probably part of the fun."

Djuna looked at her. The expression was appreciative, congratulatory almost. "You can see headlights from a long way off," she said.

"What if someone is driving without headlights? Michael told me his friends who grew up in the suburbs used to do that. When there was a full moon."

"I never thought of that."

"And never mind that everyone's high."

"I'm not high."

"You're not?"

"I'm afraid of it. Sometimes I might be a little tipsy though."

"So you're sort of like the designated driver."

"Yeah. I guess. Mostly for Jamie."

Nisha thought about *I'm afraid of it*. She thought about it when she hugged Djuna goodnight. She felt as though a sliver of ice had been slipped into her heart. It occurred to her that when their parents died, in Djuna's mind, they had not become ash, they had become fear. A quality, a belief.

The look of that road stayed with her too. She pictured it littered with the bodies of children. When she saw the mug shots of drug offenders in the county newspaper, that road was in their eyes, flat, empty, running to nowhere.

Two of these boys were famous (if that was the word) because they got high, drove down to Jacksonville, robbed a mini-mart and shot the owner and her son—Indians from Agra who had joined their family in the U.S. six months before. Four and a half minutes caught on the store's videotape, the boys pumped up, breathless, a little woozy. The pointed gun, the open register—not much in it. You could see that, and then how angry the boys were. In the last frame, the boys had looked at each other, and the camera was right there. So everybody could see it, their mix of terror and resignation. How strange that the human visage could accommodate both at once, Janus-like but not divided.

Djuna's friends all smelled of marijuana, peppermint and Febreze. Nisha thought someone ought to bottle that scent and call it "Controlled Substance." Or "But, Officer." It was almost funny—except that it wasn't—that they thought she wouldn't notice, wouldn't see right through their feeble attempts at covering up. And in some ways, the scent was a relief because opioid users didn't need to cover up any smells. Almost a relief. They usually forgot about their hair—all of Djuna's friends wore their hair in long, thick braids, and so often when Nisha hugged them, the sweetness of burnt rope filled her nostrils.

Still, marijuana wasn't legal—not anywhere in the south, and seemed like it wouldn't be anytime soon. Nisha reminded Djuna of this again and again and believed her when Djuna said she didn't smoke with them.

"But you're the driver," Nisha said. "You're almost 18. Their parents could charge you."

"For what?" Djuna said, laughing. "Contributing to the delinquency of a minor?"

"Exactly."

"Really?"

"Look it up. Oh—and by the way, you're brown. You look like all those immigrants people want to send back to their own countries."

Nisha could see Djuna was thinking, calculating the risks, past and future.

"I will look it up, "Djuna said. "At least it's not fentanyl."

"It's a gateway drug."

"No it's not. You don't even believe that."

"I work in a pharmacy. It doesn't matter what I *believe*. I know what I see."

"What's that supposed to mean?"

"I know what I know about these kids who come in to try to fill prescriptions for their grandparents. You know them too."

"Not really."

"I think you probably do know them. The kid who rushed in waving his grandfather's pain prescription the day of the funeral. That one."

"He was never a pothead."

"He was messed up in a lot of ways."

"A lot of people are messed up."

"You get my point."

"Actually." Djuna closed her eyes as she spoke. "Jamie wanted to do that, her grandmother's pills, but I talked her out of it."

"See?"

"But what do you want me to do? Not hang out with my friends?"

"In a perfect world," Nisha said, "the answer to that question would be yes."

"We don't live in a perfect world."

"I know. So be careful. I mean really, really, excruciatingly careful."

"So what you're saying is don't hang out with them."

Nisha stood up, crossed the room, eased herself in between the arm of the sofa and Djuna, slid her arm behind Djuna's head. Djuna stiffened and tried to pull away, but Nisha held on, drawing her closer.

"I feel so bad for Jamie. She needs you. But you've got this big future. I couldn't bear for anything to mess it up."

"I know," Djuna said. "Turning 18 seems so…like this huge empty field ahead of me. But I sort of dread the actual day."

Djuna's birthday was always hard, a reminder of their missing parents. Their mother couldn't tell the birth story. Their father couldn't load the table with Djuna's favorite dishes. Nisha planned to try some version of that, Djuna's particular international palate: *shawarma* and *arroz con pollo*, roast potatoes, a savory rice pudding. Djuna had told her not to bother with a cake. She hadn't really meant that, Nisha knew. Without an American style birthday cake, from the grocery store bakery, abundantly decorated with butter-cream roses, her name written in the baker's shaky cursive, the birthday would be a disaster, ruined, not a birthday at all. Maybe without the birthday cake, Djuna would not age, and so time could stop and she wouldn't go off to college, and Nisha would not leave Michael, and they would all be caught together in the more or less adequate present.

On the day, Nisha and Michael planned to meet Djuna and her friends in New Bern for Mexican food. The girls—in Djuna's car—were late. Nisha and Michael waited, drank a beer, and when the girls still had not arrived, there was nothing to do but order another round. They ran out of things to comment on, other diners to comment on, the menu, the past, the future. Michael seemed out of sorts, some disappointment flattening his speech until he was nearly mute. Around them, the somewhat frantic gaiety of Mexican restaurants, salsa music and sombreros and huge steaming plates of food. And a surreal touch: Djuna's 4th grade teacher, who had been so warm and welcoming to the newly orphaned Djuna, moved from table to table, greeting her former students or their parents. "I'm just proud as I can be of your baby sister," she said when Nisha stood to embrace her. "She's a wonder. She's going to go far."

Djuna arrived just then, apologizing a bit sheepishly, but jubilant, ready to celebrate. The waiter crowned her with a huge sombrero. Her three friends, Jamie, Kat and Erin, were obviously high as kites. Nisha glanced at Michael, who seemed not to notice.

The girls ordered *arroz con pollo* by its initials, ACP, and wolfed it down. Nisha studied them when she thought they weren't looking (they were never looking; they were incapable of looking). She considered their private stories: Erin's parents had not wanted her to go to prom with Djuna last year when neither of them had dates. Her mother had said she didn't like *how it would look.* Nisha was enraged, but Djuna had explained that they were small town people who didn't know any better. She was loyal, Djuna was, and she was grateful for these American girlfriends.

Kat's brother was in a drug rehabilitation facility in Fayetteville, but she was smart and pretty and athletic and would probably be okay. She was very close to her mother, Djuna said. Her mother would like you, she told Nisha, if she ever got to know you.

Jamie was the puzzle. Her mother was in prison, so she lived with her grandparents, but upstairs, in what was really her own apartment. She was pretty and lively and talked openly—even there in the restaurant, in front of Nisha and Michael, about what she did with the boys she dated—the kind of storytelling in which little was said, but much was implied. The boys were always in college, or at least out of high school. While she spoke, she looked pointedly at Nisha, but her expression was more pleading than arch. What she wanted most, Nisha believed, was a mother. Probably not anyone in particular, maybe not even her own mother. Jamie probably spoke exactly this way to the mothers of all her friends, her female teachers, the guidance counselor at school, the postmistress, bank tellers.

Today, especially, Nisha felt a lurch of pain for Jamie. She was one of them, and so was Djuna. A motherless girl.

In honor of graduation and the start of college, Djuna wanted to get a tattoo. On the American Independence Day, she decided it was time. She had been scrolling through designs online. She left off setting the table for dinner, sat down in front of the computer, clicked the mouse.

"What do you think about this one?" she said.

Djuna lifted a piece of paper out of the printer tray and brought it to the table. She laid the paper in front of Nisha with a one-handed flourish, as if she were serving a plate of delectable food. What Nisha saw was a naked woman, her legs tucked around her artfully, her head lowered, black hair flowing halfway down her back. Above the woman's bent head, a straight horizontal line suggested some sort of division. Above the line, connected through it to the woman's head, was a plant, a new shoot with two leaves.

"I get it," Nisha said. "She's the roots for this plant."

"Sort of," Djuna said. "But how does she look?"

"Tired. Like she's sleeping."

"No. People sleep on their sides or on their backs. She's sitting up. Her head is down."

"Right. Okay. She's—I'm afraid I'm going to say something stupid. Maybe you should just tell me."

"No. I want you to think about it."

"Give me a hint."

"No hints. Think."

All right. She would play along. "She's in the dark."

"Why?"

"She's underground."

"That's true."

"She's probably cold. She doesn't have any clothes on. Maybe she's poor. She can't afford clothes."

"Maybe."

"Or she's lost them."

"Maybe. Keep going."

"I have to check the oven."

"No, you don't. When you sit like that, how do you feel?"

"I feel sad. In pain."

"Bingo. And then look up."

Nisha looked up at the ceiling.

Djuna laughed, shook her head. Michael came in from working downstairs, stood behind Nisha, bent over the design.

"She's having an idea about growth?" Michael said.

Djuna drew her finger slowly along the line above the woman's head. "Underground."

"Didn't I say that already? She's the root."

"Just tell us," Michael said.

"Are you being clueless on purpose?" Djuna tapped her finger on the design.

Nisha could see this conversation marching toward an argument.

"Maybe it needs words," Nisha said.

Michael agreed. "Definitely."

Djuna whisked the paper away to the end of the table and went to get a pen from the splay of pens in a cup on the kitchen counter. She wrote something above and then below the design, brought the page back.

The line above read *From Your Pain*, and the line below, under the woman's feet, read *Came Your Planting*.

"I get it," Nisha said. "I like it."

"Me too," Michael said. "But honestly, I don't know if you're old enough to have experienced that much pain."

Djuna and Nisha looked at each other.

"That's harsh," Djuna said.

"Only the death of her parents, Michael," Nisha said. "Our parents."

Michael dropped into the chair at the end of the dining table. "I'm sorry," he said. "I'm an idiot. I was just thinking about your age. The number of years."

"Maybe you were trying to be hopeful," Djuna said.

"I think I was," Michael said. "Thank you for giving me the benefit of the doubt anyway."

Nisha turned away toward the windows, watched the wind move the water, ragged lines like a child's finger painting. Crisis of hurt averted, she thought. She wanted to curl herself up like the woman in Djuna's design. It would feel good. But what if you took off all your clothes and buried yourself, and then nothing grew?

"I don't know if I really want words," Djuna was saying.

"You might save yourself some money," Michael said.

"True," Djuna said. "So when should I do it?"

"Tomorrow," Nisha said. "Before you lose your nerve."

"I was thinking that."

"Can I come along?" Michael asked.

"Sure," Djuna said. "My sister will need you to carry her when she faints."

"I'm not going to faint."

"You used to cry whenever I'd get a shot."

"I just don't like needles."

"Ahem," Michael said.

The rest of July Fourth was a nice day—mostly. Nisha and Djuna inflated the two rafts and then dumped them in the river, unceremoniously off the dock, clambered in, tied them to the pilings. They lay, one on each, sunning themselves, then grew bored and attempted the pillaging of each other's rafts. "Permission to board not granted!" Nisha shouted, but Djuna flung herself into Nisha's raft anyway, grabbed Nisha's water shoe to use as a bailing bucket. She rammed Nisha's raft with her own. They'd played this way years ago, but not last summer or the summer before, the mermaid game, in which Djuna was Ariel and Nisha the sea witch Ursula. This year there was a kind of frenzy, almost hysteria. The specter of departure loomed.

Michael did not go inside or busy himself weeding or moving boats across the lawn and then moving them back. He brought out the single kayak, let it down over the rocks and climbed in. He paddled around the rafts, never coming in very close, then under the docks to the west and back to the east, never completely out of sight. North, towards Minnesott, the sky darkened and a storm spread towards them. Nisha heard thunder but thought the storm might pass around or beyond them, as often happened. A spattering of rain, then nothing. When the thunder grew too loud to talk over, she ordered Djuna out of the water, and they made their way, miraculously unharmed, through a school of jellyfish, up over the rocks and onto the grass. They shared a towel and settled into the bench swing. Michael paddled in, put the kayak away, disappeared into the house and returned with two beers and a bottle of water for Djuna. Still no rain, though the sky blackened and the thunder pounded. Across the river, lightning streaked from the clouds to the ground. They told silly jokes, Djuna made tender fun of Michael's windblown hair, and he didn't seem to mind. They were a relaxed, happy threesome.

Why would I want to leave this, Nisha thought? This is so nice. The rain found them, finally, drove them upstairs, inside. Nisha and Djuna showered off the salt and sunscreen and took naps. They ate cheeseburgers and watermelon, watched the fireworks over the National Mall in Washington, D.C., listened to John Stamos remind Americans what immigrants have done for the country. White men in white shirts sat on the front row smiling for the television cameras. Republican congressmen, probably, Djuna said, the ones who had not gone home to face their angry constituents.

By 9 p.m., Michael had inexplicably descended into a foul mood, cursing the neighbor's dog for drifting over into their yard, mocking the fireworks over the Capitol.

"Who rained on your parade?" Djuna asked him. She went into

the bathroom, closed the door.

Michael sat for a moment, staring straight ahead, then he rose from his chair and walked toward the bedroom, kicking the bathroom door as he passed by.

A little while later, the rental agent called to tell her the apartment in town was available.

Nisha's independence day.

Lucky Street Tattoos was 20 miles north of Jacksonville, the base, Camp LeJeune—you said "Le Jern" if you were native enough to know—where there must be at least ten such establishments. Michael had stayed in his dark mood and decided he didn't want to go with them. Djuna shrugged this off and asked Felicity, who professed to be charmed by the invitation.

Inside there was a Japanese theme going on, Samurai warriors, dragons, masks of mythological beasts with long, curved tusks. On the far wall ran a slow-moving video of a tattooed woman who was modeling for a male painter. He appeared not to be interested at all in her body, only the designs. Nisha was struck by that, a sort of de-objectification. The videographer seemed to be doing the same, and so close ups of the woman's body were completely disorienting. Nisha saw what appeared to be a dahlia, which she finally realized had at its center the woman's nipple. What kind of transformation was that? Was it good or bad? Or neither?

How could you not see the woman? Felicity wanted to know.

The tattooist was working on a man's upper arm. A large man, shirt off, lying on his back on a massage table. The tattooist appeared to be young. He was inking in a design that matched the woman's in the video. He looked up and smiled at the three of them in turn. No guile, no attitude.

"Give me an hour," he said. He called Djuna "man." He called

Nisha "your mom." He didn't call Felicity anything.

An hour to use up on this road. The possibilities were nearly endless. It was, Felicity said, like all the roads you see running perpendicular to the interstates in America: Burger King, Pizza Hut, Walmart, Pep Boys, Speedway Gas Mart. Contemporary America. Cracker Barrel, Red Lobster, the ABC store, a failed strip mall, Ace Hardware.

In the MacDonald's, they ordered specialty coffee drinks, just for fun. Djuna wanted a latte, Nisha a mocha. Felicity ordered plain black coffee. The high school girl at the counter stared and blinked, leaned forward as if she was sure she hadn't heard correctly. Felicity repeated her order. She brought their coffees. They carried them to a booth by the side door where the AC whined fiercely.

"I'm kind of nervous," Djuna said.

"You can change your mind," Felicity told her.

"She's not going to change her mind," Nisha said.

Djuna looked—it was a disturbing thought—caught between worlds. That was the only way Nisha could think to describe the distance in her sister's gaze in this hour between unmarked and marked.

"It tastes just like Starbucks," Djuna said. "Isn't that crazy?"

"Saves you a lot of money," Nisha said.

"You sound like Michael," Djuna said.

"More to spend on tattoos," Felicity said. "You know," she continued, nodding her head in the direction of the girl who took their order, "I'm just realizing why she looked at me like that."

"Like what?" Djuna said.

"Like I was crazy. I thought it was because I didn't want a fancy coffee drink like you two did."

"I thought it was that," Nisha said.

"It was because I'm white."

"And you have that accent," Djuna said.

"I bet they see white people here all the time," Nisha said.

"And I'm with you two. And the accent."

"But you know what?" Djuna said. "It's still the same thing. You still don't know *why*. You still don't know *what* she thinks. Does she think you're a good person for not ordering some fancy thing to drink, or does she think you're a total freak for hanging out with two brown women? Or maybe she thinks you're some posh granny?"

Felicity shook her head so imperceptibly it might have been a tremor, a movement over which she had no control. "No idea," she said.

Nisha wondered what point Djuna was trying to make. It was that same between worlds, really. Was she theirs, the girl she and Michael had mostly raised and Felicity had taken an interest in, or had she already struck out on her own and left them all in the dust?

"I decided not to do words," Djuna said to the tattooist while he was adjusting the design on the inside of her forearm. He wore a black t-shirt that read NIKE 1972.

"That's good," he said. "I'm not a typewriter."

"How many times have you had to write *Semper Fi*?" Felicity asked.

Nisha thought she would crash through the floor, but the tattooist seemed to consider the question reasonable.

"Not that much," he said. "For one thing, I'm fairly new on the scene. Guys who want that go to the old timers in Havelock and Jacksonville. If you want words, get a charm bracelet or some other piece of jewelry."

"What do you mean?" Djuna said.

"My sister-in-law has a necklace that says Nevertheless She Persisted. You might not want to be wearing that all the time."

"Or you might," Djuna said.

"Fair enough," the tattooist said. "Words are moods. Images are personality."

"I like that," Djuna said.

"Yeah," the tattooist said. "Sounds pretty smart for a 24-year-old with a needle."

"What's your name?"

"Troy. What's yours?"

Djuna told him.

"Troy," Felicity said. "How did you get to be named after an ancient city?"

"My mom was convinced I was going to be a girl. She convinced herself. She wanted a girl after having my three brothers. She wanted to name a girl Helen. But she got another boy. And so she did this sort of sideways thing. This wink-wink kind of thing so she'd always remember."

"That's great," Djuna said. "That's so…warm."

"It is," Troy said. He looked up from his work, into Djuna's eyes.

It's like a date, Nisha thought. A first date. Troy had hundreds of first dates. That seemed rather wonderful, a beautiful surprise. He'd probably told the story of his name over and over, but it sounded fresh and sudden just now. Intimate. Nisha felt she should look away.

A diploma hung on the wall just to the right of Troy's workspace. Nisha had to squint to read it, discovering it did not belong to Troy but to someone named Suzanne Franklin. A female tattoo artist. Nisha had never imagined such a thing. She wondered how Suzanne Franklin's work was different, dreamy, like a Burne-Jones painting. She wondered why Michael had decided not to come with them.

Nisha reached into her pocket for her phone, turned on the camera. She took some still shots of Troy and Djuna, and a couple of videos. Djuna would want these, she thought. Somewhere, from the great beyond, she heard her mother's voice. *You're letting a stranger stab a needle into your sister's arm?* A bell jangled. When the front door

198

opened behind her, the hot air rushing in was her mother's disapproval. A man's voice asked who was next in line.

Troy lifted the needle, turned to look. Something shifted in his face. Curiosity or concern. Nisha watched Djuna, saw a tiny flash of relief that the needle had stopped, a grimace. Nisha offered her mother a silent apology.

Troy negotiated for a minute with the man. He wanted a sleeve. He had the kind of voice that sounded as if it were just about to get much louder. For some reason, Nisha did not want to look at him. She had no idea why this was so. Maybe if she took her eyes off Djuna, she would miss something important and some spell would be broken, and she really would be derelict in her duties. Her mother would be right. It was a powerful sensation—as if she were physically incapable of turning her head. She was not supposed to see this man.

The man asked if he needed to take a painkiller before. Troy said yes. The man went out the door, jangling the bell again. It sounded different, a warning.

"If they have to ask about the painkiller," Troy said, "then the answer is always yes."

Troy went back to work. He changed needles, explaining he used a different size for the shading on the woman's hair and on the edges of the leaves above her head. He was so calm, so steady. In a crisis, you would want Troy.

"How long have you been doing tattoos?" Djuna said.

"Five years, "Troy said. "I used to write some poetry. But then I got into this."

"I write poems sometimes," Djuna said, "but art is art, right?"

"That's right," Felicity said.

"Exactly," Troy said. "Make something with your hands. It's all good."

Then he was done. He squeezed a dab of skin cream on the new tattoo, rubbed it in gently. He folded a paper towel and with cello tape fixed it over the design.

"It'll be red for a few days," he said. "But don't scratch it. Tap it with your hand. Make a sound like applause."

"Like I'm saying great job, Troy."

"That would be nice," Troy said.

In the car, Djuna declared that she felt different, changed somehow. Then she fell asleep. Nisha glanced in the rear-view mirror and believed that her sister was smiling.

The person who wanted the sleeve, Felicity said quietly, he was a vision out of a nightmare. His left eye was gone, just a sunken hole. When he held up his right arm, the hand was missing two fingers.

Djuna rarely came into CVS during shifts, so Nisha felt a quick pinch of fear when she saw her sister winding her way through the aisles toward the pharmacy, not exactly hurrying but clearly filled with some purpose. She waved to Nisha, motioned for her to come out from behind the counter.

"I found a family," she said. "An Indian family. And we found a house."

A family. That was good, Nisha thought. A little painful to hear, but it sounded safe. A brother and a sister, Kasim and Sariah. He was a graduate student, she a sophomore. From Raleigh. They had joined a Facebook group, people looking for housemates. Felicity had already put her touch with a rental agent. Djuna had pictures on her phone. A sweet little house, three bedrooms. Devin Graham lived down the street. Felicity said she thought he worked for a cable company. Maybe he'd do the installation for them.

"What do you think?" Djuna said. "Kasim is asking for a deposit."

"Let's talk to Michael tonight."

"Why do we have to talk to Michael? It's our money. From Mommy and Daddy."

"That's true, but…."

"But what?"

Djuna was right. It was their money, most of it intended to be used for Djuna's education. Nisha took in this picture of her sister, there in an aisle filled with remedies for foot problems, fairly levitating with excitement, happier than she'd been in a long time. Ready to go, to leave, to get on with her one wild and precious life.

"What do you know about the parents?"

"One is in real estate, and one is a banker. I forget which is which."

"Funny that either could be either."

Djuna looked blank, and Nisha suddenly felt the gulf of years between them.

"Should I call their mom, do you think?" Nisha said.

"Email."

"OK. But what about getting to campus? Won't you need a car?"

"Kasim has one. But he says a campus bus stops right at the end of the street."

"OK."

"Please, Nisha. I don't want to lose this place."

Nisha drew her sister into her arms. "All right," she whispered. "You probably want me to write a check right this instant, don't you?"

"Venmo."

Something about that word, a transaction into the mysteries of the modern world, the city, out of this sleepy place and into the future. Nisha's eyes filled with tears, her breath caught in a sob.

"It's OK," Djuna said. "I won't be that far away. You won't lose me, not really."

And Nisha had her own new living quarters: the apartment was eight miles from the river house, two former school buildings that had been converted to condos. This unit was furnished, though all Nisha could see in the pictures was a bed, a sofa, two bar stools and a dining table. She hoped there would be room for that chair and footstool from her study. The ad said there were two bathrooms, which seemed odd, but probably there was some structural explanation. A school would have had boys' and girls' bathrooms. Perhaps they were right next to each other and difficult to un-plumb.

She would lose the view. No ritual gauging of the river's mood in the early morning, no shaded deck, leaves on the pecan tree trembling in a breeze. No garden, no gardenia, no gladiolas, crape myrtle, iris. She would have to walk to see the river, not far, but some planning and effort would be required. That was the hardest to let go.

So make a new ritual, a voice said. Go find a view of other water: Charles, Liffey, Thames, Seine. Or views you've never seen: Arno, Danube, Rhine, Rhone, Potomac. What she never liked about San Francisco when they visited: no river. A bay is too much, a glut, a surfeit. A bit out of control, especially that one, with its sinister winds, dangerous bridges, the possibility, friends had told her, that a baseball flying out of AT&T park could crack the hull of your boat or rip through your sail.

Maybe Michael would find some friends. Maybe this was the biggest favor she could do for him—force him to have a larger social and intellectual life. She could tell herself that, anyway.

When Nisha saw the apartment, she knew she had found her place. Parking and entrance on the back of the building, lovely modest landscaping. She could come and go without being seen or watched. Inside—exposed brick, 13-foot ceilings, 6-foot-high windows with views of nothing but trees and sky. So much light, all day long. A sofa bed and a full bath enclosed off the front hallway, so when Djuna stayed with her, she could have her own space. A large master bed-room and bath, stacked washer and dryer. She imagined her things there, on the dresser and the wide window sills. Her clothes in the two closets. Her photographs. Her dishes, the pottery she had bought years ago on a trip to Maine and never used. It seemed her life would be returned to her. She had done a good job of raising Djuna and taking care of Michael, and now she would be rewarded.

Was it crazy to think Michael might be happier too? That every-one might be happier?

But then there was the waiting to move in and the constant chat-ter in her mind about how to tell Michael and when to go. The day after they dropped Djuna in Chapel Hill? Though in some ways that seemed cruel, hasty, like she wasn't even going to give their new life a chance. Why not? Because she already knew how it would be. They'd already had plenty of nights when Djuna slept over at friends' houses or went away for school events. A whole month the summer she was at camp in Virginia, the trial run for their new life. It had been a postcard sent from their old age, only lonelier.

People talk about the empty nest as if it's fun or funny or some kind of joke. Or they say it with a wink, now you can have sex at all hours of the day, in any room in the house, with the doors open. No. Nisha believed the empty nest would only make their nakedness more startling, more embarrassing. More fallen, as the western religions would have it. Cast out of the garden, That's it. That paradise once inhabited by the perfumed, indulged, overfed, somewhat despotic but beloved child. Not cast out. Woken from the dream of it, bereft, the garden suddenly vanished around them. Poof! Had it ever been there, really?

Nisha knew that Michael didn't have any idea she would leave, that he would be completely blind-sided. Sometimes she felt terrible guilt—how could she do this to him, to this innocent and really fundamentally good man? But one morning, watching him get into his car and drive away, her thinking shifted. How could he *not* know? How could he think everything was just fine? Why did he not examine his life, or their life together, more fully? Nisha believed he was afraid to peer too deeply into his life, afraid of what he would find there.

So these thoughts battled with each other, day after day, as she waited to hear from the property manager about her rental application.

A breeze frittered in the leaves of the pecan tree. The river appeared not to move in either direction but rather to tremble. The crabbers' boats began their morning passage, heading upriver, the engines whining for a long time after the boats had disappeared from sight, maybe a full minute, until it seemed that somehow the boats had entered some fold in the universe, into some eternity of sound. And then the growling motor was just gone, silenced. Nisha knew it was because the boat had rounded the bend at Minnesott, but she liked her own supernatural explanation better than the hard physics. Nisha waited for the boat that always slowed in front of their stretch of docks.

Another boat now, the one farther out. Sometimes they sounded like bass-voiced mosquitoes. Crab pots in the bow looking like a shack, a transparent wheelhouse. The wake opened a clear, still space in the water, like a pool of milk or a patch of ice. Or the apron of a stage, and some drama would take place there, or some creature rise out of that still space in the water. Or land there from above. Nisha liked to imagine Mommy descending from heaven, her sari fluttering, her dark hair spread out around her head. Drifting, floating there, gazing at the dock, Mommy on the half shell. Nisha would take up the binoculars and fix her in the sights and be able to see her face again. Mommy's expression, its judgment about Nisha's leaving, about the apartment in the village. She had to close one eye to see it clearly. There. Good: approving. Concerned but approving.

Soon it would be time to wake Djuna and get breakfast, pack her lunch, send her off to work in the Village, stop this pointless agonizing, this tortured waiting. Nothing ever happens here, Djuna had said last night. Nisha wondered if that was what she—Nisha—wanted: to make something happen, shake up her world. A voice said, Can't you do that without ruining someone else's life?

But the answer came back loud and clear: You can't ruin someone else's life. All you can do is end it. The worst you can do is end it.

Would she miss this, the shushing of the river against the riprap, the passage of fishing boats, white hulls silvered by the morning sunlight, the sun rising behind the pecan tree, hidden at first by the trunk, then striking her though the leaves? The quiet, birdsong, dolphin visitations. Something on the fishing boat passing now glittered like Morse Code, long glow followed by short flash, language from motion rather than from intent. Maybe. The boat had moved farther out, away. But still the flashing, persistent as memory.

Nisha met Kasim's family finally, in August, when she and Michael moved Djuna into the Carrboro house. Before that, there were emails from Gauri, the mother, but it was hard to tell anything for certain from the few brief exchanges about the neighborhood and the rent. Gauri always referred to Djuna, Kasim and his sister as *our children*. Nisha didn't know whether this was a kindness or a bit of overreaching, but she didn't want any misunderstanding, so she gave in to the idea. It takes a village, she said, to reassure herself.

At the move-in, Nisha felt awed and intimidated by Gauri, who was the real estate agent, and her husband, Maninder, the children's father, a vice-president at Wells Fargo. Even dressed casually and hefting boxes and suitcases, they appeared refined and aloof. Nisha finally understood the English phrase about butter not melting in someone's mouth.

But then, Gauri carried two boxes straight into the kitchen and began to cook. Vindaloo, she said. My sister's recipe. She cooks for a restaurant in Atlanta. The house began to smell good, familiar, like home. Gauri sent Sariah out to buy naan and yogurt at Trader Joe's. They all ate lunch together, and then Gauri clapped her hands and declared they would leave the children to wash the dishes and organize their household.

Nisha was not ready to go, but Gauri reminded her of Mommy, and so she felt she had to do as Gauri suggested. They kissed and hugged their children, then each other's children, then their own once more. Nisha felt a hole burning in her chest and widening by the second. She pictured it as a flame in the center of a white page and burning outward until everything was black ash. Outside the adults shook hands, promising to be in touch. Nisha could see Djuna standing just inside the open front door. She didn't know whether she could wave, call Djuna outside for one more hug. Michael steered her toward their car, and she opened the door. Her limbs and hands moved mechanically, slowly, as if they weren't sure of the foldings and bendings involved. Kasim's parents' car, ahead of them, pulled away from the curb and sped off, heartless, a machine going about its business, turned the corner and disappeared. Nisha's eyes filled with tears.

"Wait," she said. "I forgot something."

"What?" Michael said.

Nisha opened the car door, stepped into the street. I'm not sure," she said. "I'll be right back."

Djuna was standing in the same spot, frozen inside the front door. "I knew you'd come back," she said. "I hoped you'd come back."

"Do you have everything you need? Do you want to go get anything? Groceries? Anything?"

"I'll have to see. We'll make a list. Right now—I just...."

"I know," Nisha said. She had no idea what she knew or didn't know. They held each other, held on.

Djuna began to cry.

"It's just three hours," Nisha said. "We'll see you for fall break."

"Maybe you can drive over before that?"

"Labor Day? But we'll see if by then you even want us."

"Okay."

"Okay."

"You probably have to go. You know how Michael gets."

"And you need to go help them get settled."

Kasim and his sister appeared briefly in the hallway, as if summoned. They paused, then returned to the kitchen. Water ran in the sink. Dishes and cutlery clattered and rang.

"I know. This is hard."

"We just have to do it."

"I know."

Something across the street caught Djuna's attention. "Look," she said. "There's Devin."

Nisha turned. Devin Graham stood in his driveway, leaning against a green pickup truck. Nisha waved, but she could feel Djuna waving even more enthusiastically behind her. Devin Graham never moved or seemed to change his expression. But maybe it was too far away to be sure.

"Odd," Nisha said.

"Maybe he doesn't know it's us."

"Probably not." Nisha didn't want to make this moment any harder. "Last hug," she said. "Make it a good one."

"It's just three hours."

"I know."

In Nisha's arms, Djuna's body felt taut, a spring coiled and ready. The scent of Djuna's hair, the silky feel of it on Nisha's cheek. Not to have this every single day, this attachment. How would she do it?

And then somehow, Nisha had stepped outside, crossed the lawn, let herself back into the car, tuned, waved, blew a kiss. At the corner, she wanted to tell Michael to go back, but she kept quiet. She thought she would never stop crying.

She'll be fine," Michael said. "You? Not so much."

Nisha remembered the phrase from that dreadful movie, *Borat*. They'd watched it during their first visit to Chapel Hill, in fact, with dear friends. Nisha thought it was stupid. Their hosts felt bad. Djuna was little—she had just come to live with them. Nisha saw everything through the haze of her parents' violent deaths. Their hosts lived out in the woods, but just off the interstate, and had that spring built a climbing wall. Djuna sometimes slept out on the trampoline with a gaggle of daughters and cousins visiting for Easter. Djuna remembered those visits later as Going to Shangri-La. No one wore shoes. There were, in fact, snakes everywhere, and sometimes their host would capture small ones so the children could get a closer look at the cool skin, the pulsing wave of muscle that moved the snake along.

Once they all hiked back through the property to an in-wash of Jordan Lake and a growth of cedar knees. Nisha didn't walk into the water, but their host did, with Djuna riding on his shoulders. Nisha was terrified that he might trip and fall and lose track of Djuna, who didn't swim well, but she kept herself quiet and still, while fear sat heavily inside her.

She recalled the feeling as they left Djuna inside the house. Fear of Chapel Hill. She distracted herself by making up a Latin phrase for it: *cappella collis phobia* arranging and then rearranging the three words for maximum linguistic authenticity, the medical diagnosis.

What were they driving back to now? What empty place? The apartment in town wouldn't be ready for another week.

"I think I might…" Nisha began. She couldn't get through the sentence without crying. "I might go to the beach. Rent a place for a couple of days. Get away."

"Okay," said Michael, his voice rising into the second syllable. It was an inquiry, really: *without me?*

"Yes," Nisha said, answering the question that had not been asked.

Michael had broken her heart. By accident, By neglect. By selfishness. By himself. She imagined him looking up from what he'd done, her heart fractured in his hands, stony pieces of it (because before he broke it, he'd hardened it). He might wonder if such a wreck of a thing could ever be put back together. A thousand pieces, and still he would ask himself that question. He might think of similar breakages and fixes, recoveries. What on earth was the word? Surgeries? He might imagine a mirror. Was that what he held now? A broken mirror? Maybe he would want to rip out his own heart and hand it over to Nisha, but what would she do with it now?

Nisha did not regret a single word in the letter.

She began with *Dear.*

I have been thinking in this last year of Djuna-centric living that we have neglected each other. Probably mostly my fault. I'd like to work to fix it if you think that's possible.

She'd decided that was enough at first. If Michael wasn't interested, then why say more?

By the time you read this:

She left the house, drove to the ferry landing, waited to cross to the other side.

Once she got off the ferry, Nisha drove slowly toward the coast, keeping below the speed limit. She stopped at the Dollar General in Jarrett's Bay and bought milk and eggs and a cheap bottle of wine, crackers, chips, cookies, but not too many, a good brand of pasta, picked everything out slowly, in 18 years, the first groceries she would buy only for herself. Ice. She didn't have an ice chest and thought about investing in a cheap Styrofoam cooler, but decided against it. She didn't turn on the radio. She thought about Michael's shock and sadness and wept for Djuna, listened to an old voicemail. She didn't feel better. She didn't know what she felt. Just before Morehead city, traffic was stopped, a policewoman directed cars with one green dayglo hand. Fifty yards ahead, blue lights flashed, and a firetruck stretched across both lanes. A man in the basket of a cherry-picker worked at the top of a utility pole. At the end of the short detour, Nisha looked in the rear-view mirror and saw a Suburban wrapped around the pole, the driver's side crushed. She guessed the ambulance was long gone.

She passed the exit for the Atlantic Beach causeway and drove on to the grocery store. With a too-large cart, she wandered back and forth in the produce aisle. Tomatoes. What kind? How many? The heirlooms looked hideously misshapen. She thought she had never seen such ugly tomatoes. They made her sad, as if they were homely children. No, they made her *sadder*, which she didn't think was possible. Yogurt, olives, hummus, beer, grapes, spinach, cheese, sweet potato, corn, jalapeno. Maybe she would try Gauri's vindaloo. Spaghetti with garlic; a frittata. She would cook. She had not cooked for just herself in years.

She did not regret leaving.

On the causeway bridge, left on Beach Road. Right on the driveway of the last group of condos before Fort Macon. A gated community. She was glad for that. It would keep Michael out. Of course, he could jump the fence or ram it with his car. Wait until someone else was coming in or out.

She brought in her bags and groceries, ate a handful of grapes, put perishables in the fridge, carried her duffel upstairs. She remembered when Michael had hugged her goodbye that morning, he had pressed his cheek against the top of her head. He had never done that before.

She tried not to picture him reading the letter. She sat outside on the deck for a while and looked at the ocean, and then it was too hot. She wanted more clouds, more shadow. She watched the fishing boats. Presumably moving parallel to shore, they looked like they would run aground. A trick of perspective. She wondered where these boats were headed. To the north was the bottom of the Outer Banks, Oregon Inlet.

She wanted not to have arrived at this place, or anywhere, really. She wanted loneliness to make a kind of vacuum, like a diving bell. The way a diving bell worked, that dangerous miracle.

When Djuna texted that Kasim and Sariah were going home for Labor Day weekend, Nisha understood that this was a request for a visit rather than a statement of fact. She wondered if Djuna meant a visit from just her or from Michael too. Reading her mind, Djuna texted. Michael can come too. I don't want to hurt his feelings.

Nisha had been living in the apartment for almost two weeks. She had seen Michael for part of the first evening, to talk, but then he'd smashed the wall with his fist, and Nisha thought *this is when I get out of here*. She gathered her phone and her keys and said goodbye. If he wanted to talk, there would have to be a third party. A witness. What did it mean that most human truth-telling these days involved witnesses? That was another question for another day.

They communicated otherwise by text. Some evenings, Nisha would go over to the house, drink a beer, and watch News Hour. She would hug Michael, cry and leave. Michael waved from the deck. Nisha waved back. As soon as she rounded the bend, bumped out of the first pothole in the road, she felt all right. On the bridge, she was better. Unlocking the door to her apartment, immense relief but sadness for Michael.

"This isn't about Michael's feelings," Felicity said. "It's about yours."

"It seems so selfish."

"It's not."

"Isn't marriage about giving up what you have for the other person? Aren't you supposed to lose yourself to become a couple?"

"Do you hear how perfectly mad that sounds? Not to mention saintly. You do know what happens to saints, don't you?"

Nisha arrived to pick Michael up at 8 a.m. the Sunday morning before Labor Day to drive to Carrboro, parked, and edged past the terrible overgrown garden, reproachful weeds, choked herbs, angry mosquitoes. Abandoned was the word. She had abandoned gardening three months ago, in June.

The back door was locked—a shock. She could see through the house to the river side deck and the back of Michael's head. He was no doubt reading the *Times* on his iPad and drinking coffee—what they always did on a Sunday morning, even when Djuna was living there. She felt nothing like nostalgia for those mornings, only the slap of the symbolic: locked out of the house because she had left it. And why should the place be open for her? She deserved to be locked out. She knocked on the window glass, texted Michael I'm here, watched him read the text, rise from the chair, bring in the chair cushions, slowly, before he looked up and saw her outside. His face was empty.

"You have a key," he said as he opened the door.

"I left it in the car."

Nisha held up the travel mug she'd brought. "Can I have some coffee?"

"Of course. I have tea if you'd prefer."

"No thanks. Coffee's fine."

"Do you want some sweet potato pie?"

"Are you going to have any?"

"It's too early for me to eat."

"Me too."

"Take some with."

"Do you want a piece too?"

"I don't think so."

Nisha opened the refrigerator. It was still full of food, plastic containers of leftovers, packaged for Michael's lunches next week. Meals she would not be putting into his lunchbox with notes she would not be writing. She brought out the pie in its heart-shaped dish, cut out a ventricle.

Michael was putting on his shoes, gathering his wallet and sunglasses.

They drove mostly in silence, commenting now and then on the weather, the route. She considered every sentence carefully before speaking. She didn't want Michael to deduce she was living in the Village. It still surprised her that he didn't ask—though maybe he knew. Maybe she was a fool to think that in such a small town no one knew where she was living, no one had casually mentioned it to Michael as the faux friendliness that was really gossip. *Bless your heart.*

Miles of quiet. A vague storminess in her brain. She wasn't going to take on the entire burden of making conversation.

"I don't know," she said finally, "if there's anything on the radio now."

Michael pressed power, dialed in the news. North Korea was misbehaving, as well as Iran and the Saudis. The advisors were assembling, the President was tweeting about immigrants, who were dying in his camps. The winds of the next storm, 500 miles from Cuba, had been clocked at 60 miles per hour. Our little problems, Nisha thought the line from *Casablanca,* don't amount to a hill of beans in this crazy world.

They listened for forty minutes. Then to a TED talk. The subject was silence. Stillness. Introverts. Behind her sunglasses, Nisha began to cry. She hoped Michael was paying attention. She didn't dare speak.

"That was really good," he said when the talk had ended.

"It was great."

Michael said he'd dreamed that he and Nisha were back in college. They were trying to get to the classroom where the exam for Rationalist Philosophers would be given. But they were lost. They kept walking around Harvard Yard, on the periphery, inside the gate beside Mass Ave. Up to the Science Center and Memorial Hall. But they couldn't find the building. They saw the section leader, but he didn't recognize them. Michael turned to walk back to the Yard, and when he glanced back, Nisha was gone. He knew she had found her way to the exam without him. He knew she was fine, but he would never get to where she was. He would fail this test and then other tests, and finally he would be asked to leave college.

Maybe he would get it. Maybe he would understand. They might work it out.

What was 'it'?

Ten minutes of *Wait, Wait Don't Tell Me*. That narcissist fool in the White House, surrounded by all his *best people*, had given the guests on this show the easiest job in radio.

The passage from I-40 towards Chapel Hill was travel between two universes. From flat glare of highway buzz to hilly green, dappled light. An exhalation. Djuna's neighborhood was still shaded and serene. Djuna waiting on the front steps, in her bare feet, beautiful. Taller, Nisha thought, slimmer. Those long legs. They couldn't stop hugging. That body, that body, pressed tight to Nisha's. How to make up for two weeks without this? Keep trying. Keep holding. Djuna did not pull away either.

"I missed you so much," she whispered.

"I know."

214

When they could bear to let go, Djuna turned to Michael.

"I haven't hugged you yet."

And they did.

"Where should we go?" Michael said.

"Do you want to see my house?" Djuna said. "I mean now that I've decorated."

Djuna's room, done in gray and teal, had a calm, somewhat austere feeling to it, but the effect was surprisingly warmed by a print of Van Gogh's "Starry Night" and Magritte's "Empire of Light." Nisha would never have guessed Djuna liked these images. She wanted to ask her sister about them. What do you see here? What do you get from these? But maybe the answer was something private, or maybe Djuna didn't really know. Maybe—no, certainly—not everything Djuna would do from now on could or would be explained.

Kasim's and Sariah's bedroom doors were closed, and Djuna honored this privacy.

The kitchen was small but bright and orderly. The table was set for three. The air smelled of cumin and frying.

"Kasim made a rule," Djuna said, laughing. "No frozen pizza, only delivery pizza."

"Seems like a good rule," Nisha said. "Is he the rule maker?"

Djuna looked away, maybe at something behind Nisha's head. "No," she said gently. "Not at all. He's really sweet. And funny."

"Like a big brother?" Michael said.

"Not really," Djuna said. "Something else." She shook her head. "I mean I never had a brother, so how would I know?"

"Funny," Nisha said. "None of us did."

"I guess I don't count then," Michael said. He turned and walked out of the kitchen ahead of them.

"Sorry," Djuna called after him. "I just meant, you know…."

"It's okay," Nisha said. She lowered her voice. "You know how he gets."

"I guess I forgot."

They followed Michael into the living room, bare except for a couch and a flat screen television. "We're still trying to figure out what to do in here. When we're all at home, we're in the kitchen."

"Which sounds like it must be nice," Nisha said.

"It is."

Michael was impatient, maybe to get away from the vision of another life he was not a part of. Nisha couldn't be sure what he felt. "Take us on a campus tour," he said. "Where do you go? Where are your classes? Where do you hang out?"

Outside, Devin Graham was standing beside Michael's car.

"You can't park here," he called to them. "You can't park in the street without a permit."

Michael walked toward the car. Nisha noticed that Djuna stayed where she was, on the front porch. "He's actually not very nice," Djuna said. "Michael shouldn't get into it with him."

Nisha crossed the front lawn to stand beside Michael.

"Hi, Devin," she said. "I'm Nisha Malik. I'm a friend of your mom's."

"I didn't think my mom had any friends."

What does a person say to something like that?

"We won't park here anymore," Michael said. "We're about to leave now anyway." He called to Djuna, who had disappeared inside the house. Nisha walked back to find her, but she heard Devin say to Michael, "Those people are just irresponsible."

"What people?" Michael said.

"Them," Devin said. "You know who I mean."

They drove to Franklin Street and Djuna took them into the Cosmic Cantina, where they ordered giant burritos and Mexican beer. Then

216

back to the art museum for a quick look, and after that to Target and Trader Joe's. Nisha and Michael bought bottles of wine and olive oil, pasta and beans, as if all of these groceries would be going to the same house to be cooked and consumed together by Nisha and Michael. Nisha wondered how they would ever tell Djuna that she had moved out, though she knew that Michael would leave it to her to break that awful news.

The campus was empty and green, shady and lush—and a little sad. Nisha had never seen the place like this: orientation had been wall-to-wall excited students and apprehensive parents. Before that, Admitted Students Day was a frightening crush, claustrophobic, a strange buzz in the air—it was a courtship. The students felt both excitement and withholding, as the campus played a proud but nervous suitor.

Djuna called to a man coming out of Wilson Library. Mr. McFadden, she said, then made introductions among them: English teacher, sister, brother-in-law. My *English* teacher, Djuna said, is *Irish.* Go figure. They all laughed. She's quite a good writer, Mr. McFadden said. We're very proud of her, Nisha replied. All this time, Djuna held Nisha's hand, an iron grip really, against floundering or drowning.

#6

Describe a place you love by detailing its destruction.

Fall arrived fully, signaled by the pecan trees, their leaves the last to turn. Noon sunlight changed, flattened, as if worn out. Nisha missed Djuna. She walked to the park by the river, and she felt Djuna in the gradually dropping temperature, the thinning atmosphere, Djuna fading out of this local universe, her presence growing fainter, the cold wind in Nisha's heart leaking out of her body, filling up the space between her and everyone else in the park. She tried to convince herself that it was good, that separation. It felt like how normal missing someone should feel, not like grief. Not like the awful regret and absence after her parents died. She stared at the little moons on the ground below a Japanese maple. Ordinarily the shadows would be frilly and jagged like the edges of the leaves. She remembered watching the eclipse with Djuna at the high school two years before, how the eclipsing moon could change the physical shape of a leaf, of a familiar natural object. Eclipsing changes nature—it changed the order of the universe. She remembered how after the eclipse was over, the air thickened and warmed. The smaller schoolchildren, who had been frozen in place, re-animated. Why had they been so still? What force had spoken to their bodies? They already knew something about weather. And now, it was the height of hurricane season.

In the beginning, a hurricane is called an *invest*. That's right. A clarion call. *Invest* in tarp, *invest* in sandbags, *invest* in bottled water before it all disappears from the shelves, *invest* in a generator and flashlight batteries. Invest, invest, invest.

Next, unbelievably, is *depression*. Or maybe that's to be expected after so much investment.

After that, the rain, the wind, the destruction, the loss.

So it went: invest, depression, storm. Nisha thought the progress of a hurricane sounded all too human—and the NOAA graphic was like a child's drawing: big, round red and yellow cross-hatched baubles rolling from the west coast of Africa across the Atlantic Ocean. The passage over all that water seemed to give them time to think, ruminate on the problem, grow more and more disturbed, and then finally enraged, spinning themselves into a frenzy, a whirling dervish of weather.

The storms were named in advance each season, the full list announced in June.

Anna, Boris, Colette, Dominic, Ellis, Fred, Gabrielle, Hendrik, Ismene

Djuna kept track from Chapel Hill and called every day to check in. "The I storms," she said one morning, "when they're women, they're trouble. When do you think Ivanka will be added to the list?"

"I hope never."

"Don't bet on it."

"You missed Isabel, but you were here for Irene," Nisha said.

Those two brought three feet of water into the house. Isabel rushed in and out in 45 minutes, but tore off the bathroom door, tipped over the refrigerator, upended the chest freezer, spilling out gallons of homemade tomato sauce. Eight years later, Irene churned through the neighborhood, found it to her liking and stayed six hours. They'd lost everything. Books, CDs, unopened boxes of Riedel wine glasses. Nearly every stick of furniture.

"Remember the poor piano," Djuna said.

Nisha remembered. For a few days after the storm, Djuna could still play it, and they all felt better. Hopeful. But then the strings and dampers dried, and the salt water turned to glue, and all she could do was bang, bang, thump, thump, no music, just percussion.

Nisha and Felicity met again at the restaurant by the town dock, but the rain drove them inside. They took seats at the bar, next to a man Felicity knew, who was slurring and swaying, clearly drunk. The bartender was talking about the hurricane.

"Come and get me, baby," the man yelled. "I'm not afraid. Or as they say around here, 'I ain't skeered!' Where I come from, we call this wind a *williwaw*."

"Let's not invite trouble," Felicity said, and then the man began his hurricane autobiography. Floyd, Dennis. He'd retired from Alaska to Florida, but then to get away from storms, he decided Raleigh was a pretty safe bet. Nope. Then he'd really let his guard down or lost his mind, he didn't know which, and moved here, just in time for the weird sisters Isabelle, Ophelia and Irene.

"I think I'm good now though," he said. He'd raised his house fourteen feet, got rid of almost everything when his wife left him. He leaned in, gazed down the bar. "You ladies would be safe with me."

And Nisha believed him. He was a tall, powerful looking man, probably in his late sixties. He had a sweet expression. She thought Djuna would love that word, *williwaw.*

For a few weeks, they—Djuna, Kasim, and his sister Sariah—didn't see much of Devin. Then he began to park his truck in the street so that it half blocked their driveway. The first time this happened, Kasim knocked on Devin's door and asked if he could move his truck a couple of feet forward. Devin seemed irritated, stared at Kasim for longer than was necessary, then disappeared inside to get his keys. He moved the truck without speaking a single word. You probably woke him up, Sariah had said. You know how out of it some people are if they've been asleep.

In the evenings, Devin smoked and drank beer on his front porch, still wearing his cable company uniform shirt. Kasim wondered if that would be bad for business, if Devin could get fired. Kasim was a kind person, a worrier. He wanted to say something to Devin, but Djuna and Sariah talked him out of it.

"Maybe you could mention something to Felicity," Djuna said

over the phone.

"I don't think so," Nisha said. "I mean what would she tell him? 'The neighbors say you're giving The Man a bad name'?"

"*The Man*? Wow, Nisha. When did you get so twenty years ago woke?"

"I've been working on it."

"You go, girl."

"You wouldn't believe how I'm growing and changing," Nisha said.

"It's hard to imagine growing up with Felicity wouldn't have rubbed off on him at all."

"You know what they say about skipping a generation."

"He kind of looks like there might be drugs involved," Djuna said.

"Felicity says he's clean now. He was in pretty bad shape in his 20's."

"I guess he's OK. I'm not afraid of him or anything. Just paying attention."

Ismene moved north and west. Djuna read the forecasts and reported back what Nisha already knew. The forecasters had tired of "moved" and "pushed," and so they worked to find new verbs: marched, pressed, churned. One of them, the unfortunately named Forecaster Slaughter, was given to the more fanciful *danced* and *spun*, or when the wind speed slowed, *dallied, lazed, lolly-gagged*.

"It's like the NOAA people are characters in a book," Djuna said. "You invent their personalities by what they say." She told Nisha she pictured all of them as men. Slaughter infuriated and intrigued her. She found herself thinking there was nothing poetic about a hurricane, but then coming to the idea that a hurricane was in fact all poetry, all fury and intensity in the place of complaisance. People go along and go along, thinking their lives are okay, deluding themselves, making do. And then this ravaging force comes at them out of nowhere, comes slowly enough so that they have time to fall for the next delusion, which is that they can maybe sidestep the storm, get out of her way, live through it.

And then Devin killed them all.

Grief is a hurricane.

That sound Nisha made, her arms around Djuna's body. Mrs. Achebo's arms around her. Their two voices, keening, the sound like a knife breaking the bond between living and dead, a dull knife that must saw away at the cords of connection. And outside, the loud screaming of the air, and the churning of the ocean, its voice of destruction, of windows, doors, walls, all of it, breaking, breaking.

I held onto Nisha and raged against all those daft remedies for grief: do your raging alone, and only for a little while. Then take a Valium, go for a run. I'll be fine, no, I'm just grand. But I heard my mam telling me, Go away outta that, Liam, you've not even started your raging. But did I listen, no, I fled the scene in Dublin, then put myself in the way of these young people, trying to make them into little versions of Shamus. And hadn't I almost done it with Djuna Malik. And then, she was gone too. Like losing Shamus twice, it was. But now—let the waves crash over me, crash through. A hurricane of grief. A hurricane *and* grief, to show I was wrong about everything.

About a hurricane, if I'd given that prompt, I knew what Djuna would write.

She enters your house and moves your things around to suit herself. No, she says, this doesn't go here, this table goes over there, this sofa goes behind it, china teacups belong on the floor, CDs too. Those wine glasses—how *rational* they are!—know they've hit the ground. And they also know they really want to be in seven or eight pieces

223

each. Those dresses in the closet have longed from their origins as bolls in flooded cotton fields years ago, to smell now so brackish you finally throw them away. That bedroom door belongs in the bathtub. How could you not have known that the small folding desk wanted to be caught by one of its slender legs just outside the front door? Why did it never occur to you that the books ought to be lying covers off, spines broken in that tangled wreck of a garden?

Because you're a bloody fool. For wanting anything. For thinking you had any control.

The Christmas decorations don't need to be neatly wrapped up in their boxes, the piano keys don't need to make any sound, the windows don't need to be snug in their frames. *You* need that, you small, selfish human.

Not only do you see the truth of your foolishness, but the neighbors see it too. There are all your belongings, in your vegetable patch, in theirs. Poker chips, skeins of cassette tapes you can follow like slimy black breadcrumbs back to the plastic housing. Where you see it's an hours-long inspirational workshop by a Zen master. Which you could certainly use right now. A waterlogged box of plastic straws in five colors. A cork board with push pins holding onto triangles of blank paper. What reminders had you posted there? What was it you wanted to remember? A small mermaid, made of cloth and raffia, who couldn't manage to swim away and hide in a grotto. If only she could have sprouted legs.

The neighbor's hot tub. His dog bowls, wine bottles from the recycling. Or maybe not. Maybe the storm forced them open and drank deeply and, like certain other small humans you know, got meaner. A travel mug with its lid still on, a ceramic coffee cup emblazoned with #1 MOM. All these vessels huddled behind the flooded car. Why didn't you move the car to higher ground? Because you're a fecking eejit.

But that's not Djuna writing. That would be me, the now one and only Liam McFadden. Not fooling anyone, am I? No one can write Djuna Malik but her very own self.

If only if only if only. The day of the college rejections came back, sharp and hard with a more terrible regret.

"Fuck the Ivy League and the horse it rode in on," Nisha said out loud, even though she was alone in the schoolhouse condo. Maybe Djuna would have been safe at one of those goddamn schools that rejected her. From the green armchair, she could see skeins of cloud and the upthrust arms of trees, nearly bare. *Help us*, they could be calling, the branches waving, hysterical, confused. Why did everything seem like a message from the great beyond? And where was that anyway?

Rain had been falling for days. The National Weather Service had issued a flash flood warning. Three potential hurricanes now lined up in the Atlantic Ocean, the storm called Ismene sure to come ashore nearby. Everyone in the village seemed still and pale, went even silent if it was Nisha walking into the store or the bar. Trouble, Nisha thought. That's what they see. I'm like the storm arriving. And all the storms before. All around them, trouble past and future.

She had dreamed—or maybe she wasn't completely asleep—of driving on the river road near Camp Don Lee, and coming to a section of pavement that had been completely washed out and deciding she would cross it anyway. Voices blasted at her from the radio: if you can't see how deep it is, find another way. The slogan was *don't drown, go around.*

But as everyone knew, there was no way out but through, she thought, conscious of mixing the metaphors, mixing up life and death, death and life. All the same anyway, without Djuna.

And so, in the dream, she drove on. The tires caught the submerged pavement for a few seconds, and Nisha exhaled. But then she sensed a kind of falling away, and the car seemed to gather itself, hold its breath and drift to the right, towards the river. In the logic of dreams, she understood perfectly that the river *was* the road, but only right here in this spot, and if she kept going, she would meet the road again—there, just ahead, 10 or 15 feet. She could see the slick, gray pavement and the bright yellow line, looking like—the image came to her oddly, suddenly, a trail of egg yolk.

In the dream, or whatever it was, the car began to float, south, towards Adams Creek, six miles away, gently, the way almost nothing floats in real life. Nisha gripped the wheel, steering slightly left, back toward the big house east of the camp on the river road, the house with four outbuildings and no central cooling. When they looked at this place, years ago, Nisha had imagined a playhouse for Djuna, who was not with them yet, and a workshop, a root cellar, a guest cottage for her parents and Djuna when they visited from Mumbai. A whole world for people who no longer existed. In this dream, the flooded river was taking her there, to this sanctuary for the dead. They, Djuna, Mommy, Daddy, all gone to ashes. From such deafening noise, all that gunfire, now not a whisper. It was as if her ears were stopped with cotton wool. Except that really, they were everywhere, Djuna and Mommy and Daddy, they were the stillness and the silence of this dream.

The refrigerator cycled off now, and so Nisha heard only the cries of birds, intermittent and searching. The rain seemed to tapered off. Another of the AC units went still. The silence was absolute. More birds then. Djuna would never again hear birdsong. That was the most awful thing, wasn't it? No. It was just the newest most awful thing.

There was work to be done today, out in the world. The car need-ed an oil change, tire rotation. Nisha had an eye exam. She would get new glasses. She'd been wearing this pair for fifteen years. Maybe that would make a difference. She lifted the metal urn, a shiny cube, from the coffee table, gathered her car keys and wallet. Everywhere she went these days, Nisha carried Djuna's ashes. She couldn't bear for her sister to be alone.

Of course something would have to be done about them, these ashes. Eventually, they would have to be let go somewhere. Nisha believed Djuna would want to be with Mommy and Daddy, and that meant Mumbai, but she knew she could never go home again, to that home.

And yet. The idea of Djuna's ashes with her parents' ashes was becoming a kind of obsession.

Not possible, Michael had said. Said it gently, she had to admit.

She had expected such a reaction. Ten years ago, he said, her parents' ashes had been swallowed by fish in the harbor or drifted to the ocean floor or washed back in, to the beach and stuck on the bottom of some tourist's sandal. Stop it, she'd told him. Stop dishonoring the dead. It's true, though, he said. You know it's true. He thought she'd feel less pain if she could see the situation realistically.

And now they had nearly the same conversation.

"It's a symbol," she said, weeping. "A metaphor. Don't you get it?"

He tried to put his arms around her, but she shook him off.

"Can we try to find a less exhausting metaphor? A less expensive metaphor? Less dangerous?"

"You don't get it. She's not your sister."

Michael slammed the door on his way out.

But she'd done what he suggested, planned it. Less expensive anyway. She'd chosen a day: her parents' wedding anniversary. October 15. So in some way they could all be together. And she'd worked herself around to a different place. Tiny steps, nearly imperceptible realignments, exchanges, *deals*. How she hated that word now. The President of the United States had caused her to hate a perfectly good, useful word. Bargaining: it was one of those famous five steps, though she seemed to be getting them out of order. Bargaining combined with revelation: one day, Nisha woke up and knew that she wanted to have Djuna nearby, that she wanted this all along. Djuna in her river. Djuna a mermaid, both real and not.

On October 15, at noon, Sunday, Nisha would row out to the middle of the river and, drifting or rowing along toward the village, pour the ashes overboard, most of them, saving a few to seal inside the heart locket Nisha had given ten years ago when she first came to live with them.

As the day approached, so did Ismene. It didn't matter. Even in the hurricane, she'd still do it, scatter the ashes. The promise of that storm on this day seemed fitting.

"Maybe it's the opposite," Michael said. "Maybe it's telling you not to. That it's a bad idea."

"I don't think so," Nisha said. "I think it's a test."

"The universe is benign."

"I can't talk about this with you."

"If you drown, you won't be able to talk about it with anybody," Michael said. "What about a compromise? The day after. The week after is probably when it will be safe."

"I want it to be a day that means something."

"Stand out on the deck."

"It's not the same."

"You're being stubborn."

"*You* think I'm being stubborn. Why can't you understand I have to do this?"

"Even if you drown?"

"Maybe I want to drown."

Conversations like these.

This was Friday. By Saturday night, Ismene would make landfall, and Michael behind all that glass, facing into the wind off the river and the rising water and Nisha in the village, safe in her bunker, far enough from the water's edge, just high enough (so the landlord told her) and protected by brick and the ghosts of willful, imperious school teachers.

She offered to go over to the river house to help bring plants inside, haul sandbags, move the cars to higher ground, even though she knew two facts. First, there was so little that could be done in preparation. It would all take about 20 minutes. Second, Michael would say yes because he wanted her company. She wondered if he was getting any better at being alone. She hoped he was, but she doubted it. So she'd asked, and he'd said yes, but that she didn't have to come over, that he understood if she felt safer where she was. Which was perhaps code for what was likely his hope: you might get stuck here.

She went, to make him happy, at least temporarily. It was a strange power, and she hated to use it.

They stood downstairs, crowded inside the old shell of the house, surveying the jumble of their lives. Every square inch was piled with boxes of—she didn't know what anymore. Books, extra kitchen equipment, dishes, two leather couches they'd got for free from a friend, now coated with dust and probably filled with mice and their droppings. Michael's tools, from tiny screwdrivers to power saws and a lathe, tucked or wedged into any open space, half of them rusted from the last two floods (Isabel and Irene). It looked like madness: the handiwork of a hoarder, who would perish when 40 years of saved newspapers caught fire.

"I can't move it," Michael said. "It's all going to get ruined. Again."

"We bought the trailer for exactly this," Nisha said. "It can go in the trailer. Or some of it can."

"The trailer is already full."

"We don't need this stuff, Michael."

"How do you know?" His tone was meditative, almost tender.

"It's been sitting down here for how many years now? Six?"

"I know. But I was thinking we would build that extra room. And now maybe you need…."

"My place came furnished."

"I wondered about that."

"We can take some of this upstairs probably."

"But what?" He waved his arms in a gesture of frantic helplessness.

"I know," Nisha said. "Maybe those little boxes?"

"Your stuff."

"I don't mean it that way."

"What about books?"

"Books definitely."

"But where will we put them?"

"Isn't there one more shelf in the bedroom?"

"You obviously haven't been in the bedroom lately."

Nisha sighed. She held her tongue. She wanted to say it back to him. *Obviously.* But what would that accomplish?

"We could move some of these boxes up higher," she said. "In the other rooms."

"There's no space, even Djuna's old room."

"Don't say old."

"What am I supposed to say?"

"I don't know. I really don't know."

"Anyway, those shelves are packed to the gills. Every shelf in this whole goddamn house."

She saw that Michael had stepped closer. She felt fear enter her heart like a needle, a cold, thin piercing. She couldn't move. He slid his arm around her waist, moved his hip against hers. She didn't know what this gesture meant or what it could become. Last weekend when she was dropping off the mail, he'd come up behind her suddenly and wrapped his arms over her shoulders, around her neck, against her throat. "Are you trying to kill me?" she'd asked, choking out a laugh. In the moment, it had seemed entirely possible. He'd just come inside from cutting the grass and had moved toward her quickly, without saying a word.

"It's so sad," he said now, pulling her closer. "All this."

"I know." She hugged him back.

"I wish we didn't have so much shit, but we needed it all."

"We did," Nisha said. "And now we don't. How does that happen? That you stop needing things?"

Michael dropped his arm and stepped away. "I don't have a fucking clue," he said.

What had she really meant? Nisha wondered. This was the sort of moment, a sudden mood shift when she would have exchanged a look with Djuna or moved out of Michael's reach and gone to find Djuna and hugged her or stroked her hair. That's the one thing she did need. And now it wasn't there.

"Remember that time," he said. "I threatened to break Djuna's computer?"

"Yes."

"I feel like I want to do it now." He said he wanted her to come screaming at him through the keyboard, through the separated keys, through the bedroom window, through the door. He wanted her body to come down from the loft bed as if she'd just been asleep up there the whole time. "I'm sorry I get like this sometimes," he said.

Later, they sat in their chairs, waiting, the lamp burning between them, the steady wind punctuated by gusts that shook the house, rattled the windows. They heard a slicing sound, and then a clatter in the yard below.

"That was a shingle," Michael said.

"I thought so."

"It's early to lose a shingle."

"I wonder how long before the power…. I don't even want to say it."

"I know. Don't say it."

"I have to admit I'm worried about Felicity," Nisha said.

Michael's expression softened, and he reached across the table between them, patted Nisha's hand. "You're a good person," he said.

"Thanks for saying so."

Michael sighed, withdrew his hand. "Why don't you believe anything I say? Jesus."

"I didn't mean it that way, Michael. I meant thank you. That's all. Why do you assume every word out of my mouth is somehow a slight?"

"Because it usually is."

"I don't know if I should stay here."

"Well, you can't leave now."

Nisha leaned back, closed her eyes. Mommy, Daddy, I need you now, she thought. Djuna. Why does he hate me? Make him not hate me. Or lift me out of this house and into my car and fly my car back to town where I'll be safer anyway.

Michael heaved himself out of his chair and headed into their bedroom. On the way, he banged the wall with his fist. A small voice in Nisha's head told her *go now*. Not even the words exactly, more like a convulsive gathering of viscera and will. Nisha stood up, lifted her raincoat off the peg by the door, stepped into her boots. She waited. She heard the toilet flush and the bathroom light snap off, a sound like a dry cough.

When he saw her, Michael's eyes went wide. He started toward her, then stopped.

"I can't let you," he said. "It's too dangerous."

"I'll be safer in town actually," Nisha said. "You know I will."

"On the way, though. The bridge. You can't do it."

"I'm afraid of you. I'm more afraid of you than of the storm."

You are the storm was what she wanted to say. *I thought my sister was the storm but now I understand she's not it at all.* She saw Michael's hands curl into fists. She stared at his hands until he jammed them into his pockets.

"At least hug me," he said.

"I'll hug you tomorrow or whenever this is all over." She did not know what she meant by *this*.

Michael stayed where he was, on the other side of the kitchen table. Nisha let herself out into the rain. When she glanced back, she saw he was right there, on the other side of the glass. He looked destroyed, impossibly old.

In a few seconds, she was drenched. Her hood blew back, the rain rushed inside the collar of her coat and down into her boots, soaking her pants legs, even though the house blocked most of the wind off the river. Still, this wind drove her down the stairs, the crazy combined forces of gravity and wind, nearly knocking her into the tomato plants. She fought her way to the car, wrestled the door open. Finally she was inside. Quiet, relatively. Not dry. She started the car, backed out, waved up at Michael as was their custom, even though she couldn't see his form in the window.

Michael had been right about the bridge.

There was a smaller lower bridge before it, over the mouth of Dawson Creek where it flowed into the Neuse. You could fish from this bridge, you could even jump from it, though signs warned against such recklessness. Nisha had to steer hard to the right to keep from being blown into the cement guardrail. The road beyond, open to the river on one side and the creek on the other, had already begun to flood. She drove through slowly, as the public service announcements always advised, even though she could see the water wasn't very deep, had not joined the river's current. It was brackish, though, she reminded herself, the salt likely to make a mess of the car's undercarriage. She thought of Boston in winter, DOT trucks spewing salt. Michael always said the damage here was just the same as from salted roads.

Two hundred feet beyond, houses at the river's edge sheltered the road, took the brunt of the wind, their lawns absorbing the rising river, at least for now, until the saturation point. The driving was easier here. Nisha knew there was one more open stretch, just before China Grove, where Lana Turner had a summer home. She wondered if Lana ever rode out any hurricanes, watching the water rise in the big house on the bend. In Hurricane Irene, all these houses had been wrecked. Two of them actually traded decks that had washed out into the river and then washed back, slowly crossing paths, while the two sets of owners tracked their progress. Neck and neck like a horse race, they said later, when people could laugh a little about things like that.

Why was she thinking about this now? For comfort? Just drive, she told herself. Concentrate. The wind behind her as she passed the acre of soybean a rogue developer once planned to flood in order to build a marina. That work was about to be done for him now. Across the road was the gate into a creek-front community planned in 2007 and abandoned the next year in the financial crisis. One house built and sold. She wondered if anyone lived there. What isolation. Terrifying right now.

She came to the right turn at Mariana Road. She could go straight, the long way around, and avoid the bridge. Nisha knew this was probably the wiser course, but she turned anyway, or the car turned itself. She felt a strange giving up, giving in, and at the same time a powerful desire. She wanted to know. She wanted to have crossed the bridge and survived.

The odd thing about Walnut Grove Marina, on the near side of the bridge, was that it was quiet—no lines singing against their masts in this wind—and almost empty. People had moved their boats deep into the smaller creeks, Green or Blount's, their hurricane holes. They tied the boats between the largest, strongest trees on either shore, loosely, so when the water rose, the boat did too. Braver, more experienced—maybe more foolish?—owners stayed on the boats, literally rose out the storm, fighting their way out on deck to adjust the lines.

On the low end of the bridge, she knew she'd made a mistake, and she slowed the car, wondering if it would be wiser to turn back, or to get out of the car and walk across. *How would that be smarter?* Her mother's voice asked.

"I'm in trouble, Mommy," Nisha said aloud. "I'm so sad. I don't know what I'm doing here."

She inched the car forward. The wind seemed to rush down from the top of the bridge, pushing her backwards. And wind came at her from the east too, wind and rising tide driving the river toward the village. This doubled force was confusing, it seemed to confuse the car, as if the car were sentient, an animal. I'm going to flood the engine, Nisha thought. Well, that's ironic. You could still just back up, downhill, drive around, she told herself.

She locked her elbows to keep the steering wheel steady and continued the ascent. She wondered, almost absently, as if she were not in her body, if her arms would break. The wind pushed the car across the center line and into the left bike lane. The left side mirror scraped along the concrete railing and folded inward. Why had she not thought to do that in the first place? It seemed now as if she might slam into the concrete and then through it and fall into the river.

Then the gust fell away, and she didn't crash. The view from the top of the bridge was exhilarating, shocking, terrible. The river had already washed over the docks in the marina. A small sailboat, a 25-footer Nisha guessed, had broken loose from its starboard dock lines and nestled into the boat beside it, hulls grinding together with every wave that came in. An owner who lived out of town. Bad luck to berth next to an absentee. Water covered the parking lot and the first step of the condos. Those people would have a rough night. If they had stayed.

No lights on in the village. Nisha wondered how long the power had been out. Another whistling gust of wind hauled the car back against the railing. The side mirror broke off and blew away over the bridge. Nisha pulled the wheel right as hard as she could.

"Idiot," she said. "Mommy, I'm so stupid." But she knew she would be all right. She was on the downward slope now. The dock master's office and the yacht club sheltered this side of the bridge from the wind, a little anyway.

Water lapped in the road at the corner of Main Street, maybe about a foot deep. Nisha thought she could make it, even though the tires would be completely underwater. She could feel the car begin to float, drifting left, over the curb into the driveway between the bank and the veterinary clinic. And then, just as suddenly, the wheels caught, rolled forward. Here the road ran slightly uphill, just enough for traction.

Thirty feet ahead, there was almost no standing water. Nisha turned right onto Church Street, drove past the town hall. She could see flashlights inside, moving figures. Branches littered the gravel drive into her parking area. She worried that a tree might come down on her car and wondered if she should park in the street. Plenty of trees there too. She would take her chances. The car was insured. Seemed like this would fall under the category Acts of God.

She looked at her phone. A text from Michael. She hadn't even heard it.

For the smallest fraction of a second, Nisha thought she ought to text Djuna.

Made it, she typed. *I'm fine.*

Thank goodness, came the reply, immediately, as if Michael had already typed the words. *I love you. I'm sorry. Be in touch. I will too.*

Fifteen seconds from the car, the wind and rain driving harder than when she'd left the river house, up the steps and under the portico, inside the apartment.

Inside, dry, cool, fuzzy gray storm light illuminated the windows, as if through thin drapery. No power. Nisha had two phone chargers—the small one would charge the phone once, the larger one was good for two, maybe three charges. After that she knew she could charge the phone in the car.

Right now, though, that main thing was to make it through landfall, probably in the next few hours. She checked the NOAA website: Ismene's eye had clocked south. Wilmington would take the direct hit.

Nisha knew the safest place away from the windows would be the bathroom, but she wanted to watch the sky, the tops of the trees, their shadows, see the branches snap off if that's what was going to happen. She pulled the cushions off the couch and made a bed on the floor of the galley kitchen, between the oven and the sink. Then she dragged the rocking chair halfway behind the tall counter. She sat and rocked and listened, scanned the sky.

She imagined the fury outside was Djuna, Djuna's rage at missing everything, the entire rest of her life. A dervish without religion or reason—weren't those opposites anyway? Djuna's rage and the earth's one and the same. You stupid selfish people. The same people who caused these storms and fires to be so fierce, those people had murdered Djuna. Djuna *was* the storm. Not Michael. Michael was maybe a gust of wind. Djuna was the whole spinning williwaw.

A gunshot. No, a splintering. Then silence again, except for the wind. A tree, Nisha knew, had come down very close. Not a gunshot really. Oh, Djuna. Howling. Who is that? She wondered. Djuna or me or the wind?

Somewhere behind the storm or above it, the sun set and the full-on hurricane became only sound, a constant rushing, sometimes a keening punctuated by the crack and thump of branches breaking nearby. At midnight, Nisha opened the door and aimed the phone's flashlight into the yard. Water had reached almost halfway up the steps, probably two feet. That would be all right if it didn't go much higher. She wedged bath towels at the bottom of the door just in case.

Landfall, the town website reported. Good that their generator was still running. Wilmington is inundated, wrecked. Closer, though, people were being rescued from the roofs of houses in New Bern.

Nisha slept, woke in complete darkness, slept again, The rain kept up all night, then on through the morning, the wind too, diminished but still a force. Texts came in from Michael.

Fine, here, he wrote. *The river's in the yard though. Haven't tried to go downstairs. What about you?*

Fine, she wrote.

Any damage?

I haven't been outside yet.

She ate an apple, a few pretzels. She drank warm seltzer. She didn't want to open the refrigerator—there wasn't much inside anyway. She thought about having a real drink—there was a bottle of Irish whiskey in the cabinet above the sink, but in the end, she was frightened of losing reflexes, attention, what little control she had. Trees could still come down-the two trees she could see outside the tall windows, their roots loosened by all the rain, would fall onto her end of the building. Already, there was a different open space in the early morning view: the tree across the parking lot, that must have been the splintering she'd heard—when? Was that yesterday? Yes.

How many hours ago? She wasn't sure. Time moved oddly, swam as if waterlogged.

But now the briefest silence itself was a sound. Nisha listened carefully, for changes, breaks, modulations. She wondered if she'd developed some sort of odd seeing blindness, so acute was her hearing, so completely did she depend upon it. Silence always so cherished in this apartment. Some lines about *a fine and quiet place.* Maybe this is what Djuna heard now, how Djuna listened now. And so, in this sense, Nisha felt the storm was another way to be closer to Djuna, to understand Djuna's death. The storm was sitting shiva, the storm was a wake, the letting go of the body. But in elemental terms, the storm was the opposite of immolation. Water and wind would always be the ruin of a funeral pyre.

Nisha wanted the storm to last forever.

On Sunday morning, the fifteenth of October, she heard a car on Church Street, one car churning through floodwater, and then hours later it seemed, another. More vehicles splashed by in the afternoon, so many that she stopped counting. This storm will end, she told herself. *Is* ending. It has to. That's how it works. Later, she heard human voices, hushed but steady. The town website reported that the police said it was safe enough for residents to come back and check on their homes, their boats. She wondered how many people had left and how many stayed. Around 6 p.m., a neighbor knocked, called her name. I'm here, Nisha called out, I'm fine. She stood up from the rocking chair and went to the door. When she opened it no one was there. Twenty yards away, on Church Street, a man rode past on a red bicycle. The color seemed extraordinarily bright, almost painful to look at.

She stepped out onto the porch. Debris had washed halfway up the steps—two more inches and there would have been water in the house. A branch from the crape myrtle lay along the top step, as if it had been a barrier. Heroic. Maybe an offering. She thought it was a beautiful artifact—in some unforeseeable future, it might be varnished into a Christmas decoration.

Pools of water still stood in the yard between the old school buildings. Tree branches and leaves covered both parking lots. Nisha wondered if it was safe to walk around out here—if the shingles, branches, entire trees had stopped falling. Maybe if she kept away from all of that, walked in the middle of the street? She picked a path through the parking lot, past the tree fallen on the neighbor's garage, turned right on Factory Street, heading toward the river. Some houses seemed to have been moved off their foundations. Debris everywhere. Someone's shed had come loose and floated to the river's edge. Farther along, an uprooted oak tree blocked the storm-driven progress of wooden fencing and potted plants and a twisted Adirondack chair.

The fishing pier was gone, reduced to broken spikes of pilings and half-submerged boards. Two blocks to the east, the storm surge had broken the concrete roadway into an archipelago. The intersection with High Street was a beach, sand built up like a two-foot-tall speed bump. At the corner of Front Street, rip rap and boulders blocked the road. Nisha thought of the barricade scene in *Les Misérables*. All that stuff piled up and still no defense. She did not see another person. The scene was post-apocalyptic. It wasn't hard to imagine she was the only person left on earth.

Michael texted *the downstairs is a mess, windows broken door smashed in but Felicity's place looks like a bomb went off.*

Nisha remembered the sheared-open façade of Uncle Raj's house in Cambridge.

This must be what my heart looks like, she thought.

She retraced her path back to the apartment and picked up the urn, walked back through the ruin to the river. She stepped carefully across the scattered riprap, along the new spit of rubble that had formed, as far into the river as she could go.

#7

The past is never dead; it is not even past.

"But I just stood there," Nisha told me. "Trying to balance on the rocks and keep hold of the urn. I couldn't do it. I wasn't ready to let her go. I'm not sure I'll ever be ready."

I wanted to tell her that someday she would be ready, but I knew that kind of reassurance was empty—the word came to me in the voice of Shamus—*gobshite*.

"I feel stuck," she said. "I want to sit somewhere and read this journal until…I'm afraid it might start to fall apart in my hands."

"I feel that way too, about certain books."

She knew instantly what I was talking about.

"Your parents' novels?"

"Yes."

"Because you think if you read them, you're going to still hear their voices. And you might find something you didn't see before. Some clue."

"True enough."

Nisha was quiet for a minute, watching me. "Which one the most?" she said finally.

"My father's. There's a novel called *The Bungalow*."

"May I read it?"

"It's hard to find, that one."

"Don't you have a copy?"

When I put the book in her hands, she stared at it, then looked up at me, disbelieving.

"The cover," she said. "This house. We're in it."

I had known, I think, even without looking at the book to be sure. This bungalow, on Rosemary Street. On my father's novel, in water-color, the trees darkening the long front porch in the same way, the tangle of a back garden just visible, a storm brewing in the distance.

"We are, yes." I said. "I'm curious to know what you think."

"I'm curious to know what I'll think." Nisha said this slowly, as if she were trying not to disturb something fragile, some uncertain emotional weather.

She finished the coffee, gathered her coat. I offered to walk her to her car, but she said no, she'd paid to park just down the road—but I could watch that she got there safely.

As Nisha disappeared into the Rosemary Street parking deck, I had two thoughts. She'll bring the book back and that will be grand. She won't bring the book back, and then it will be gone out of my hands for good.

Liam broke the key in the door. He's not sure how it happened. Nisha was standing right there. He wanted to get her inside and get her into bed, but now that would have to wait. What was a person supposed to do? Call a locksmith? Stand there with half a key? Go to the back door, which was opened with the same key? Use a credit card? In American movies, that always worked. Everyone had a credit card.

Break a window? Can't. It's a rental. Windows can be replaced. Fix a break with another break, that's the ticket.

Liam broke his brother's nose. He said it was an accident, but he knew and Shamus knew and their parents knew. He wanted to say that the rage blinded him—that was something that happened, didn't it? Also in American movies…. He was so enraged that he couldn't see straight, and so he couldn't exactly tell that it was Shamus whose face loomed there, grinning, drunken, gloating over his book contract. Liam made a fist and pulled his arm back.

Liam dreamed that Shamus appeared on television in the robes of a monk and threatened to hurt anyone who didn't believe in God. And the way he would inflict the hurt was this: he would give you the runs, a case of the shits so bad it could kill you. And, Shamus the monk said, even if you're at death's door and still won't admit that you believe in God, I won't make you well. I won't have mercy. You'll die sunk in your own shite.

When Liam woke, he had not decided anything

Felicity said they should meet in public. When she said the words, over the telephone, her voice shook, as if she were cold or in some weakened state. Nisha understood: in the secrecy of their homes, one of them might kill the other. They would have good reason. Murderer son. Murdered sister. Fear and revenge and loyalty, the truest, deepest feelings a person could have, everything that had driven this country to its knees in the last few years. They were a droplet of it, siphoned away from the ugly mass, but still poisonous as a shiny ball of mercury.

Nisha suggested the river, where they could walk or sit privately. Maybe the view would calm them both, though Nisha wondered how that could be so: the ruined pier, riprap washed into the road. And if that went all right, Felicity said, they might move indoors for coffee. Tea. Maybe. No. Felicity was not a taker of tea, as she had said, when they first met last spring.

They settled on a Friday morning at seven, after intricate, unspoken calculations about who might be out walking, even in December, who would be at the gym, enjoying breakfast in the Village. The sun would be bright, perhaps still breaking through the dawn mist. The southern end of the park, by the Stallings House fence, would be in shadow. Below them, rocks and riprap, a few incurious birds.

Nisha arrived ten minutes early, on purpose. She stood at the farthest corner, by the water's edge, knowing she was partly obscured from view at certain angles. She might appear to be a post, or mistaken for a channel marker: solitary out there, apart from land, vaguely helpful. At the last minute, she'd made up two silver travel mugs, one of coffee and one of tea with honey and milk, the way Djuna liked it.

As she waited, she cursed her impulse for the conciliatory gesture, and now had no place to put these idiotic mugs, growing warm in her hands. The heat was good though, traveling up her arms, into her heart, boiling up in her brain. Djuna! She wanted to shout her sister's name over the water. God fucking damn it! He killed my sister! Djuna, Djuna! Where are you? I've brought you tea. Do you hate me for making his mother a cup of coffee?

She tried to calm herself, but by the time she heard the shush and glide of footsteps over the grass behind her, she hadn't succeeded.

I won't look at her, she thought. I can't look at her.

There was Felicity, coming around the corner, towards her. Nisha could see there were tears on her face already.

Would it be easier, Nisha thought suddenly, if I just lost my mind? Now she was glad for the coffee and tea to fill up her hands, giving some other purpose to her arms. Otherwise she might have torn out Felicity's hair, dashed her head against the Stallings House fence.

"Please, Felicity," she said. "Please stop crying."

"All right," Felicity said, wiping her eyes with her gloved fingers. "I'll try."

"I brought you coffee."

"Thank you." Felicity tried to smile. "Not poisoned, I trust."

"If I wanted to poison someone, it wouldn't be you."

Felicity bowed her head. They stood side by side, not quite touching, staring out across the river. Mist drifted at the far shore. A ruffle. That's what it would look like from the air, Nisha thought, a lace edging. The trees must have produced this effect, the expanse of them over there in the Croatan National Forest, their warm exhalation.

"I know it doesn't help to say I'm sorry."

"I don't think anything will help," Nisha said. "But thank you for trying. And I'm sorry about your house."

"You don't have to be polite."

"No." Nisha listened to the echo of the word. It sounded as if she were asking a question. No, no, no, no, no. How many times had she said it in the past weeks? Her mind seemed to break away, break off from itself. Had she ever stood here in just this spot with the living Djuna? Maybe. Yes. Sharing a Styrofoam cup of ice cream after school. Strawberry. She could almost taste the sweet of it on her tongue right now, the pale pink color, which almost had a taste itself, that color, and the white plastic spoon passed back and forth between them, taking the ice cream from it a kind of kiss. The overwhelming tenderness of that, how ice cream shared with her sister could make (how *could* it?) Djuna feel better after a day when someone at school had bothered her, wronged her, shamed her.

Nisha realized this sort of thinking happened every day, all day, this drifting toward the memory of Djuna when she was supposed to be doing something else, be present in some other context.

"Do you want to talk?" Felicity said.

"I think so."

"Devin is sorry too."

"No, he isn't."

"He's sorry in his own way."

Nisha pressed the silver mug hard against her forehead.

"I don't know if this is going to work," she said. "Us talking."

Felicity sighed, the breath popping and stuttering in her throat. "I don't either."

They sipped at their mugs and watched the river move, the wind driving the water north towards Craven County. A green pickup truck rattled towards the park, pulled in beside what was left of the pier. The door creaked open and an elderly black man stepped onto the pavement, walked to the truck bed, lifted out two fishing rods and a small red cooler. He started toward the park, then noticed Nisha and Felicity.

"Y'all mind?" he called to them.

"Of course not," Felicity called back. She raised her mug. "Good luck."

"I need it," he said.

They watched as the man settled into a corner of the bulkhead, facing away from them. He opened the cooler, took out a plastic container of bait, set it on the ground. Next a can of Diet Coke and something round, wrapped in foil. He popped open the Diet Coke and took a long swallow, then unwrapped the foil. A ham biscuit. Nisha could smell it. He ate and drank, contemplating the river, not in a hurry, the day stretching before him. She could almost hear him sigh. Maybe he would catch his dinner, but more likely he wouldn't. Why was he even fishing this time of year? She wondered if he was a visitation, a message.

After he'd finished eating, the man crushed the foil into a ball and dropped it into the cooler. He pried open the container of bait, lifted out a wriggling worm. Before he could wind it onto the hook, Nisha glanced away, then back. They watched the old man cast again and again, a smooth, rhythmic motion, as if he were taking an arrow out of a quiver and offering it to the fish.

"Two o'clock to ten o'clock," Felicity said. "I remember teaching Devin to fish."

What should I say to that? Nisha wondered. She'd drained her mug, but Felicity was taking a long time. Djuna had fished with Michael. Not often, but there was one day when she caught a flounder, and then another, and then a third, each bigger than the last. Even though she wanted to be out on the dock with them, Nisha had stayed inside and watched from the window. It thrilled her that Michael and Djuna were doing something together, having a good time, without seeming to argue. Michael looked as though he was being very patient. Maybe he was even proud and telling her so.

"Djuna," Felicity said, then stopped. "Is it all right for me to say her name?"

Nisha considered. Was it all right? Maybe. It had just happened. Felicity had said her sister's name, and the world had not shattered into a million pieces.

"Say it again."

"Djuna," Felicity said. "Djuna. Djuna."

"Djuna," Nisha said.

And then they were saying the name together, half shouting, choking on their tears. The old man on the pier stopped casting, went completely still, turning toward them just slightly.

"I have to go now," Nisha said.

Felicity handed her the silver travel mug. There was coffee left inside. "All right," she said. "Anyway, we've made a start."

"About your father's book," Nisha said the next week.

She lifted *The Bungalow* out of her bag and brought it to me. "It's really lovely," she said. "Very different from the first one."

"That was the consensus among critics."

"Is it true?"

"Do you mean autobiographical?"

"Yes," Nisha said.

"Which part?"

"The plagiarism. The father steals his son's work."

"It is."

"The marriage. You told me. He forbids his wife to write after her first book was published. But she writes in secret."

"I did tell you."

"How do you feel about this novel?"

"Well, I left Ireland, didn't I, to avoid those questions."

"The questions tend to follow you anyway."

"I've noticed."

"And there's a good bit of my culture too."

In the years before he died, so I told Nisha, my father developed a certain fascination with India. Mostly the modern country, but also the British colonial world, how the British had taken advantage, what they'd run off with and what damage they'd left behind. My father thought he could do that, write about that world, comment on it with impunity because he was Irish, and his was another culture the British tried to dominate. The Irish were just trying to crawl out of their filthy peat bogs while the British were enslaving Indians and taking their raw materials. So, I told her, my father's book is a novel about taking things that don't belong to you. The real question, how I felt about it, I couldn't answer yet. Too soon, as the Americans say. As Djuna said when I proposed writing about the campus troubles. The trouble has to sink in, doesn't it, then drive a person to some action, some decision.

Nisha returned to Chapel Hill, and we rode together out to Jordan Lake, hiked along one of the steams, the place where, ten years ago, their friend walked into the water with Djuna riding on his shoulders, as if she were Parvati, riding on Dawon, her tiger. Djuna, above the dark element, fearless in her new life on the other side of the world. Nisha opened the mouth of the urn over the water and shook it. The wind found its way inside and lifted Djuna's ashes into the air, carrying them upward, south toward the opposite shore, down to the water's surface and then up again, a swirl, a somersault. The ashes glittered a little in the weak sunlight, like mica, like light on water, above the water.

Aspara. *Aspara.*

"I don't want to go back yet," she said. "Is that alright?"

I told her it was fine with me. We sat on a fallen log, close together for warmth. All day the sky shone a flat gray, crowded at the horizon with soft round clouds. The snow came now, softly, just a ticking in the trees, like a lazy clock marking off the seconds.

"What exactly happened to your brother?' she said.

The snow came a little harder. White flakes flashed in her hair, then disappeared.

"They were out at a pub. The last people to see them said they were arguing about my father's new novel, which was due out the next month, and about me. Shamus said I was lucky to be going away, and Da pressed him on the question. *Away from what?* He wanted to know, and Shamus was heard to have said, *away from you.* And my brother went on raging, roaring his head off. *You never loved me as much as you loved him. You only wanted me to be a writer so you could be a better writer than I am. You like it when people say, well, he's good, but he's no Liam McFadden. I had a chance, but you took it away from me. And it's the same thing you did to our mammy. You made her stop writing her novels.* Our da got as far as out the door and collapsed. Shamus thought he'd killed him.

"Oh no," Nisha said.

"He did, so. He drowned after, but was it by accident or on purpose, I don't know."

"Then you can decide," she said. "How you want to make your peace. It's your decision."

#8

Describe an item you've stolen and never told anyone about.

When Nisha turned away from the pill separator and saw Jamie at the prescription pick-up counter, she flinched, and then some weight in her chest dropped lower. She felt sick. She knew what Jamie wanted.

"Gram sent me," Jamie said. "She needs a refill." She opened her clenched fist. The magician's gesture of *voilà*. The bottle lay there like a thing fallen over, a dead soldier. Percocet.

"Let's see," Nisha said, reaching for the bottle, but Jamie closed her hand.

"It's in the system," she said. "Opal Lee. That's Gram."

"Okay," Nisha said. "Let me take a look." She opened the scrips program on the computer, typed in Gram's name.

"It's for her back," Jamie said. "All the hurricane clean-up. They lost like twenty trees." Something twisted in Jamie's expression. She was trying not to cry. "There's broken stuff everywhere."

"That's awful," Nisha said. "I'm so sorry, Jamie." She read the message on the scrips page. I'm seeing no more refills." Nisha looked up. Jamie was staring at her, that expression she remembered from the birthday meal: defiant at first, then pleading, wanting. "We've got to call her doctor."

"She already has an appointment. But she's out of the pills. She just needs a few to get by until then."

"When is the appointment?" Nisha took up a pen, as if she would write down the number of days. But she knew what Jamie would say.

"She didn't tell me. Maybe two weeks?"

"Can she get the doctor's office to give us a call?"

"I guess." Jamie leaned in closer. "But I think she's really in pain. She kind of needs them today."

What if she's telling the truth? The words came to Nisha in Djuna's voice, so forcefully that Nisha had to rest her body against the counter in front of her. She resisted the temptation to turn around. Djuna would not be standing there. She would never be there.

"I can call the doctor's office now if you want."

"No, thanks," Jamie said. "I'll just tell her you're too hard-hearted."

"Jamie, you know that's not fair."

"Yeah. *Fair*. Tell me about it."

In the years she'd worked at CVS, Nisha noticed the store was exceptionally busy the day before Christmas Eve and the Friday before Father's Day. Funny and a little sad: even a picked-over selection of Christmas cards and Father's Day cards at a drugstore was still pretty good because everybody knew that people didn't really read Christmas cards and fathers around here didn't read their cards as closely as mothers did. Nisha marveled that what she felt were the worst cards sold out first—the messages inside about Santa's drunk reindeer and lewd suggestions about Mrs. Claus or, for the fathers, about flatulence or laziness or the hoarding of the television remote.

A gift from CVS was acceptable, hard sticky bricks of fruitcake or bottles of cheap champagne. Not flowers for Christmas except poinsettias from the grocery store. And fathers didn't want flowers or could never say so if they did. Chocolates, beer or maybe wine, small gadgets, barbecue tools, travel mugs. Sometimes health products as gag gifts to go along with the cards: foot powder, compression socks, caffeine supplements, adult diapers.

On the eve of Christmas eve, from her perch in the back of the store, Nisha observed Jamie's surreptitious entrance, slouched into a black leather jacket that was too big for her. Maybe a little sad to be without a father or a mother at this time of the year, eyes cast down. Nisha started to move toward her, but then something stopped her. Jamie, she knew, would be galled and angered by unasked-for sympathy or any looming adult presence. She wouldn't know what to say about Djuna. Let her have her privacy, Nisha told herself. And let me have mine.

Jamie appeared to have time to kill. She began a slow meander to the right, past the ice cream, the milk, and the juices, to the beer case, where she paused, perhaps calculating some illegal act—she was 16. Djuna said she'd skipped a grade somewhere along the way. She looked older, world-weary. Nisha was sure she'd had sex—beyond what she said, all the innuendo, there was an air of experience about her, even from this distance. The way she held herself, her shoulders. She didn't really breathe, instead she seemed to sigh with a constant impatience. Nisha hoped she would find a way to leave the county before she got pregnant and thus trapped.

The store stocked stationery items right next to the cold beer—in case someone set out to get drunk and write a novel, or slightly more likely, a letter. Jamie stopped here too, picked up a pocket-sized notebook, riffled though the pages, and—Nisha could hardly believe her eyes—slipped it deftly inside her jacket. A notebook! Nisha was amazed, a little pleased even. Not lip gloss or mascara or a packet of mints.

Jamie moved closer to the pharmacy, weaving slowly but steadily through medical supplies, foot care, cough and cold, vitamins, miming perfectly the distraction of someone filling the minutes before an appointment, waiting for some more important thing to begin. In the next aisle, she paused just slightly to palm a hot pink contact lens case out of a bin and into her jacket pocket. Then she passed, like a puff of black smoke, by the pharmacy window but did not look up.

There was premeditation, a deft consciousness, Nisha thought, in that move. Surely Jamie knew Nisha was there, watching. Jamie was proving or testing something, maybe both at the same time. Nisha stayed where she was, motionless as if she were afraid of being seen.

She wondered that everyone else in the store didn't feel it or hear it, the angry vibration of Jamie, the jangling of bells and chains.

Jamie meandered through feminine products, to the far wall. Hair coloring. Nisha thought that display was the loveliest part of the store, what makeup could be if all lipstick, foundation, eyeshadow, blush were arrayed not by brand but by color, moving through the spectrum. She saw the hair color display as a kind of perpetual autumn, shades of platinum, red, and brown edging toward darkness. And lately, all the newly fashionable washes had been added, jewel-toned: garnet and deep green, ruby red and silver-white, amethyst, topaz, all of it represented by small, identical loops of synthetic hair dyed in the particular color. From a distance, the wall looked like a hand-tied quilt, the kind your granny would unpack from a battered footlocker and drape over the back of the sofa when the weather started to turn towards winter.

Standing still in the middle of this display, Jamie seemed taken with it too. Her shoulders straightened, and her head moved slowly left to right, as if she were appreciating the expanse of color. She stepped closer and began to touch the loops of hair, rubbing them gently between her thumb and forefinger. Nisha wondered what Jamie was thinking. Do the colors feel different? For the first time—she was a little surprised it had taken her so long—she considered the possibility that Jamie was high. The thought made her go cold all over, an ache deep in her bones, as if the temperature in the store had suddenly dropped thirty degrees.

Jamie stepped back and crossed her arms as if she felt the change too. She glanced over her shoulder to the pharmacy, but at the questions window, not the intake window where Nisha stood. Nisha wondered if this, too, was part of Jamie's game.

Heaving a dramatic sigh, Jamie wandered back towards the middle of the store, tight rows of aisles mostly shielded from Nisha's view. She paused only once—Nisha could just see the top of her head—in front of the bins of travel-sized items. Pocket-sized, Nisha thought. What would it be, when Jamie had to empty her pockets? Toothpaste? Deodorant? Shampoo? Because eventually Jamie would have to empty her pockets. The alarm system at the front door would read all the bar codes, and Jamie would be caught. How could she not know this noisy discovery would be how the game ended?

As Jamie moved toward the front of the store, Nisha wondered how she could save her from detection. Or from the rest of her life. She stepped off her stool and to the door between the pharmacy and the rest of the store. She opened her mouth to call Jamie's name, but she felt submerged in the landscape of nightmare, when you try to call out but your voice is lost to you. Jamie was moving too fast. She steeled herself for the blare of the alarm, the confusion, the confrontation, maybe a chase. Jamie could easily outrun Tonya, the cashier, and disappear into the woods behind the store, wait there until dark. Maybe call a friend on her cellphone, most likely a boy who would be happy to play partner in crime or hero. It was all so infuriating, so stupid, such a waste.

But Jamie stopped, two feet from the door, stood motionless for a few seconds, then turned and retraced her steps toward the back of the store. She disappeared from Nisha's view into the hallway that led to the restroom, the break room, storage, the emergency exit. Nisha heard the restroom door whine open and closed. The lock clicked. After a minute or two, the toilet flushed, water ran in the sink, the hand dryer whooshed.

Nisha waited just past the sign that read *no unpaid merchandise beyond this point*, blocking the doorway. When Jamie opened the restroom door, Nisha could see that she had already arranged her features into a look of mild surprise.

"Oh! Hi!" Jamie said, pushing her hands inside her jacket pockets. "I forgot you worked here."

"Hi, Jamie," Nisha said. "What's up?"

"Not much. I was looking for something for Gramps for Christmas, but I can't make up my mind."

"Would he like a card?" Nisha said.

"I doubt it. But I'll look."

"Or chocolates?"

"He actually loves Mounds bars. Isn't that weird?"

"Not really. I love them too."

"What he'd really like is a case of Bud Lite, but of course I can't get that."

"Jamie," Nisha said. "Can I see what you have in your pockets?"

"In my pockets?"

"In your jacket pockets."

Jamie took out her cellphone, car keys. "Here."

Nisha opened her hand. She hated the gesture. Jamie slapped the phone and keys onto her open palm. From the other pocket, she brought out a wad of Kleenex, a tube of Chapstick, a pencil stub.

"That's to write on the offering envelope," she said. "I stole it. From church."

"Anything else?"

"Nope." She pulled out both pocket linings, the yellow material garish against the black leather, like the stain of some awful sickness.

"What about the inside pocket?"

"Do you want to pat me down? That's pretty weird. I could report you. Stranger Danger."

"I'm not a stranger."

Jamie unzipped the jacket, opened it wide. "Check for yourself," she said.

Nisha slid her hands into the pockets, two on each side. She was careful not to touch Jamie through the fabric. Nothing.

"Maybe I should just take the whole thing off. Shake it out. You can reach up the sleeves. Then my shirt. My pants. Whatever."

"I was watching you, Jamie. I'm not going to say anything. I don't want you to get caught for doing something dumb."

"Do you want me to get caught for doing something smart?"

"I don't want you to get caught at all. I don't want you to ruin your life."

"How about if I remind you that it's my life?"

"Okay. I'm reminded." She handed Jamie her phone and all the rest.

"I hate this fucking store. There's never anything decent here." She brushed past Nisha, clipping her with some force, stormed toward the exit. Nisha held her breath.

No sound. The two sets of doors parted as if Jamie were just another beloved customer. *Guest* was the word. Other guests hummed in the aisles, spoke into their phones. Went on with their buying of beer and chocolates, liter bottles of Mondavi, heating pads, *Wanna Play Some Reindeer Games?* t-shirts.

Nisha turned back, pushed the restroom door open. She stared at her face in the mirror. The same face as always. Older. She washed her hands. Moved across the small room to the hand dryer. In the waste basket below, a small notebook, a pink contact lens case, a one-ounce bottle of Cetaphil lotion lay, waiting. She pushed the waste basket aside with her foot, dried her hands, bent and picked up the notebook, lens case and lotion. She would put them aside to buy later, at the end of her shift.

She opened the notebook. On the first page, in pencil, Jamie had written *I miss Djuna like fuck-all.*

Two days later, Jamie texted: *im stuck at the high school nobodys answering their phones. Can you give me a ride home please?*

Sure. Nisha answered. *I can be there in ten minutes.*

This is not just a ride home, Nisha thought. There are plenty of other people Jamie could call. Plenty of guys in the county who would love to give Jamie a ride. Somehow, and for some reason, Jamie knew or remembered this was the end of Nisha's shift.

Jamie was sitting on the curb outside the library, her palms flat on the sidewalk behind her, head back as if she were sunning herself, her long hair lifted back off her shoulders by the wind. A gorgeous waif. She knew exactly how she looked.

Nisha parked beside her and waited, probably 15 seconds, for Jamie to open her eyes, mime a sort of smug surprise, stand up, walk toward the car. She looked Nisha in the eye but did not smile.

"Sorry you got stuck," Nisha said. "Will anybody be at your house to let you in?"

Jamie held up her keyring, shook it back and forth, a little harder than was necessary.

"Ah, right. I just wanted to be sure. I guess I worry. That mother thing."

"I'm not your child, you know," Jamie said. "You don't have any children. You have no clue what it's like to be a mother."

"And you do?" Nisha said.

"No. I'm just saying stop acting like you're trying to take care of me."

"I'm not acting like it," Nisha said. "I *am* trying to take care of you."

"That's Gram's job."

"Actually, it's your mother's job."

Nisha could hardly believe she said the words. She waited for Jamie to take hold of the door handle.

"That's not very nice," Jamie said. But she stayed in the car.

"No, it's not. You're right. I'm sorry. It just kills me...."

Nisha couldn't say any more. She felt heavy, burnt from the inside out, as if her veins had filled with molten lead.

"It just kills you," Jamie said, "that people who have children fuck it up, and you didn't have any, and you'd do a better job."

"Couldn't have any."

"Yeah, well."

The last car left the parking lot. A boy Jamie knew. She waved. He gave her the finger and she laughed.

"He's such an asshole," she said. "He just wants to get into my pants."

"Kids still say that? *Wants to get into my pants*? That's what we said in my day. I would have thought the slang moved on faster."

"I already said fuck once in this conversation. I didn't want to be repetitive. And anyway, you know time sort of stands still around here."

"I wish."

"You wish it had stood still a year ago."

"I think I do."

"Me too. What a fucking waste. Damn, that's twice."

"Oh Jamie, what are we going to do?"

"Probably mess up a lot more. Me. Not you."

"Look who's coming," Nisha said.

"I think he tracks my every move. I wonder what I did this time."

Nisha had never had much to do with Mr. Ballard, the assistant principal, because Djuna was never in trouble. She thought Jamie probably spent a lot of time in his company.

When he had walked close enough to see who was in the car, Ballard's pace slowed. He seemed to hesitate, then ducked his head and moved forward, as if into a stiff wind. He paused again, deciding, then veered right, to the driver's side window. Nisha rolled the window down halfway. Ballard bent at the waist, resting his hands on his knees. He looked at Jamie, past Nisha, as if she wasn't there.

"I saw you were still here," he said.

"I'm okay," Jamie said. "We're just talking."

Still, Ballard didn't acknowledge Nisha.

"You remember Djuna Malik's sister, right?"

"The one who was killed," Ballard said, his voice remote, mechanical. Then shifted his gaze, stared at Nisha as if he were seeing her in a line-up.

"Nisha Malik," Jamie said.

"Not sure," he said, squinting just slightly. "Maybe."

"She was a senior last year," Jamie added. "She was never in trouble."

"May," Ballard said, his voice pausing over the first syllable of the word, "be." His tone suggested he had a hard time believing *never in trouble* was possible.

"We're fine here," Nisha said.

"You know this parking lot has to be cleared out by seven," Ballard said. "Unless you have a permit."

"Yes, sir," Jamie said.

Nisha wondered how she got away with it—that tone. Obedient, and yet. An edge, a breath of sarcasm. Where did she learn to do that? And when? Nisha felt a small, vague urge to meet Jamie's mother.

"All right," Ballard said. "Have a good evening."

"You too," Jamie said.

Ballard stared at Nisha, frankly waiting for her reply. Nisha thought she must look like a slave to him. Or less.

"Have a nice night," she said.

Ballard walked away, not the way he'd come, back toward the school building. He crossed behind their parked cars, examining the back bumpers, and then moved off towards the gym. He seemed lost. Nisha felt sorry for him. Always in search of the bad, the broken, the wrong. What a terrible life.

"Does he have kids here?" she said.

"He did," Jamie said. "Jason. Hung himself two years ago."

"Oh, god."

"Yeah."

Dead teenagers everywhere. She felt their presence, profoundly, on the edges of this parking lot, half disappeared into the woods beyond the school grounds. Her vision of Ravi on the river. She wondered if they were lonely—or were they able to find each other? What did they have to talk about then, besides regrets, besides longing for their mothers. She wondered why this image came to her so vividly now. Except that she was sitting a foot away from another teenager who seemed to be headed toward those same woods.

"Do you ever want to do that, Jamie?"

"Kill myself? Sometimes. I think everybody does. Don't you?"

"Why do you want to?"

"I just get sad. I don't see the purpose in anything. School is a bunch of bullshit."

"It's a means to an end."

"Right. So you get good grades, and all the teachers love you, and you win a bunch of scholarships and go off to college, and then some racist lunatic shoots you, and that's your end."

Nisha put her hand to her chest. It felt as if someone were digging out her heart with a dull knife or a spoon.

Jamie was crying. "Why do people *do* that?" she sobbed. "What you just did. It's so ridiculous. Your heart is just a machine. It doesn't feel anything. Why don't people press on their heads? It's the thoughts that hurt. Not the stupid organ."

"Can I hug you, Jamie?" Nisha said.

"No."

"Please."

"Okay. Just not too hard. I'm breakable."

#9

What if I gave you a prompt? Nisha said.

Nisha broke the last glass Djuna used before she left home. She had not washed the glass. This was a secret. She'd put this glass in her bag when she left the river house, carried it to her new apartment and set it on the windowsill, where it had stayed, hazy with fingerprints. Kisses of lip gloss coated the rim. She was embarrassed to have kept it, as one would be ashamed of a disgusting habit. Michael would never understand. And so she was in a hurry, watering the Bodhi plant, and she knocked the glass to the floor. Now it's truly all gone, she thought. Now she's really dead. Nisha thought at first to keep the pieces, but instead she swept them into a dustpan and tipped them into the trash.

She told me this, and then she said she knew I would go back to Dublin. I protested that I wouldn't, that I had a contract and a lease. I liked the University and the students.

"You'll go, though," she said, "because you should. You know it's true."

I couldn't look at her.

"I'll think of you there," she said. "And someday I'll visit. I want to see the Liffey and…all of it."

"I won't go. I promise."

"You will."

We sat in our side-by-side chairs, our assigned seats, and took in the stillness of the bungalow on Rosemary Street, the jumble of furniture and books, papers piled on the kitchen counter, the shadows of bare tree branches falling on the carpet before us, on our bodies, a slash of shadow across Nisha's face as if she'd been marked, temple to lips, in ash. She took hold of my hand.

"Let me give you a going-away gift, Liam."

"No, no, no," I said to the emptiness of my bungalow on Rosemary Street. "It doesn't end that way."

I would try a different version, look at other sorts of endings. Poems, perhaps.

> *In my dreams you walk dripping from a sea-journey on*
> *the highway across the river in tears to*
> *the door of my cottage*

> *Holy forgiveness! mercy! charity! faith! Holy! Ours!*
> *bodies! suffering! magnanimity! Holy the supernatural extra*
> *brilliant intelligent kindness of the soul!*

> *We have lingered in the chambers of the sea*
> *By sea-girls wreathed with seaweed red and brown*
> *Till human voices wake us and we drown.*

Liam broke the water siphon in the backyard pond. He thought if he could make the fountain work again, Nisha might come back and sit outside and listen to the water and be soothed. After he'd drained the pond and tugged at the filter, cracking the plastic housing, he sat down in the long, damp grass at the edge of the pond with the two halves of the filter in his hands. Liam did not know how to fix very much and wondered why this was so. His father, old Liam, old dead Liam, had not been any good with tools and parts and broken machines. Clearly. He looked at a ruined thing, sometimes for years, and then left the wreckage for others to mend. Liam thought maybe he himself would buy a manual or watch a YouTube video. DIY, they called it.

Do it. Yourself. This time, the decision came earlier, before the breaking on purpose and the dream. He stood and rubbed the mud from his fingers and walked indoors to write a letter.

Liam broke the lease on the bungalow in Rosemary Street. He

would fulfill this semester's contract, read his students' final portfolios and turn in their grades before the due date. And then he would go home to Dublin. He would have Christmas in the house in Ringsend, and maybe he would invite Nancy Hennessy, or she would invite him to the house in Ballsbridge. They would talk about all their dead and about all the living as well. They would drink a little something, not too much, and they would tell old stories, and they would laugh. Maybe Liam would take Nancy in his arms and twirl her in a dance as his father had done the day of the first visit to Bob Hennessy, to make Nancy smile and forget her sadness, just for a moment.

Liam dreamed his own long howling in the manner of that American epic poem: in the dream he saw the best minds of the next generation destroyed by a hurricane from Washington, where white men cough all night and won't let anyone sleep, the best minds destroyed by rising sea levels, destroyed by Silent Sam on its face in the dirt, the best minds who passed through universities with radiant cool eyes hallucinating literature among the scholars of nothing, and were expelled or murdered. He dreamed he was imitating the shade of his father and his brother who were great writers on the same dreadful typewriter. He dreamed of his mother sobbing alone in the asylum of forgetfulness.

Liam woke and decided he had to let Nisha go, that he had to give up Djuna's journal. It didn't belong to him. As for Shamus, he didn't need to decide right now. *Too soon.*

But I would remember enough to write the book. I would write the book of Djuna and Nisha, their duet, the two of them mermaids, singing each to each. Anyway, I had already written it, hadn't I? Hadn't we, Nisha and I? Or had I stolen it. Whose book was it? Whose book was any book, really?

I miss my brother terribly. And my father, God love him. And,

God love her best of all, my mother. Ah, sure, look it, Nancy Hennessy would say, what can we do? I've done my crying now, Liam, haven't I?

So I am coming to understand this thing. About Nancy and Nisha Malik and about my mother, about how women make their way in the world, how they face grief. They look death in the eye, and they howl. And it makes a kind of shape. That kind of howling after a death is a kind of creation. Mostly only women do it. Or should I say: the task of howling falls mostly to women. I tried to teach the students that poetry was as close to silence as a person could come but still make a sound. But now I realize I was wrong. This howling at death is closer to silence than poetry. Because it has no words. In the face of death and its unending silence, those of us left behind are stripped of language. The living have to acknowledge that words aren't enough, that words will never be enough. We are *unworded*. Women know this. Women know how to have the last word by moving beyond words.

I heard a radio programme recently in which a woman talks about grieving for her father. She said in the cultures that she comes from, the women *ululate*, that chilling sound that rises up in the neighborhood when a death is made known to the community. I listened to her say that this howling is a kind of performance to show how hard, how nearly impossible it is to cut the bonds of love. The community helps to make this severing, this end, to separate from the loved one. I decided I would read the transcript to get it right, the words that she said. The transcript looks like this:

In the cultures that I come from, the women (unintelligible), you know, that chilling sound that rises up....

That's quite a thing, is it not? *Unintelligible*. Whoever did the transcripting got it exactly right.

In the two weeks' long reciting of the *Mahabharata*, a common theme appears: an Apsara is sent to distract a sage or spiritual master from his ascetic practices. One story embodying this theme is that recounted by a woman named Sakuntala to explain her own parentage. Sakuntala says that the sage Viswamitra generated such intense energy by means of his asceticism that the great god Indra himself became fearful. Deciding that the sage would have to be distracted from his penances, he sent the Apsara Menaka to work her charms. Menaka trembled at the thought of angering such a powerful ascetic, but she obeyed the god's order. As she approached Viswamitra, the wind god, Vayu, tore away her garments. Seeing her, thus, disrobed, the sage abandoned himself to lust. Menaka and Viswamitra sported together for some time, during which Viswamitra's asceticism was forgotten. As a consequence, Menaka gave birth to a daughter, whom she abandoned on the banks of a river. That daughter was Sakuntala herself, the narrator of the story.

Continuous recitation, Nisha said. So long as men can breathe or eyes can see. So long lives this, and this gives life to thee.

I decided I would go home and finally arrange a memorial for my da and for Shamus, a performance, night and day, until the very last sentence, of *The Bungalow,* the novel of thievery. I hoped that Nancy Hennessy would help me, because the memorial would be for Bob too. Nancy would know the people to invite to read, and where and when. Not at Neary's, which would be haunted by the last argument between my father and Shamus. She would suggest The Palace Bar, in the back room, where the *Irish Times* writers gathered. Then I would do the same for my mam's wondrous second novel, read it out loud, maybe with just Nancy, her dearest friend, passing the brittle pages back and forth between us, the quiet, dusty language brought out to air and gleam in the sunlight. Give Mam the last word. I could already see the phrases and sentences shimmering and dancing in the air above our heads, making little trembling rainbows, every word we spoke a promise that she was somehow still with us, that she, like Djuna Malik, would never be forgotten.

#10

By the time you read this:

You will have thought of my four-part prompt. Break something on purpose. That, you've done, haven't you?. Break something by accident. Dream. Decision.

You broke the glass by accident. Now what? Decide. Sometimes, the decision must come before the dream.

You will decide to rest. You will lie down and sleep and dream that Djuna is back, alive, that she is walking through the river house, from her bedroom to the bathroom. In her sleep, you will be overjoyed, ecstatic, shaking with happiness. But Djuna won't see you, she won't or can't, sitting there in your usual chair, then standing, then opening your arms. Djuna will stare with an expression that is at once puzzled and sad. Then she will say, "Is that really you?" You will try to say yes, yes of course, but no words will come. That familiar dream experience—the strangling almost to cry out, to protest, to stop some terrible confusion rushing toward you. "I would know you anywhere," Djuna will say then, even though she is staring past your face.

You will wake and sit up.

By the time you read this, or, I should say, if you're reading this you will have received the parcel I've sent. You'll be holding the contents in your hands, your sister's journal, and the parts we filled in together. You can decide what you want to do with them, this past and its future, and you'll let me know. You will sense Djuna in the room with you, actually you'll know it, as if you've heard an echo of a step, the rustle of pages turning, or laughter, or the wind. As if you've caught a trace of scent, *ginger and marine, needle and metal.*

Acknowledgments

First, deepest thanks to Joe Taylor for believing in this novel. And to Kerry D'Agostino for eight years of good advice and friendship, as well as all the fine people at Curtis Brown for helping along the way. Thank you Kelly West for the cover design, and thanks also to Savannah Beams, Trinity Cates, and Tricia Taylor.

I'm grateful for my friends and colleagues at East Carolina University, particularly The Fabulous Starlight Women, Derek Maher, Jill Jennings, Judy Whichard, and Christy Hallberg.

Farther flung friends Kathy Fagan, Alexis Khoury, Connie and John Hales, Tanya Nichols, Cheryl Huff, Jane Saunders, Carries Thies, Laura Cook, Dympna Ugwuoju, Mary Ann Williams, Dan Marcucci, Grace Cordts, Barry and Susan Saunders.

As ever, my mother listened patiently as I talked about this book before she passed away in 2021.

And finally, gratitude and love to Dan and Georgia, who lived alongside this book and made it—and me—better.

Liza Wieland has published five novels, three collections of short fiction, and a book of poems. She previously taught in New York, Pennsylvania, Colorado, California, and recently retired from East Carolina University.

www.ingramcontent.com/pod-product-compliance
Lightning Source LLC
Chambersburg PA
CBHW030358020726
47493CB00003B/866